THE EXCITING SEQUEL TO
WHEN JESUS CAME TO JERSEY
AS THE SON OF THUNDER

As usual, Aaron Adams is headed for trouble. This time, the Son of Thunder will once again summon him to assist in an endeavour that will wreck havoc on those who dare practice chicanery against the downtrodden in the little corner of the world known as the Broughton Archipelago. As usual, rivers of blood will flow as Aaron Adams refuses to bend before the winds of tyranny.

Remember how much trouble Jesus caused in New Jersey? Well, wait until you see what he is up to in Canada. He goes to a group of islands off the coast of British Columbia to incite rebellion among people who had their land stolen hundreds of years ago, and their way of life destroyed by those who looked upon them as savages. Jesus knows who the real savages are, and he will not be meek or compromising when it comes to righting the wrongs and indignities suffered by these people who have waited far too long for amends to be made.

Just like his visit to New Jersey, one day in the Broughton Archipelago, Jesus just simply appeared, seemingly out of nowhere. The only way to the island was by float plane or boat. Yet, neither was seen bringing this man to the island. He strolled on the pristine beach of Gilford Island, almost embracing it with love. He was a moderately tall, comely man, with a very irreverent countenance, such that those who saw him would respect him, but there was also an element of this man to fear, made plain by his assured manner that seemed to foretell a coming rebellious calamity.

The Place Where it Started
Gilford Island (Kwak'wala)

This area is inhabited by an indigenous group of First Nations people, numbering about 5,500 total, who live in British Columbia on northern Vancouver Island, the adjoining mainland and islands in the Broughton Archipalego. Gilford Island (Kwak'wala) was the place where Jesus was first sighted, strolling along the beach below.

Quote from the book *When Jesus Came
to Jersey as the Son of Thunder*

"Those who truly love justice will always stand with me against the evil of tyrants who wrap all of you in bondage to greed and judgemental arrogance. I have suffered mightily because in the face of deceit, truth becomes revolutionary." (*The Son of Thunder*)

J. Wayne Frye

When Jesus Came
To Canada to Lead
An Indigenous Rebellion in
The Broughton Archipelago

By
J. Wayne Frye

The Wooden Protectors of Kwak'wala
Guarding Against a Coming Armada of Greed

The Author

Wayne Frye's Aaron Adams series has been popular among Canadian mystery lovers since first appearing in 2005. He provides satirical political commentary to many Canadian newspapers, and his books on politics have created a great deal of controversy. He has written marketing/ advertising textbooks, been a successful U.S. university hockey coach, professor, university president and served as a marketing consultant to hockey teams and motion picture companies. He has been cited for his work with inner-city gang children in the Los Angeles area and been active in the anti-globalization movement. He became a Canadian citizen in 2003 and lives with his wife, Jasmine, in Ladysmith, British Columbia.

Other Fireside Books by J. Wayne Frye

When Jesus Came to Jersey as the Son of Thunder
Something Evil in the Darkness at Hopkins House
How Hockey Saved a Jew From the Holocaust:
The Rudi Ball Story
The Catastrophic Calamities of a Village Idiot
Fighting for Justice in the Land of Hypocrisy
Guide to Alternative Education (13 Editions)
Cataclysmic Dreams in Black and White
The Girl Who Stirred Up the Whirlwind
The Fall From Apocalypse
Armageddon Now
Worth

Books by J. Wayne Frye with Jasmine Falling Rain Frye

Canadian Angels of Mercy – Nurses in Times of Peril
Points of Rebellion: Aboriginals Who Fought for Justice

When Jesus Came to Canada to Lead An
Indigenous Rebellion in the Broughton Archipelago

Table of Contents

When Jesus Came to Canada to Lead An
Indigenous Rebellion in the Broughton Archipelago

TO: The First Nations people of North America, who have suffered mightily at the hands of those who looked upon them as savages. This author knows who the real savages are.

Also, I must render a special thanks to my cousin Monte Cagle, whose intention to show me the path to what he considers the light of righteousness motivated me to write *When Jesus Came to Jersey as the Son of Thunder* in 2012; and thereby, his love for me served as a catalyst for this sequel as well.   JWF

Catalogue Number: 20126196111

ISBN: 978-0-9879728-5-9

Fireside Books – Victoria, British Columbia

PROLOGUE
WITH THE SWORD OF RETRIBUTION

To thoroughly understand what is about to follow, it would be advantageous to have read the previous account of Jesus when he showed up in the small New Jersey town of Woodbury Creek in 2006, but for those who are unfamiliar with the events that were described in *When Jesus Came to Jersey as the Son of Thunder*, I shall offer some background information on just what occurred before he showed up on Kwak'wala Island in 2007.

In 2006, a man professing to be Jesus, but never claiming to be holy, appeared in the small New Jersey town of Woodbury Creek. It was there that all the forces of evil in the USA conspired against this man who dared challenge authority. The government and the church did all they could to make sure that this man, who was preaching rebellion against the powerful and wealthy, was brought to heel. Branded a terrorist by a government that was, at the time, using its own brand of terrorism in Iraq, Afghanistan and those monuments to inhumane cruelty, Abu Ghraib and Guantanamo, Jesus was whisked off to a place of sadistic evil in an abandoned mansion on the shores of the Delaware River in Camden, New Jersey. It was in that place that he would be rescued by Aaron Adams.

When Jesus Came to Canada to Lead An Indigenous Rebellion in the Broughton Archipelago

Aaron Adams and a beautiful young woman, Mary Madison, got Jesus to the Camden, New Jersey Railroad Station where they put him on a train, so that he could escape the wrath of the U.S. government and the religious establishment that feared his appeal to those who were crying for economic compassion and genuine freedom in a land where benevolence and liberty had been sacrificed at the altar of greed and expediency.

As the train started to pull out, Aaron asked him where he was going, because he felt like he was about to lose the most magnificent person he had ever known, even though he had only been with him a few hours. Jesus, his eyes twinkling like bright stars in the night, replied, "I can only take the train as far as Seattle. From there, I shall slip across the Canadian border and make my way to a small island off the British Columbia coast, where Aboriginals still live a simple life free of materialism. It is there that I will recuperate and connect with those who still know compassion. When the time is right, I shall emerge again, and try once more to bring light to the darkness."

So now, the time had come. It had been six years, and this man calling himself Jesus had been living peacefully among the Aboriginals of British Columbia, but he was about to come forth again, not with meekness, but with the sword of retribution.

CHAPTER 1
A TUMULTUOUS SEA
OF AGITATION AND BEDLAM

In New York City, Aaron Adams was a man who shouldered heavy burdens from a life in which he had battled against the tyranny of those who think the privileged and powerful should be exalted above all others. His devotion to fairness, justice, integrity and honour sat him apart from those who ruled with the iron fist of repression in a society that had been manipulated into believing it was free. He was well-known in government circles as a man who defied authority and refused to bend before any man or governmental body. He was an anomaly in an America that worshipped at the altar of greed. In fact, he was a dangerous man in a society that demanded conformity and adherence to a set of standards that codified all people into nothing but sheep who were willingly being led to the slaughter. Aaron Adams was an individual who simply refused to go quietly into the night.

Had Aaron's exploits not been so reverentially covered in best selling books by his biographer, Wayne Frye, he would have been long ago disposed of by those who feared anyone who dared question the authority and control of society exercised by the 1% who ruled America like it was their personal fiefdom. Aaron Adams was a man who could not be bought nor would he give any quarter to those who dared stand between him and true justice for the downtrodden of the world.

It was Monday morning, and at 9:00 Aaron was always at Andy's Coffee Shop that was at the far end of the first floor of the office building where he kept his combination office and apartment. While the smart set in their high dollar suits, designer dresses and Italian leather shoes were at Starbucks or Seattle's Best, sipping their $4.00 lattes, Aaron was just having a black cup of coffee in a well-worn, chipped mug while he conversed with Andy, who had long ago given up fighting the corporate coffee giants who had sold the gullible public on the trendiness of gourmet coffee. Yeah, the smart set wasn't just drinking coffee. They were making a statement about their relevance in a world where character was much less important than the clothes you wore, the car you drove and the place where you sipped your latte. Andy was just a dying anachronism of old-style capitalism that had been gobbled up and devoured by the avaricious corporate monsters that could never get enough. He was Aaron's kind of guy. Andy didn't need to be rich. He just needed to make a living to support his family. That was all he asked for, but the hand writing was on the wall for him, like most other small-time entrepreneurs. The clock was ticking toward his demise, and soon, one of the corporate giants would take over his lease when he could no longer afford the exorbitant rent charged by the real estate corporation, and a once independent businessman would become just another toiling minimum wage earner for a corporation that had no heart or soul. This was the way of the modern world of wage slavery supported and abated by a U.S. government that was bought and paid for by the wealthy who ruled mercilessly in the land of broken dreams.

Andy was a robust man of about 40 who had a great deal of reverence for the 60ish Aaron, and looked upon him as a man of integrity and compassion who represented what had been lost years ago in a country where success was judged by the things you had and the size of your bank account rather than by how many people you gave a hand up to in a world of pain. As Aaron sipped his coffee, on a tiny island in the Broughton Archipelago, the man calling himself Jesus was about to set in motion some cataclysmic events that would once again make Aaron Adams rise from the ashes of despair to stand alongside righteousness and justice in a world that had no compassion.

Jesus, who had lived a quiet, contemplative life for six years among a simple people on Kwak'wala in the Broughton Archipelago, who took him into their hearts, was about to unleash his revolutionary fury that had gotten him into so much trouble in New Jersey. This time, his rage would bring about even greater turmoil in a world where the barons of greed and their government lackeys would tolerate no one questioning their right to rule with complete and utter impunity. However, a few of them would have to reckon with the son of thunder.

Jesus, thanks to Aaron Adams, and Mary Madison, had survived an ordeal of fiery retribution by the U.S. government and the church that feared his message of defiance against those who supported the culture of greed that was enslaving 99% of the world to the avariciousness of the 1%. It had cost Mary her life and nearly cost Aaron Adams his. Fighting the forces of economic and social injustice was simply an exercise in futility, not only for Aaron Adams and Mary, but for billions of people all across the globe who pleaded for mere scraps from the table of plenty set for the wealthy. The world was a place of great abundance, but that abundance was controlled by a few corporate entities that saw people as nothing more than chattel. And it was the corporations, the wealthy and the powerful that manipulated governments run by men and women who were in bondage themselves to the culture of greed that made them turn their backs on the downtrodden to serve the needs of those who were corrupt of mind, body and spirit.

When Jesus Came to Canada to Lead An
Indigenous Rebellion in the Broughton Archipelago

Jesus, unlike his time in New Jersey, had done absolutely nothing to rile up the people of Kwak'wala. He had avoided all controversy as he sought to heal from the ordeal of the house of torture in Camden, New Jersey, where he had endured unspeakable agony at the hands of U.S. government masters of torture who had been told by the fascist-like Bush Administration that he was a terrorist. In fact, when the Inter-Tribal Health nurse came for her bi-weekly visits to the island, he simply faded into the background and usually holed up with one of the many families who gave him a place to stay, or went into the interior of the island to be alone and contemplate.

Jesus preferred to avoid any contact with the outside world that had treated him so irreverently when he had tried to motivate the people in one small New Jersey town to fight their oppressors and stand against the tyranny that kept them in invisible chains. His efforts got him arrested for terrorism and tortured by the United States government that had absolutely no tolerance for anyone who dared question authority. However, six years of meekness was about to come to a dramatic end in the little corner of the earth that had become home to a man who simply could not abide watching these people be abused once again by a society that had, in many ways, tried to make amends for the mistreatment afforded them by previous generations. Yet, just like the country south of them, there were far too many Canadian politicians and uncaring, unsympathetic citizens who still looked with disdain upon those who turned their backs on the culture of greed that was spreading its evil intentions northward. There seemed to be no escaping the corporate and religious theocracy of America that was still determined to enslave all of humanity to the evil of greed. Even under a President who, unlike his predecessor, seemed sympathetic to the plight of the poor and the middle class that struggled to keep their heads above water, there was no let up in the march of corporations toward total world domination. However, when one corporation made the mistake of casting a greedy eye on the resources of Kwak'wala Island, they found that the Son of Thunder was not one to go meekly into the night. All hell was about to break lose, and the world would quake in disbelief at just how determined a people could be when they had finally simply had enough of those whose avaricious appetite for more and more could never be satisfied. There would be no retreat and no surrender with the Son of Thunder leading the way.

In order to comprehend what led to these momentous events, it is necessary to understand a little about why Jesus had, in a way, given up hope for a world where the oppressed seemed unwilling to make a stand against the injustices that were heaped upon them day-in and day-out. Upon arrival in Seattle, Jesus had hitch-hiked to Port Angeles, Washington where he managed to get in an unlocked camper that was waiting in line for the Coho Ferry that went to Victoria, British Columbia. Without a passport or any ID papers, he faced arrest by Canadian authorities once he was in British Columbia. All he could hope for was not getting discovered in the back of the camper. If he was found, the Canadians, now with a conservative government in power, willingly deported anyone one deemed by the United States as a terrorist. And the moronic American government of George "Bring 'Um On" Bush and Dick "Waterboard" Cheney deemed anyone a terrorist who dared stand up against their tyrannical fascist policies of subjugation through militarism and economic servitude. Of course, Jesus was fairly dark skinned and had the look of a Middle Easterner; thus, he was immediately suspect in a nation that had long identified those not white as second class citizens or suspected them of being in league with those evil doers all over the world who were out to get the USA for its self-defined, superior way of life.

On the ferry, the elderly couple who had the camper were shocked when they entered it to remove some items to take on the ferry lounge with them and saw that a man had broken in. Jesus, raising his right hand and placing his index finger over his lips as to indicate they should not scream in horror, said "I will not harm you, and I am not a terrorist. I am just a man who has been marked by the U.S. government for extinction, because I encouraged people to stand against the tyranny of those who want to enslave everyone to the culture of greed and militarism promulgated by George Bush and his henchmen. I hope that you are two people who can see the folly of a government that has no respect or consideration for those who wield no religious or economic power."

The man to whom Jesus addressed his remarks was in his early 60's and had long, scraggily, thin, white hair and an unkempt white beard. He looked at his wife, who was dressed as if she were a fugitive hippie from the 1960's and said, "hey, it looks like we have an anarchist in our camper."

His wife, who, despite being dressed like a homeless street person, was strikingly attractive for her age, replied with a wink, "I don't see anybody, old man. You must be getting senile."

The man looked back at Jesus and said "yeah, you're right. I must be imaging things. Good thing he isn't there, because if he was, I'd want him to be sure and tell the authorities if he got caught that we did not know he had broken into out camper. I mean we are just two innocent old hippies." He then closed the camper door and Jesus breathed a sigh of relief. He had been lucky enough to break into a camper that belonged to two people who, he would ultimately find out, had the same disdain for authority that he did.

Myra and George Brekenridge were, in fact, both fugitives from that wonderful time when America almost changed to a more equalitarian and just society, the 1960's. Unlike their brethren who had tossed away their love beads, subdued their anarchist rhetoric and joined the establishment, they were still rebels with a cause.

After getting past the Canadian Border Service Agents without being discovered, Jesus was invited to travel to Port McNeill on northern Vancouver Island with the couple who had come to Canada in 1971 when George had been drafted to fight in the American abomination of the time, the Vietnam War. They decided to stay, even after the deserters and draft resisters were pardoned, because they had gotten used to the real freedom enjoyed by Canadians as opposed to the propagandized version that was prevalent in America. They got a good laugh when they asked Jesus his name. When he insisted that was his real name, George said, "you men Heh-soos."

"George, you can call me Heh-soos if it suits you, but I am not Latino, so I prefer Jesus. It is a name I have had for a long, long time," calmly replied Jesus as they sat by their roaring campfire.

George, looking at Myra, smiled and slowly looked back at Jesus. "O.K., we'll call you Jesus, Hey, we can remember when you were a super star on Broadway. We used to sing that song all the time. We actually were believers back then."

As George offered Jesus a joint, he indicated no by waving his right hand and with a curious tone said, "And you are no longer believers in God and his son, Jesus?"

Myra, smiling, replied "we lost our beliefs in the streets fighting for justice while getting bashed and brutalized by the cops and the National Guard. We suddenly realized that there was no evidence of a God in a world as fucked up as the one we lived in. I assume you don't agree?"

Jesus exuded calmness and an air of authority like no one they had ever met before. He pointed at the ocean that they could only hear, not see, in the darkness. "You hear the ocean, so you know it is there, right? Yet, what if I told you that it wasn't there? That you were only imaging you heard it. Would you believe me?"

George replied, "No, we know it is there because we have been here many times before.

Even if we hadn't, we know that we are on an island and that there is an ocean that surrounds it."

"Ah, then nothing I could say would change your mind?" a smiling Jesus replied.

Myrna, extremely intrigued by the comely, ruggedly handsome man said, "I doubt it. We are both pretty sure the ocean is there."

"So, your instincts tell you that even though you can't see something it is there?"

Emphatically, George replied, "yeah."

"So, I could not assuage your belief that the ocean is there, but because you see no evidence of a God, you assume he is not there? Does that really make any sense?"

George and Myra were really beginning to enjoy the philosophical discussion. George said, "O.K., so you are telling me that there is a God, and I suppose you are his son?"

"I did not say either. I am only posing a philosophical question. God? God is in every man and woman on earth. He doesn't have to be floating on some cloud in the sky, hanging around with angles that are flapping their wings. He can be everywhere there is compassion for the weary of heart, spirit and body. When you reach out to give someone a hand up, you are God. When you stand against the tyranny of the powerful and wealthy, you are God. When you refuse to bend before the winds of injustice, you are God. When you hear the ocean when it is not there, you are God."

Myra and George were speechless at the wisdom of this simple man. Jesus continued. "You are good people. I sensed that the first time I set eyes on you. Your hearts are pure with love and sympathy for the downtrodden of the world. That is a precious gift that is in short supply. So, you are both Gods."

Jesus loved it when people seemed to hang on his every word, so he continued. "God is an idea more than a deity. If God was like the one I read about in the Old Testament, I would not worship him myself. It would be distasteful to worship a deity who was as cruel as the one portrayed in the Old Testament. You don't worship that God out of love. You worship that God out of fear. What kind of God indiscriminately kills women and children, tells a father to sell his daughter to the highest bidder, says it is permissible to kill a rebellious son, urges his followers who see people so much as light a fire on the Sabbath to put them to the sword and punishes the descendents for the sins of the father. The list of admonitions by this so-called Jehovah is so long that it would take a ream of paper to list them all. People who would worship that kind of God are themselves cruel, because they cannot see the evil in a deity that knows no compassion. I tell you that I am not the son of God as much as I am the son of thunder. I roar with indignation at every single injustice I see. And some of the most heinous injustices are perpetrated by those who claim to be Christians. I stand against hypocrisy. I stand against those who worship at the altar of greed. I stand against those who carry a gun in one hand and a Bible in the other. Do not think that the Bible can do anything but wreck havoc in a world where it is used as a tool to control people and justify the most despicable acts of mankind."

Enthralled by this man, Myra and George sat in stoic silence as they contemplated just who he was. They were non-believers, but it was undeniable that this man was like no other they had ever met. He was able to succinctly crystallize all that they thought was wrong with religion. Myra, still spellbound, muttered, "What would you have the people of the world do to eliminate all the pain that most suffer."

Jesus' eyes glassed over and he stared into the darkness. "At present, I am exhausted from trying to get people in a small New Jersey town to rebel against their oppressors and from the torture I received from a government of criminals who hide behind patriotic platitudes. I have for many years gone to many places to see if there were people who would stand against the tyranny that was drowning them in a sea of despair. I did stir up a few people in New Jersey, but in the end, only two men and one dear woman really stood by me until the end. Two of them are dead, and the other is, no doubt, in deep mourning over the loss of the woman he loved. I am a pariah for all who learn to love me, and I do not want to take you two wonderful people down the path of destruction that always lies before me. I am a one-man anarchist wrecking machine who has no fear whatsoever of death, for I know he who fears death cannot truly ever live. I shall leave you tomorrow morning and make my way to the safety of a place of respite and solitude where I shall contemplate and reflect. I am a man who needs rest from the weary drudgery of trying to get people to stand up to their oppressors, rather than lining up for the invisible chains that keep them in bondage."

George reached out and touched Jesus on the right arm and was shocked at how cold he felt. Turning to Myra, he said, "Get him a blanket dear. He is like ice."

Jesus, touched by George's concern, smiled. "Thank you Myra, it would be nice to wrap myself in a blanket and get warm, for I have been cold for many days, but tonight I am warm with the affection you and George show me."

Myra came back with a thick, well-worn blanket, looked sternly at George and said, "why don't we let him sleep in the camper with us George? It wouldn't be the first time I slept with two men."

George, as he got up, laughed and looked directly at Jesus. "My friend, I think my wife is asking if you would like to share our bed. We are a product of the sixties, so we have a pretty open attitude about sex. Heck, at my age what else could you have? She has been a deprived woman for far too many years. She may be old, but she still is an incredibly attractive woman. Don't you agree?"

Jesus, flattered that she would find him appealing, replied, "I have shared many people's beds, and I appreciate the offer of the pleasures of fornication, but I am a man who simply has no libido whatsoever. I am afraid I would be a disappointment. However, I shall certainly not turn down the opportunity to stay warm in your camper."

They spent a peaceful night conversing in the warmth of the old, broken-down camper, and when George and Myra awakened early the next morning, Jesus was gone.

They went back to their home at Alert Bay on Cormorant Island and reflected back on the brief time they had spent with this extraordinary man. They were deeply saddened that he had left them, but they felt a rejuvenation of their revolutionary spirit that had died so long ago when they felt all hope for change was lost in the swelling tide of corporate theocracy that was flooding the world. In the tiny village of Alert Bay, they shared with their friends the story of Jesus and what they had learned from this extraordinary man. They were met with scepticism, except by the First Nations friends they had. It was the Aboriginals who seemed immensely interested, not because they had reverence for Jesus, as many had suffered mightily at the hands of those who professed to be doing his work, but because of the man's disdain for the culture of greed which was anathema to every thing First Nations people held dear. They were some of the last brave souls who had not bowed before the altar of selfishness. Their curiosity aroused, for years they listened in rapturous reverence as George and Myra told and retold the story of this remarkable man. Little did they know that in a few years, this very man would be at the forefront of a calamity that would engulf them all in a tumultuous sea of agitation and bedlam.

J. Wayne Frye

CHAPTER 2
IMMUNE FROM THE CULTURE
OF GREED

Jesus had quietly slipped out of the camper that night, realizing that if he stayed with Myra and George that they might well get in trouble for harbouring a fugitive from American justice. The long arm of the United States law enforcement and government agencies extended into almost every country in the world, even a more humane and compassionate society like Canada's. Yet, the place to which he was heading was so thoroughly isolated that he could effectively simply drop off the face of the earth. Although he had never been there before, he had heard about it from an elderly Canadian Aboriginal he had met while in Woodbury Creek, New Jersey where he had first called himself the son of Thunder. The old man had been captivated by his homilies delivered in a small park, and came to him with tales of a place where he was born, a place where people still lived a simple life free of the culture of greed. The old man longed to return there, but was too poor and too addicted to drink and drugs to make the journey to the place where he wanted to die. The homeless man had been killed by a government agent because of his relationship with Jesus. He had paid a price suffered by so many that dared resist a government that tolerated no one who stood against its tyranny.

When Jesus Came to Canada to Lead An
Indigenous Rebellion in the Broughton Archipelago

Jesus did not want to make trouble for Myra and George Breckenridge who represented the sanity, love and compassion of a long-ago time when the world was on the verge of a dramatic change. While their compatriots gave up the fight, they had remained true to the ideals of a movement that nearly toppled the calamitous economic and political system that was enslaving the world to the evils of corporate theocracy. The two people were simply anachronisms in a modern world that had no room for compassion and economic fairness.

Jesus made his way to the small hamlet of Sayward, British Columbia on Vancouver Island. As was customary for him, he had no money and no other clothes than those on his back. In a world where being poor is considered a crime in many countries, rather than a condition of circumstance, most people do very little to personally try to lift up those who are trapped by an unjust economic system. However, the good people of Sayward were not typical of those who want to blame the poor for their poverty. When Jesus strolled into town, it was obvious to Captain Tom Hardy that he was a man down on his luck. He offered him a meal on board his ship the Sayward Princess and allowed him to sleep on deck that night. The next day, he introduced him to Will Hampton who offered him a job as a dishwasher in his restaurant for what would be a busy weekend.

Jesus gladly accepted, and Will's wife came in with some old clothes for him. That night, Tom gave him permission to sleep in the cabin with his first mate, Derrick Peters and take a shower on board. Although most derelicts would have aroused caution and suspicion, for some reason, Tom, Derrick and Will had complete trust in this man who seemed to be much more than a roving vagabond. There was something unusual, something special about this man.

After a week in town, Jesus was told by Tom Hardy that he would have to find another place to stay, as the ship was going out to fish in the Broughton Archipelago near the Queen Charlotte Strait. Pleading with Tom, who was headed to the Broughton Archipelago with the boat's co-owner, Will, to fish for Halibut, he was offered a berth if he would assist Derrick. He gladly accepted, but told Tom and Will that he would not be returning with them, because he had to get off at a place called Gilford Island.

Tom was very stern when he said, "we won't be stopping at any of the islands, especially Gilford or as the natives call it Kwak'wala. We are going straight up the Queen Charlotte Strait, fish our limit, and then turn around and come right back. We have a standing order we have to fill, and there will be no time for detours. We have a three day limit and that is it."

When Jesus Came to Canada to Lead An Indigenous Rebellion in the Broughton Archipelago

Jesus looked sternly at Will, Tom and Derreck. "No problem, You know my name, so you know I can walk on water."

They all laughed uproariously, even Jesus. Yeah, this guy was a real jokester thought the three men who had no idea just how serious Jesus was. That night, as he lay in bed, Jesus thought to himself that he might not walk on water, but he was definitely going to get to Kwak'wala. He reached into his shirt pocket and pulled out a tattered and well-worn black and white map that he had carried all the way from Camden, New Jersy (see below).

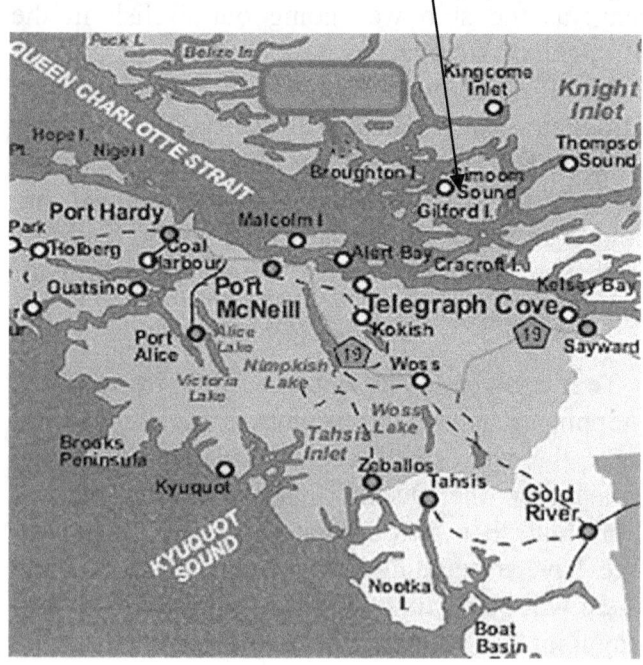

J. Wayne Frye

When Jesus Came to Canada to Lead An
Indigenous Rebellion in the Broughton Archipelago

As he looked at the map, he could see that they would be heading up the strait past Alert Bay and Malcolm Island. To the right was Gilford Island (Kwak'wala). He would stay with them until they made their catch, then on the way back, he would have to figure a way to get to Kwak'wala. He drifted off to sleep with visions of the peaceful shores of the sparsely populated, pristine island where he could escape from the turmoil of a world that simply knew no compassion and had turned its back on his message of peace and love.

Just north of Port Hardy, near Hope Island, they came upon a huge school of halibut, and within a few hours their hold was filled and they had turned around and were headed for home. As night wrapped the ocean in darkness and a slight mist started to fall, Jesus sat down with Will and Derrick for dinner, while Tom stayed at the helm. Thin sheets of fluffy clouds danced across the distant darkness, foretelling a peaceful night with no threats of any storm. The full moon peeked its subdued light through the clouds, kissing the calm seas.

Suddenly, the sounds of killer whales could be heard alongside the ship. All three men got up from the dinner table and went up to join Tom at the helm, enjoying the playfulness of the whales as they cut gracefully through the water on the left side of the ship.

When Jesus Came to Canada to Lead An
Indigenous Rebellion in the Broughton Archipelago

The whales seemed to be almost pleading, begging for attention from the men on the deck. Derrick went to the rail, leaned over and shouted at Tom, "They are so close they may ram us. Must be at least a dozen of them."

Tom, throttling back the engine, barked at Derrick: "Get a grappling hook and bang on the side of the ship."

Jesus placed his hand on Tom's wrist. He looked directly into his eyes. "We are close to Kwak'wala are we not?"

Tom, disconcerted that Jesus was more interested in their proximity to Kwak'wala than the immediate danger they were facing from a pod of whales that were getting dangerously close to the boat was rather curt with his reply. "What the hell difference does that make?"

Jesus, calmly and with deep passion in his voice, said, "I need to know."

Tom, a remorseful tone to his voice, replied "I suppose about 25 or 30 kilometres."

Just at that time, the lead whale let out a cry that seemed to reverberate all about the ocean, as if it was pleading for something from the men on the ship.

When Jesus Came to Canada to Lead An
Indigenous Rebellion in the Broughton Archipelago

Jesus, turning to Will, said "I appreciate all you have done for me. You are a kind man who is filled with compassion for those who need a helping hand. Never think that you are not revered by the many whom you have, no doubt, helped over the years." Then he turned to Tom, and placing his hand on his shoulder, softly, almost in a whisper, said "you Tom were the first to reach out to me and give me a hand up." He then strolled over toward Derrick, looked back at Will and Tom as he put his right hand on Derrick's shoulder while all the whales in a rhythmic cadence seemed to be pleading in the darkness, and in a raspy, cadent like manner he said something that would stay with the men the rest of their lives. "For I was hungry and you gave food. I was thirsty and you gave me to drink. I needed clothes and you clothed me. I had no shelter and you opened the door to warmth for me. I tell you that this day, in the book of life that dwells in my heart, I have marked all of you as the most worthy of human creatures."

With those final words, Jesus dove over the side into the water among the whales. Tom and Will frantically ran to the side of the ship, while Derrick grabbed a life vest and tossed in into the dark sea in hopes that Jesus would be nearby and grab it. The whales moved off toward Kwak'wala, their mournful sighs abating. The men could not believe that Jesus had simply committed suicide in such a dramatic fashion. Why? Why? Why?

When Jesus Came to Canada to Lead An
Indigenous Rebellion in the Broughton Archipelago

Spending the rest of the night searching for him, as the morning sun came up, the men dejectedly headed back home, despondent over losing a man they had only known for a few days, but who had affected their lives like no one else they had ever met. When they reported what happened to the authorities, the response was one of unconcern, as obviously, according to the authorities, he was despondent and had planned the action before going on the trip with the three men. He was just another derelict in a world filled with wandering souls of desperation. No search was ever conducted, but the three men, every time they went through those waters, looked longingly into the sea where he disappeared, always wondering why he had done it.

That night, Jesus became a whale rider, straddling the massive leader of the pod and being carried into the darkness toward Kwak'wala. He was never fearful, because he knew that the massive creatures were kinder and more compassionate than most humans who looked upon their fellow animals as unintelligent sub-species that were not on par with mankind. Humans were so arrogant they could not see that the creatures of the sea and the forests were often more benevolent to one another than humans. They certainly were free of that horrible greed gene that seemed to permeate among most humans much to the detriment of so-called civilization.

When Jesus Came to Canada to Lead An
Indigenous Rebellion in the Broughton Archipelago

Not wanting the whale to beach itself, Jesus climbed off as they arrived near shore just as the sun was coming up. Shivering from the cold, he bade his transportation good-bye and waded ashore, finding a small grove of trees where he undressed and hung his clothes in the sun to dry. Standing naked on the beach in the sun to get warm, he was still shivering when an old man who was strolling down the beach came upon him. Assuming from his dark skin that he might be a native, the old man said, "You aren't from around here. What band are you from and how did you get here?"

Jesus, still shivering, thought it best not to tell him the story of riding the whale ashore, as it would be too preposterous for the old man to believe. Instead, he just said "my small boat capsized and I swam ashore."

The old man, taking his jacket off and handing it to Jesus so he could get warm, replied, "I doubt that, but it is not important how you got here. What is important is that you need to get dry. I would still like to know what band you are from."

Jesus, not familiar with the term band in the way the old man was using it, said, "I am afraid that I do not know what you mean by band. You will have to clarify the term for me, before I can answer your question."

When Jesus Came to Canada to Lead An
Indigenous Rebellion in the Broughton Archipelago

"Ah, then you are not First Nations? A band is a small group within a tribe, but we are all one nation in a way, as we consider ourselves apart from those who conquered us and destroyed our way of life. My native name you would never be able to pronounce, but in English it means *Soars like an Eagle*. The name I use when addressing whites is Octave Joe. You see, the whites, when they carted us off to residential schools to beat Jesus into us, gave us last names based upon anything they just picked out of the air, and often they used what is generally a white first name for our last name. That is why many of us have last names like Frank, Harry, Joe or Bill. A nun at my school was always meeting this white farmer named Joe behind one of the barns, so she named me after him. I always wondered what they were doing behind that barn, and as I have gotten older, I have a pretty good idea of what they were up to. It sure wasn't praying to Jesus. By the way, what is your name?"

Through laughter, he replied, "I am called Jesus."

The old man smiled broadly and said, "Now ain't that a corker. I suppose the next thing you are going to tell me is that you come her to save all us heathens and get us right with God. It's been tried with me, and believe me, it didn't work. I didn't believe in fairy tales even when I was a child, and

I am certainly too old to start believing in them now."

Jesus, still slightly giggling, said, "I do not believe in fairy tales either, and I certainly don't believe any religion has a monopoly on God. I do believe, however, that all men are capable of being Gods, if they would only open their hearts and minds to the compassion that should flow from the depths of each person's soul. For example, you saw I was cold and you handed me your coat. Had I been on Wall Street, no stock broker or banker would have shared their coats with me. If I had been walking the streets of Beverley Hills, the cops would have arrested me for fear that I was there to do damage to someone's lavish monument to greed. Had I been outside the White House or the halls of Congress, the guards would have slapped handcuffs on me for fear that I might offend one of the elected officials who are supposed to be there to serve the citizens like me. If I were in Ottawa to plead for a crumb from the Prime Minister's table of plenty, he would have rebuked me as a malcontent who wanted a handout. I, sir, am here on this island for rest and respite from the evils of the world. I want to enjoy the peace, the quiet and the harmony of a place where a man is free from the harshness of a society that simply knows no compassion, and has no place for those who do not worship at the altar of greed."

When Jesus Came to Canada to Lead An
Indigenous Rebellion in the Broughton Archipelago

Otave Joe, dumfounded by Jesus' response, said, "You are a man who understands the problems caused by a society that has no place for those who do not subscribe to the idea that all things can be owned. Come with me to the village, where we do not own our houses, but share shelter with all, where we cannot eat when we know another villager hungers, where we have no material wealth, but are all rich with the knowledge that we love one another."

Jesus, looking down between his legs, smiled and meekly replied, "I think I should put on some clothes first, before going into the village."

Smiling, the old man could not resist a little levity. "With what you have between your legs, going into the village that way will make you a lot of friends with the women."

Jesus, never one to be shy about sex, even though he had no interest in it, replied, "yes, but their boyfriends and husbands are what concerns me, and I wouldn't want to get off on the wrong foot with them."

Still smiling, the old man could not abstain from one more act of levity. "Well, we have several two-spirited people, so you might find the boyfriends and even some husbands willing to become very close friends with you, too."

Jesus, now laughing out loud again, could only shake his head as he reached over to the tree and took his clothes off the tree limb. "I believe I shall abstain from all sex, if you do not mind, whether it be with male or female. I recognize that it is a great recreational activity, but I am not one who is particularly interested in it. I have other recreational pursuits.

The old man once again could not restrain himself. "Damn, maybe you are the real Jesus. If I had equipment like yours and was your age, I'd be fornicating like a 16 year old."

Jesus, looking a bit more serious, said, "I am an awful lot older than I look – a lot older, believe me."

The two men strolled back to the village and Jesus' demeanour and manor endeared him to everyone in the village. As time passed, he became like a member of the band, and was treated as such by all.

It was in the fall of 2012, when a medical student of Aboriginal ancestry came to the island with the nurse who visited bi-weekly to assess the health needs of the hand full of people who called their part of the large island home. This nurse had only heard of Jesus during the years he had been there, never actually seeing him.

When Jesus Came to Canada to Lead An Indigenous Rebellion in the Broughton Archipelago

On this occasion, he came in to get a flu shot during his fifth year on the island, because, having contracted the flu the previous winter and spending nearly two weeks in agony in his little cabin that had been so generously donated to him by the band, he decided it prudent to get immunized.

At that meeting, Nurse Jane Drummond was particularly taken with a man who, unlike everyone else on the island, she did not know personally. Jesus was a relatively tall man, comely, with a strong countenance, so that those who saw him could immediately distinguish him as a charismatic individual whose very appearance gave him an air of authority, although it was with a quiet assurance that was not abrasive. His chestnut hair was long, flowing and full, falling over his ears and, in the back, resting on his shoulders. He appeared to be a man of perhaps 35. His forehead was only slightly wrinkled and it had somewhat symmetrical pock marks across the front, seeming to indicate that he had suffered an injury there at one time. His beard was mildly thick, and in colour, like his hair. It was not very long. His look was innocent but mature. Ah, but his eyes, they seemed to penetrate to the very soul of the person upon whom he looked or addressed. There was an intensity of purpose in his gaze, and his voice was moderately modulated, courteous, temperate, modest, wise and fair with inflective intensity that seemed to exude sincerity and acuteness of purpose. It demanded your attention.

Jane was a woman of considerable charm, who, at 40, was not only competent at what she did, but highly revered as a person who genuinely cared for the people on the island who were dependent on her for their healthcare needs. To comprehend why she was particularly taken with Jesus, it is important to understand that the first meeting with him in his fifth year on the island was nothing that could be considered commonplace, because anyone who was in his presence felt a certain celestial glow that seemed to emanate from him. Well, that is anyone with a compassionate gene. Those who lacked compassion felt a sort of coldness from his presence, because he was not one who looked kindly upon those who displayed arrogance, judgemental disdain, indifference and insensitivity to those mired in a marginalized existence in a world of abundance. Nor did he suffer genially those who felt superior because of their Christian faith. He was a man who rarely mentioned faith, as he always said that it was a personal thing and that having it or not, had nothing to do with serving the genuine needs of humanity. In fact, he had often said that the kindest, most caring people he met on his numerous journeys all over the world were often atheists. In his own words, he once said before a meeting in the village square, "be careful of calling yourself a Christian, for it is a word that had been used to kill, maim and subjugate throughout history. It is better to simply be known as a compassionate person who bends down to lift up those who have fallen.

At that first meeting, Jane almost trembled when she raised the needle to inject him, so overcome was she with his magnificence. That was just one of many propitious examples of the profound influence this man had on everyone with whom he came in contact.

After administering the shot, a boy of about 11 was brought in. He, as described by his own mother, was "hell on wheels." Seeing the needle, Robert Blackwater immediately started screaming in fear, and all those standing in line for their shots just shook their heads, because they were used to his reaction every time he saw a needle. Jesus, smiling at the student who came with Jane said to her, as she stood there with a needle in her hand, almost fearful to attempt a step toward Robert, "are you afraid?"

The medical student let a mischievous smile creep across her ripe, full red lips that seemed to be begging for a kiss from a willing lover. She was tall, big-busted and as shapely as an hourglass sitting on a mantel. Winking at Jesus, as they both moved toward Robert, her thick, lustrous dark hair

J. Wayne Frye

that cascaded down her back fluttered in slow motion, forming a seemingly perfect symetry of softness that made you want to reach out and touch it.

Jane watched cautiously, because she knew how much trouble Robert could be in these situations. Thinking it would be good experience for her charge to tangle with an unruly child, she stood watching what was transpiring. It was not the medical student who spoke first, but Jesus. "My man, you mean that you are afraid of this beautiful lady? Why, I would consider it a privilege to be protected from a horrible illness by getting a little shot from this woman." He then reached out his right hand to the boy, as if to say, take my hand and I will give you strength. He said, "Take my hand and I will tell you a story about a rock."

As they walked over to a chair, Jesus sat with the boy, who seemed enthralled by this remarkable man whom he had seen about the village, but never really talked to at length. Jesus turned to the medical student and said, "And what is your name?"

"I am Huyana Patrick," replied the vivacious lady.

Jesus said, "Robert, meet Huyana, who is going to gently roll up your sleeve and give you a shot while I tell you an interesting story about how important it is to always look beyond what is on the surface. You see, many times we have to suffer a bit for the greater good that will come."

As Robert listened intently, so did the other 20 to 25 people in the room. No one seemed to notice Huyana gently rolling up his sleeve and dabbing his upper left arm with alcohol, not even Robert, so mesmerized were they all by the hypnotic voice that offered strength and peace in its soft, restful, melodic tone. "In ancient times, right here on this island, a wise chief wanted to see just how resourceful his people were in caring for one another. So, he placed a huge boulder in the middle of the road. Then he hid himself and watched to see if anyone would remove the huge rock from the middle of the road, so others might travel through the area more easily."

Jesus paused just a bit and smiled at Huyana, who was about to administer the shot. Then he harmoniously continued. "Some of the wealthiest tribal members were walking together and they simply walked around it, showing no concern over the many people who were made to stop and walk around it. Many loudly blamed the chief for not keeping the roads clear, but none did anything about getting the stone out of the way. Then a few really poor tribal members came by on their way back from a hunt for meat in the forest. Upon approaching the boulder, they lay down their game and after much pushing and straining; they finally succeeded in rolling the boulder to the side of the road. As they started to leave, they noticed a bag lying in the road where the boulder had been. The bag contained many gold coins and a note from the chief indicating that the coins were for those who worked together to remove an obstacle that was preventing the people from freely travelling the road. These people learned what many of us never understand in life. Every obstacle presents an opportunity to improve conditions, and if people work together, there is nothing that they cannot accomplish. They all shared the coins with one another and used them to buy food for all the poor of the tribe, rather than just keeping it for themselves. You see, you and I are working together, sharing our time which is as valuable as any gold coins, and you didn't even notice Huyana giving you a shot."

Robert perked up, looked over at a smiling Huyana and said, "You two tricked me!"

Huyana, reaching into her lab smock, came out with a piece of chocolate and said, "sometimes being tricked pays off."

Robert took the candy, smiled and sauntered off with his friends. The room was enthralled with what had happened, as it was the first time that

Robert was ever given a shot without having to be held down by two or three adults. Then, as Jesus waved good-bye to Robert, Huyana looked at his right wrist that seemed to have a large scar on it. Glancing at his left wrist, she saw a similar scar in almost the same place. She thought to herself that this was a man who had endured torture. In the back of her mind, she wondered if he had been at that chamber of horrors in Guantanamo, where heinous acts were carried out by the brutal overlords of mayhem in the USA.

Jane also noticed the scars and wondered if they might be from a botched suicide attempt, but they were more like two holes, driven by a spike than a cut from a sharp object. No she thought, those scars were definitely not from an attempt to end his own life.

Huyana was left at the station on her own, where she would grow ever more fond of the man calling himself Jesus and of the simple life lived by individuals who refused to join the march toward selfishness in a world where people were taught to pursue materialistic pleasures as a worthy ambition for all who wanted to enjoy the fruits of that great and wonderful life of excess that was touted as the only true happiness. She had long ago turned her back on that ideal and pursued the simple contentment of a life free of self-gratification through indulgent excess.

When Jesus Came to Canada to Lead An
Indigenous Rebellion in the Broughton Archipelago

She and Jesus became great friends as time passed and the clock of turmoil relentlessly ticked toward a catastrophic confrontation between good and evil. The cataclysmic storms of conflict were brewing nearby, but the peaceful occupants of the village were unaware that they were about to be propelled into an encounter with malignant forces that were determined to destroy their peaceful way of life in a corner of the world that had been, to date, mostly immune from the culture of greed.

CHAPTER 3
THIS IS DISASTROUS

If there is something which devours,
I will leap within its belly
and fight it to the death,
though I bring the world to ruins.
The earth, which bulks between me
and the dark abyss of death,
I will smash to pieces by enduring curses,
forever refusing to meekly submit.
I will throw my arms around harsh reality,
embracing anarchy to defeat evil.
The world may pass away,
and then sink down to utter nothingness.
Rather than living in chains,
I choose to perish, having no existence.
But my spirit will burn brightly,
though I am gone.

The day that the helicopter passed over the village, heading toward the interior of the island, the people shrugged their shoulders and assumed it was just another group of government bureaucrats sent to photograph the island and present it as an example of how the government in Ottawa was dedicated to treating the Aboriginals fairly and protecting their environment. Yeah, they were really looking after the environment; the paper mill spewing out toxins on the other side of the island was proof of that.

When Jesus Came to Canada to Lead An Indigenous Rebellion in the Broughton Archipelago

For years the Aboriginals had watched helplessly as the mill, run by a multinational company based in the USA, had consistently dumped toxins into the streams of the island and sent smoke laden with chemical substances of a questionable nature bellowing into the misty air that hung over the island. They had managed to stop the wholesale clear cutting of their forests by the paper company through legal injunctions, but it only slowed the environmental damage. It did not alleviate it altogether. Battling the corporate behemoths was a daunting task that cost millions of dollars, and the corporations always had many more millions than the people who were forced to fight for their existence.

It had been almost five years since the last battle over environmental damage was fought, and the Aboriginals had been compensated a few million dollars, most of which went to pay the legal fees. Anyway, why would the corporations worry about a few million dollars in fines and compensatory damages when they were reaping billions by ignoring the plight of those they exploited for profit? However, this time, the rising storm of subjugation would encounter a man whom the powerful and wealthy would laugh at for using the name Jesus. He never claimed divinity, but he did assert divine purpose in his commitment to protect those who suffered indignity.

When Jesus Came to Canada to Lead An
Indigenous Rebellion in the Broughton Archipelago

Jesus was a man who trembled with rage at any injustice perpetrated by those who had no compassion and were obsessed with the accumulation of more and more at the expense of the meek who pleaded for survival in a world of corporate connivance and subterfuge. He was about to stand against, not only a powerful corporation, but two powerful countries that were controlled by those who had designs to enslave all of humanity to avaricious greed of the foulest kind. Although he had been meek and unassuming, the man who called himself more the son of thunder than the son of God, was about to go toe-to-toe with the United States of America, and its enabler, the government of Canada.

The helicopter landed in the interior once it found a clearing among the vast forests that covered 80% of the island. Out of the chopper bounded Patterson McCord and Alton Jordan, of Trans-World Industries, a conglomerate that included everything from gambling casinos to paper mills, and, of course mineral extraction. They had come to the spot about 25 kilometres inland to take a look at something that had been picked up on the company's satellite. With a GPS monitor in his hand, McCord, a bio-chemist, moved carefully through the thick forest toward an area that was of intense interest to the executives back in Seattle. Alton Jordan, a mining engineer, was ecstatic with excitement over what they were looking for in the isolated paradise. He had been to the far side of the island once before to assess the possibilities of mining some biotite deposits that were found near the paper mill, but the amount found and the cost to extract it simply made the prospect economically unfeasible. However, what had been detected here was something that was worth any cost to extract.

After two days of running tests, the two men could not wait to get back to Seattle and share the news that there were indeed vast deposits of polonium in the centre of the island. As the helicopter once again soared over the tiny village where Jesus was living, he and several elders, with whom he was walking, looked skyward at the whirling rotors, and Jesus sensed that those blades cutting through the air were like daggers of discontent searing the flesh of the people who were now so dear to him. Looking at the helicopter move eerily like a great bird of prey into the light of the autumn sun and cast a dark shadow against the amber glow, it was as if the light of hope was being extinguished. There was an ill, bitterly cold wind of destructive force about to descend from the heights of the mountain of evil called Trans World Industries and rain carnage upon those who revered the land of their fathers.

When Jesus Came to Canada to Lead An Indigenous Rebellion in the Broughton Archipelago

Polonium is the most radioactive substance on earth. In fact, the little spot on Kwak'wala, where minute deposits were found, had been detected because even beneath the surface among the thicket of trees it was radiating a blue glow that was picked up by satellite. Despite the small amount that was found, its value to the U.S. government would make it nothing less than a multi-billion dollar bonanza for a corporation that had laid waste to pristine places all across the globe in its relentless pursuit of profits. The CEO of Trans World, Harold Frommer, greeted the confirmation of polonium deposits with enthusiasm, as the dollar signs were performing a marionette of delight in his warped soul that judged everything based upon how much material wealth could be fostered.

Some knowledge in regards to polonium is critical to understanding what followed in the board room of Trans World Industries in Seattle. Polonium was discovered in 1898 by Marie and Pierre Curie. Ironically, their daughter, Irène Joliot-Curie, was the first person to die from the radiation effects of polonium. She was accidentally exposed to polonium in 1946, when a sealed capsule of the element exploded on her laboratory bench. She died from leukemia, paying a price that led many countries, including the USA, to see the potential of the material as a killing agent in the constant battle between various forces for control of the planet. Although it is rare and difficult to find, its potential for use as weapon were unlimited. It was essential as a trigger element for nuclear weapons that were the backbone of the American arsenal that kept the evildoers, as defined by them, of the world at bay, so there was no price too high to pay, and TWI saw the potential for billions to flow into their corporate coffers.

Several deaths between 1957 and 1969 were caused by polonium. A polonium leak was discovered at Rohovot, Israel's Weizmann Institute laboratory in 1957. Traces of polonium were found on the hands of a professor and a physicist who researched radioactive materials. Medical tests indicated no harm, but the tests did not include bone marrow. Over the next few years, there was a rash of deaths from cancer. The issue was investigated secretly, and there was never any formal admission that a connection between the leak and the deaths had existed. However, the truth often suffers from the expediency of purpose, and the truth never gets in the way of those with nefarious intentions.

Alexander Valterovich Litvinenko was an officer who served in the Soviet KGB and its Russian successor, the Federal Security Service (FSB) who defected to the United Kingdom. During his time in London, Litvinenko accused

Russian secret services of staging terrorism acts in an effort to bring Vladimir Putin to power. He also accused Putin of ordering the murder of Russian journalist Anna Politkovskaya. Like all people who dare stand against authority, he would pay a price, and polonium would be used to exact revenge.

On 1 November 2006, Litvinenko suddenly fell ill and was hospitalized. His illness was later attributed to poisoning with radionuclide polonium-210, after the Health Protection Agency found significant amounts of the rare and highly toxic element in his body. In interviews, Litvinenko stated that he met with two former KGB agents early on the day he fell ill, and traces of polonium were in the house and car the agents had used in Hamburg, Germany.

Abnormally high concentrations of polonium were detected in July of 2012 in clothes and personal belongings of the Palestinian leader Yasser Arafat, who died in 2004 of undetermined causes. On 27 November 2012 Arafat's body was exhumed and samples were taken for separate analysis by experts from France, Switzerland and Russia. So, as this book is being written, polonium is suspect in his death as well.

The evil of corporate culture is well-documented, but in a world where they control the politicians and the ability of most people to make a living, have a roof over their heads, water to drink, food to eat, a car to drive and the gas to put in it and all the wonderful baubles that are promoted as the only things that will make life worthwhile, is it any wonder they are in a position of dominance?

Upon receiving the report, Harold Frommer, a robust man of about 60, congratulated the two men on their superb work and enthusiastically shouted, "Let's get this show on the road. Time is money. I will fly to Washington and meet with the officials who will be in our corner and see to it that we get what is necessary to bring this product to market, so we can continue to defend this country from those who would do us harm. And if we make some money in the process, isn't that what this nation is all about, anyway." Then, pointing at his Vice- President for International Affairs, Lon Corcoran, he sternly said, "You, get to Ottawa and make sure that the Canadian government is on board with fast-tracking our concession to start mining as soon as possible. We don't want any regulations tying out hands."

Corcoran, a close confidant of many in the corporate friendly conservative government that had been governing Canada since 2006 replied, "gotcha chief. Should be a piece of cake. I'm on it!"

When Jesus Came to Canada to Lead An
Indigenous Rebellion in the Broughton Archipelago

Then, there was the one member of the board who was always the point man when dealing with indigenous populations no matter where in the world they were. He was a ruthless negotiator who had conned and cajoled leaders of indigenous communities all over the world with promises of wealth if they abrogated their commitment to their people. Unfortunately, there were a few ignoble people in the Aboriginal community who had bought into the culture of greed and were willing to sell out for material gain. It was Corcoran's job to locate them and use them to TWI's advantage.

Thus, all the elements that were about to lead to a rising tide of indignation among the First Nations people in one small part of Canada were taking form, and TWI and the governments of both Canada and the USA assumed that, as always, the interests of progress, as defined by the corporate theocracy and by two willing governments, would be served in the long run.

When Lon Corcoran showed up to talk to the chief of the tiny village, he had no idea that he was about to rile up a man who had no fear of a corporation, nor the governments that enabled them. This man was by the chief's side when Corcoran, said, "chief, we will do absolutely no environmental damage, and this mineral extraction will be a great opportunity to put money in the pockets of your people. They can build new homes. They can buy those big flat screen televisions. Why they might even want to put roads on the island so they can drive the new cars they are going to be able to afford from one end of the island to the other. There is no limit to what they will be able to buy. The benefits are beyond your wildest dreams."

The chief, Marvin Harry, turned to the despondent-looking Jesus, who had sat quietly in the home of the chief, along with six village elders, listening to what Corcoran had to say. Marvin did not say anything, just gave him a quizzical look. Jesus, ever respectful of the traditions of those around him, asked of them, "May I speak to this gentleman who offers great material wealth, but has absolutely nothing to uplift the soul of a great nation that has more abundance than any amount that could be offered by the corporation he represents."

All nodded their heads in affirmation that he should share what he had to say. Thus began a discourse that would make Corcoran realize that TWI was about to encounter trouble like it had never experienced before in its pursuit of the mineral wealth of an area they wanted to exploit, because they were going to have to deal with a man who was not only eloquent, but determined to not give into the greed that was so easy to use as a manipulative ploy to get people to open their lands to exploitation.

Jesus stood in order to make Corcoran feel at a disadvantage, as Corcoran was a large man of about 40, with a muscular build and broad shoulders. Just his size, no doubt, intimated most people with whom he came in contact. At six feet five inches and about 225 pounds, he was a formable figure of a man. Meanwhile, Jesus, who was tall, but not as tall as Corcoran, and a bit frail looking, was certainly not a physical match for Corcoran. However, his air of charismatic confidence made him appear totally unafraid of anybody or anything. He started his discourse by striding in front of the long conference table that had been set up in the living room of the chief. He leaned on the edge of the table, his back to the elders and facing Corcoran, who was sitting in a well-worn leather chair. Jesus was silent for several seconds and then scratched his right cheek and began. "Mr. Corcoran, you have one of those marvels of modern technology called a smart phone. We both know that there is no cell coverage in this little spot of the universe, but I suggest you take the phone out and turn on the recorder, so you can get my words down as exactly as possible, because you need to let the people back in Seattle know just who you are dealing with here as the good people of this village are not like any you have encountered before. I have been among them for several years, and I can assure you that they will not bend before giants of economic terror as have so many others who have faced off against you over the years."

Somewhat surprised at what he perceived as complete unmitigated arrogance and bravado, Corcoran, who had not even been introduced to Jesus, who had arrived late to the meeting after Corcoran had already began his presentation, took out his cell phone and held it up, recording a video of the man who was about to throw down a the gauntlet on behalf of the people he had grown to respect and admire. This would be only the beginning indignant defiance.

"You have not told these people what mineral it is you want to extract from this sacred land that they call home. Your lack of willingness to share the information is indicative of nefarious intentions to keep it a secret from them, and even from the world at large. My guess is that it is a mineral that is vital to the interests of those who make war in America. I assure you that I will find out just what it is, regardless of your attempts to keep it secret, and I shall share that information with these people."

Now, knowing he had managed to get Corcoran's undivided attention, he let a smile slowly creep across his lips and said, "I am called Jesus."

Sitting up straighter in his chair, Corcoran fought back laughter. He was dealing with an egomaniacal buffoon who thought he was Jesus Christ. This man wasn't a threat at all. He was a lunatic who could simply be disposed of by going before a judge and getting an order to have him institutionalized. Corcoran shut off his phone and got up. Standing before the chief and elders he said, "You guys better get this nut-case out of here before all hell breaks lose. This isn't Jonestown and he isn't Jim Jones."

Jesus, in his typical calm demeanour said, "No, this is not Jonestown. Unlike those people who solved their problem by committing suicide, these people will fight against insurmountable odds to protect that which they love. You cannot buy their birthright with your big screen televisions and your promise of monetary riches. They are already richer than you are. They just don't know it any more than you know deep within your heart that you are morally bankrupt."

Corcoran instinctively turned his cell phone back on, so he could get audio of what was occurring. Jesus, moving slightly toward Corcoran continued. "Go ahead; turn the cell-phone back on. Even video me if you want. You

think because of my name that I am some fugitive
from a mental hospital, but the only thing I am a
fugitive from is a world where people like you
have sacrificed your souls at the altar of greed. I
will not stand idly by and watch these people lose
all that is dear to them without a fight. If you
want to be honest and tell them what it is that you
want to mine, and the purposes for which it will
be used, I am sure they will entertain further
discussions."

Now Corcoran was beginning to lose his
patience. He ignored Jesus and addressed the
chief and elders directly. "You people going to
listen to this rebel-rousing fool, or are you going
to deal with me? Believe me; if you don't deal
with me, you are going to deal with some high
powered attorneys and your government that will
be on our side. They will not be as merciful as I
am.""

The chief replied, "Jesus is our friend and our
spokesman. We have complete confidence in him
to guide us down the right path to protect our
scared land that has already been defiled on one
side of the island with that abominable paper mill
that spews toxins into the air and fouls one of our
streams, making the water in it undrinkable."

Corcoran was beginning to turn red with anger,
the veins in his neck pulsating and growing

larger. Jesus, enjoying the sparing continued. "I am the son of man. I am a root that clutches into the rich earth and my braches spread and grow strong. These people of the branches of that tree with roots that reach deep into the soil. Out of what you would call rubbish, a great people will emerge to stand against tyranny. You cannot understand, because you live in the squalor of broken images. You are trapped in a dungeon of despair, but cannot fathom your own enslavement. Were you a man of character, you would go back to your bosses, resign in disgust and tell them that you could no longer serve a master with no heart and no soul."

Jesus, moved so close to Corcoran that he could, for the first time, see the pock marks on his forehead. "Go back and tell those who pull your strings like a puppet that these people will not part with the land where their forefathers are buried. You cannot buy land. It belongs to all, and he who thinks he can own the land is like sand on the beach trying to stay dry at high tide. There is a whirlwind stirring and it is about to sweep those who have an unquenchable appetite for more and more into its funnel and carry them to destruction. These are people who will stand their ground. It will take more than a piece of paper issued by a judge who is in the pocket of the corporate thugs who rule the world to dislodge them from their birthright."

When Jesus Came to Canada to Lead An
Indigenous Rebellion in the Broughton Archipelago

A discombobulated Corcoran shook his head in complete, total confusion, as he had never been talked to in that manner before, especially by a man like Jesus whom he considered his extreme inferior. He looked directly into Jesus' eyes with cold calculating determination. "You've made an enemy here today; this will be a big mistake. We are not people with whom you can trifle. This is a battle that you cannot and will not win."

Jesus, as always, was enjoying the verbal sparing; although, even an impartial observer, would deem it a mismatch of monumental proportions. Jesus continued his discourse. "Your modern world, for all its technological marvels, can be an uncomfortable, unfulfilling place to live because it is hollow. Capitalism spews out products, but it has no core values. The conservatives decry the loss of old time values, but still embrace the modern technology that makes a mockery of those values they want to protect. Anyway, what are they protecting? You are what they protect, and you represent the same system that let the feudal lords of the manner enslave people in service to an idea that only the privileged were worthy. You and your kind represent the evolution of despair."

Corcoran threw up his hands and turned to leave just as Jesus asked, "Are you not going to stay and have lunch with us? We can forget the acrimony and enjoy some smoked salmon and fry bread."

Shaking his head as he stormed out, Corcoran shouted back over his shoulder, "you are fucking crazy, all of you!"

Jesus, the chief and the elders laughed in unison, feeling that they had made it plain that they would not yield to those who wanted to rape and pillage the land. A stand had been made, and those who had suffered the indignity of the paper mill that had been forced on them by the government, felt invigorated that they had made a stand for justice.

Knowing that he must find out exactly what there was in the interior of the island that was so important, Jesus realized it was imperative to arrange for a mining engineer to assess the situation for the band, and there would be only one man who could find the right engineer. It was at this time that Jesus made a decision that would once again bring him into contact with that champion of justice, Aaron Adams.

Explaining what they needed to do, the chief told him to use the his phone, but Jesus, ever wary of the long reach of the corporate thugs and their government enablers wanted to use a more secure line that would likely be free of a tap.

When Jesus Came to Canada to Lead An
Indigenous Rebellion in the Broughton Archipelago

There was only one place on the island with a line that was secure and that was in the medical office, where Huyana Patrick would certainly agree to let him use her secure line. Thus it was that Huyana, who routed Jesus' call through the main medical headquarters in Victoria, B.C. became privy to what was going on. Although she asked if Jesus wanted privacy, the answer was a firm, "no, I want you to be privy to what is going on. Listen to the conversation, as the time will come when you will be a part of all that is about to occur here. You are as much a part of this community as those who were born here."

What follows is not a verbatim record of what was said. However, it approximates the conversation as nearly as possible.

When Aaron's phone rang, he was enjoying a noon-time cup of coffee at Andy's. Hearing the ring, he jumped up and headed across the hall to his office for the surprise of his life. "Adams Investigations," was said with a determined voice that seemed to exude confidence."

Jesus, thrilled to hear the voice of the man who rescued him from a house of evil, could not help but smile, knowing he was once again connecting with someone who, like him, was committed to justice and fairness. "My dear Aaron, how good to hear your voice."

Aaron immediately knew who it was. A smile creped across his lips as he said, "Oh no, I know I am headed for trouble. How the hell are you, or dare I ask? You locked up somewhere?"

"No my friend, I am still a free man, at least for the present." He then looked at Huyana and continued. "I am currently in a medical office with a beautiful young woman, whom I am sure you would love to cast your eyes upon; although, I know you are much too old for her. I am on a place called by the whites, Gilford Island. I need two things from you to assist me in helping a noble people stand against tyranny."

"Only two things?" sarcastically replied Aaron.

"Well, there might be some more down the road."

Aaron, almost laughing, replied, "Now that is the old Jesus I know. And I am sure you have no money to reimburse me."

Jesus, enjoying the banter, but realizing that time was of the essence, became more serious. "Have you ever known me to have any money? I may be able to get the band to reimburse you for your expenses, but I can't promise anything. We are in a critical situation here and need some answers fast."

"I am at your disposal and ready to help anyway I can," replied a now serious Aaron.

Jesus recounted, in front of a surprised Huyana, all that had recently occurred and ask if he could arrange for a reliable geologist to come to the island, and that if he could do some background checking on Trans World Industries before coming to the island for another assignment that would only be discussed with him in person.

Aaron got the phone number where Jesus could be reached and assured him that a geologist would be contacting Huyana within hours. As he hung up the phone, Aaron stared at the floor where he had lay with his beloved Mary dying in his arms, while he, himself, was almost near death, bleeding profusely from gunshot wounds. That had been six years ago – the last time he had seen Jesus. He had survived, but his beloved Mary had faded into oblivion. He had never believed in Jesus' divinity. Hell, he didn't believe in any religion period, but he did perceive the goodness of this man, and when Jesus had said that he was more the son of thunder than the son of God, Aaron had felt a simpatico with him, because Aaron knew that you could not defeat evil through peaceful means. Aaron understood that the poor and the oppressed of the world would never get justice by begging for it from the politicians. They would only achieve justice if they were willing to take up arms and fight to the death for it.

A call to a friend in Vancouver, British Columbia named Eric Hindle, who just happened to be a geologist and engineer, involved a few pleasantries before Aaron got down to business, and asked if he would be willing to make a trip to a place called Gilford Island. Hindle, a gruff and rugged man in his middle 60's had worked with Aaron years before when Aaron was investigating a coal company in Montana that had been ignoring safety measures and paying off government mining inspectors. Reminding Aaron that the correct name was Kwak'wala, he then said, "and I suppose as usual, you will expect me to do this gratis?"

"Eric, when I get paid, you'll get paid, but the person I am doing this for is not a man who parts with money easily, because I don't think he has ever had more than a few dollars in his pocket his whole life. However, we are doing this for a First Nations band, and I have been assured that he will try to secure some funding from them. I hope I am not imposing on you too much, old friend,"

Rather sarcastically, Eric replied, "yeah, you had to throw that old friend in there didn't you? I'm on it, Aaron. Will contact this Huyana woman when I get there. Any idea what I am looking for?"

"It's something big, something that the U.S. government is interested in, which means it can't be anything that will benefit mankind, but rather hinder it. The company involved is Trans World Industries."

Now immensely interested, Hindle shouted, "goddamn, it can't be good. Those bastards have left a wasteland of toxic materials all across the globe. They rape the land and leave the mess behind while they saunter off to their next environmental disaster."

"I am running a check on them. You know anything about their top echelon? Anything at all would help. Right now I am pretty much in the dark about the while thing."

Eric replied with candour and frankness. "CEO is Harold Frommer. The guy is a major billionaire asshole born with a silver spoon in his mouth who thinks the privilege of birth makes him something special. He has big-time connections all over Washington. Can't say the President is in his pocket, but plenty of the President's advisers are. Pick the Senator and Frommer is connected, except for a hand full that are in nobody's pocket, and I do mean a hand full – the ones who have no clout anyway, because they are actually there to serve the people."

Aaron, always one who enjoyed facing off against the powerful and wealthy who thought they should be exalted, asked, "anyone else I should know about?"

There are a slew of assholes that lick Frommer's boots. Guy named Lon Corcoran is a VP and is persona non grata in indigenous communities all over the world, because he is the lead man who opens up the exploitation. Gets signatures on the dotted line by hook and crook, never revealing the truth of the company's intentions. Alton Jordon and Patterson McCord, two demons of darkness who lead the raping of the land. Plenty of others, but those are the primary culprits of corruption who run the show."

"O.K. I am off to Seattle to run a few checks, and I may see you on the island if you stick around until I get there. Share whatever you have, and please don't laugh when I tell you this, with a man named Jesus."

Eric nearly fell off his chair as he said through laughter, "You do mean Heh-soos, don't you?"

A flustered Aaron expected the reaction he got. "Eric, call him whatever you want. When you meet him, believe me, you will understand. The name is of little importance. It is the man who uses it who will impress you."

Eric could not refrain from saying, "sure, good-bye Moses," as he hung up.

Aaron knew that he could depend on Eric. He packed a bag and got a ticket for Seattle, where he planned to see Harold Frommer and find out just what was really up. He could not explain why he was doing all this, but he knew that he simply couldn't say no to the man calling himself Jesus. He had tried it before, and it just didn't work.

As Aaron was winging his way to Seattle, Eric had gotten an old pilot buddy with a float plane, Ben Freeman, in Campbell River on Vancouver Island to make the forty minute flight to Kwak'wala where the two men strolled into the medical clinic and there sat the viciously beautiful Huyana Patrick. Delighted at the magnificence of the woman before them, the two older men were acting like giddy teenage boys who had just gotten their first glimpse of real, live titties. They were fumbling their words, but finally Eric managed to get out, "we are here to see a man calling himself Jesus about checking out a part of the island that Trans World Industries is interested in mining."

Huyana, who was used to men fawning over her, especially over her voluminous breasts, smiled and said, "come with me and I will take you to him. I assume that the man named Aaron Adams is not with you?"

Eric, taken with her mischievously provocative smile, while Ben remained silently mesmerized, said, "No, he will be coming shortly, but I am to meet Jesus and arrange to be taken to the site. I have a few tools with me in the plane for assessing what is there."

Huyana, standing and picking up her keys, said, "I will take you to Jesus."

As always, meeting Jesus the first time was an experience that you simply never got over. After getting materials from the plane, Eric and Ben followed Huyana to Jesus' small cabin. Huyana had grown fond of Jesus, and although she had great reverence for him as a man of compassion, integrity and honour, she felt that he was more of a rebel-rouser than anything else, and that he was, perhaps, leading the good people of Kwak'wala into a quagmire of trouble by encouraging them to stand against a powerful corporation like TWI. She was a woman who had great reverence for the lifestyle lived by these people who had not fallen prey to the evils of greed, but she feared the path upon which they were now headed.

When Jesus Came to Canada to Lead An
Indigenous Rebellion in the Broughton Archipelago

Standing against a corporation with powerful
allies in both governments was tantamount to
economic and social suicide.

When he opened the well-worn door, Eric and
Ben's fascination with Huyana came to an abrupt
end. Before the two was a simple looking man,
but there was an aura about him as he stood there
in the doorway smiling at the three of them.
"Come in, please," he said as he made a swift,
determined turn with an air of confidence. There
seemed to be a celestial glow about him, not
physically, but psychologically. He pointed at the
sofa, urging the men to take a seat. He looked at
Eric and said, "You are Aaron's friend?"

"Yes, I am extremely privileged to call him my
friend."

Jesus said, "You could not have a better friend,
Eric. He is a man who rescued me from a den of
evil, when all others had given up hope. He is
relentless in the fight against tyranny. And who is
this with you?"

"This is my pilot, Ben Freeman."

"I appreciate you gentleman coming so quickly.
Time is critical in finding out what lies out there
in the wilderness that is so important to Trans
World Industries. I will arrange for you to be

taken to the place of interest. I hope you can solve the mystery for us."

Eric, a self-assured man when it came to his field of endeavour, was determined in his response. "I absolutely assure you that if the answer is within the purview of a geologist or an engineer, I am the man for the job. Get me to this place, and I will have a definitive answer for you as quickly as possible. I have no doubt that if Trans World is interested it is of major importance and probably worth billions."

Looking at Huyana, Jesus asked "would you get the chief? There is enough daylight left for him to lead Eric to the place of interest."

Jesus stayed behind but the three men hiked into the forested wilderness, while the bright sunshine that covered the usually fog shrouded island offered an opportunity to get the answer sooner than expected.

After about four hours of intense walking, they arrived at the clearing where the helicopter had landed. The sun began to fade below the horizon, and a full moon hung high in the heavens with a red glow dancing about it from the descending sun's reflection. The exhausted men stood in the clearing and were preparing to camp for the night when the sun disappeared and the bright, white light of the moon disappeared behind a dark cloud, bathing the whole area in a subdued darkness. Eric saw it first, then the other two. It was like a mass of fireflies flittering about on the hillside; only their luminous glow was a light blue, not white, that twinkled incessantly in the darkness. However, it was Eric who knew what it was. He ecstatically cried, "I don't need any gauges or metres. Good god-almighty, I have never seen the blue glow that luminous. Gentlemen, emanating from the hillside is the most radio-active substance in the world. That hillside has an incredibly intense seam of polonium in it."

Chief Harry was bewildered by what they were seeing. "And just what in the hell is polonium?"

"Polonium my dear chief, is a trigger. Without it, there could be no atomic blast. You are looking at what ignites a nuclear bomb!"

Ben, mesmerized by the glowing blue particles that seemed to be dancing about on the hill, said, "Are we in any danger?"

"No, that is only miniscule tailings emanating through the ground, about the size of a pin head, but they glow as a result of the intense heat from the radiation. The real vein would be much deeper, but this is an incredible find, as the triggers for nuclear weapons have to be constantly replaced. They have a very short life span, so there is always a search on for polonium. Chief, this could be worth billions to your tribe. I mean billions.

The chief, not at all impressed with the word billions, had another take on what they had discovered. "Or, it could mean an end to our way of life and the desecration of this place that we hold sacred. It could mean that our people bend to the will of those who want to destroy rather than preserve."

Ben interjected, "yes, the world has enough nuclear weapons. The United States can destroy the world 10 times over. Does it need to double that to feel safe? Is there no end to the madness?"

Eric, the cold, calculating scientist, said, "That is far beyond my realm of expertise. All I know is there is obviously a huge vein of polonium in that hillside, and once it is cut open, there can be no containment. The island is doomed when the hillside is breeched. Gentleman, Trans World Industries supplies all the nuclear triggers for the nuclear weapons in both the USA and the UK. They and the U.S. government, probably supported by the Canadian government, will do anything possible to procure this polonium that is so close to the USA."

When Jesus Came to Canada to Lead An
Indigenous Rebellion in the Broughton Archipelago

A dejected chief unrolled his blanket, and while most people would be in a state of euphoria with dollar signs dancing in their heads, all he could say was, "we will start back early in the morning and share the bad news with my people. This is disastrous."

CHAPTER 4
WE FIGHT! WE FIGHT! WE FIGHT!

Workers of the world awaken!
Break your chains, demand your rights.
All the wealth you make is taken
by tyrannical, exploiting parasites.
Shall you kneel in deep submission
from your cradle to your grave?
Is the height of your ambition
to be a good and willing slave?

While the news of what was in the interior flowed through the village like a raging wildfire, Aaron Adams had arrived in Seattle. He immediately called Huyana, who, by now, had already developed an affinity for Aaron just from the stories she had heard from Eric and Jesus about his exploits in defence of the downtrodden of the world. Although he was a man in his sixties and she was not even 30, she felt like he must be a man who cut a dashing figure. She had no need of a man in her life, especially one as old as Aaron, but she did, with great anticipation, look forward to meeting an individual who had garnered so much respect from two men she knew, one of whom she looked upon as a true defender of the people she loved. Jesus was an individual who could arouse the emotions of all with whom he came in contact, and Huyana was a woman who had become physically and emotionally attracted to him. However, Jesus was quick to rebuff her with an explanation that he was a man who was beyond physical attraction to either sex. It did not mean he did not find her attractive and appealing, but he had other priorities that made physical love of no interest to him. He was a wanderer in search of causes to serve, and that precluded any entanglements of a romantic nature.

In fact, Huyana was not the only village woman attracted to Jesus. Several had indicated their interest, but found that he was a man who transcended the carnal instincts, while, at the same time, making those women, and even one man, who was attracted to him, feel that he was not rebuking them because they were not alluring, but because he had other, more important things, to accomplish. His refusal of carnal pleasures perplexed the people of the village, who were sexually well-adjusted, especially since he only mildly intonated that he was more than a mere mortal man. He never once said that he was the son of God, only that he was the Son of Thunder, who would bow before no man, and do all he could to protect those on the island who stood with him against the tyranny of a world where those who were economically well-off ruled mercilessly.

The chief had called a meeting in the long house that following night so everyone would have an opportunity to discuss what should be done. Huyana, who had very quickly become a respected member of the community, was invited, as was Eric Hindle and Ben Freeman.

On the phone, Huyana, after telling Aaron what had been discovered by Hindle and its significance, encouraged him to get to the island for the meeting of the people, as they might well decide to take TWI up on an offer for the land and; therefore, any further investigation might be unnecessary.

Aaron with a note of sarcasm in his voice, said, "And what does Jesus think?"

Sighing a bit, Huyana hesitated and then answered rather tepidly. "We both know that his powers of persuasion will always win out with people who are genuinely compassionate and caring. Yet, there are those here who have been affected by the greed that is so prevalent in the world outside of this island. Money is a great inducement, even to those who proclaim fealty to a higher calling."

"I haven't met any of the people of Kwak'wala, but I bet they will stand against TWI in defence of their homeland."

"I hope you are right," replied Huyana.

Aaron said that he would try to make it in time for the meeting. He hung up, and after a call to TWI, headed toward a meeting with the Vice President for International Affairs. Although Lon Corcoran had just flew back in, he had agreed to see Aaron, because when he mentioned it was in reference to what had been discovered on the island, Corcoran saw it, as perhaps, a possibility to get some leverage he could use in negotiations.

The TWI Tower dominated the downtown Seattle landscape. Yet, Aaron could barely see it peeping through the dense fog that enveloped the city, almost as if the building was trying to hide from the inquisitiveness of a man who might somehow penetrate the veneer of respectability and expose the heartless souls of the people who lived a life of luxury off the labour of those whom they looked upon as chattel in their pursuit of profits.

Only the top tower was visible in the distance as Aaron felt an almost demonic manifestation lay before him in the thick, dark fog. There was life-destroying decay that seemed to be emanating from the small green part of the tower that peeked though the fog, the decay promulgated by those who preyed on the weary. There was an inherent evil in the building. It reminded Aaron of the time he had to face the evil in the darkness at Hopkins House in one of his most famous cases.

When Jesus Came to Canada to Lead An Indigenous Rebellion in the Broughton Archipelago

The implacable Seattle weather was almost Dickens-like in its presence. The fog was now so thick that it could have, indeed, been the London of Charles Dickens. Aaron felt as if he was in the same dense fog described in the Dickens novel, *Bleak House*, as he seemed to have to almost feel his way in through the thick mist. He kept blinking his eyes to clear the mist from them.

In the intense, almost sullen darkness, the bright, flittering red tips of cigarettes could be distinguished, but only as the smokers sucked the poisonous fumes into their lungs, yielding, like most Americans, to the manipulations of just another of the many malfeasant corporations that dispensed misery in products that were manufactured to be addictive. The drug dealers were evil, because they dispensed their death on street corners, but corporations did it in bright shiny stores with the approval of the government they controlled.

People were beginning to bump into one another in a general infection of ill temper, and losing their foot-hold on the street. The fog was everywhere and it seemed to be actually scaling the buildings, slowly inching upward as if it was going to engulf everything in the city. Yes, the fog was creeping into every nook and cranny, fog on the sidewalk, fog on the building, fog slithering into taxis when the doors were opened, fog lying out on the grass of the nearby park and hovering in the doorways and alleyway, fog drooping on the expensive topcoats worn by all the executives on their way to their little cubicles that defined their lives of quiet desperation, fog in the eyes and throats of the old people forced out of retirement scurrying to their jobs of anguish caused by a government that had no heart or soul, fog in the archways of buildings, where those who lived on the streets in the land of plenty were wearily gathering up all their worldly belongings and tossing them into a shopping cart for another day of scavenging, fog cruelly pinching the rosy cheeks of the young women headed to work in the clothing stores where they could not afford to buy the clothes they sold to the privileged, fog peeping over the bridge in the distance in front of the TWI Tower, which now was coming into view. The fog around it seemed to beckon to Aaron, beckon him to enter into the portal of despicable evil of the foulest kind. It was the kind of evil perpetrated by a succubus that devoured all before it. This was the evil of a society that promoted greed as an enviable trait; the evil of a society that had no compassion and no depth of character. Yes, the fog was dirty and malevolent.

As Aaron opened the huge gold encrusted door to enter the building, it seemed a fitting trophy of excess to that which signified the very worst in all of men's basest instincts.

When Jesus Came to Canada to Lead An
Indigenous Rebellion in the Broughton Archipelago

In the opulently decorated lobby with glittering lights that shielded the building from the darkness, Aaron turned to look out the huge plate glass windows at the thick, never-ending fog of despair that engulfed the poor people out there in the muck and mire of tribulation. Still, he had rather be out there with the real people, rather than in a monument to ravenous avarice. One of the minimum wage slaves who served the lords of finance greeted Aaron gregariously and asked if she could be of any assistance. She was just another throw-away commodity in a society dedicated to the preservation of privilege.

She called to see if it was alright for him to see one of the gods of the corporation on the 38th floor. Pointing him toward the executive elevator, in the typical insincere way that all corporate flunkies are instructed to act, she said, "Have a nice day, sir."

.

The greatest evil is not done in the sordid places that are described as seedy, squalid and disreputable, but in the opulent, well-appointed offices of those who run the corporations of America. In these clean, carpeted, warmed, well-lighted offices are efficient, confident men and women with finely tailored clothes and manicured nails who are somehow considered the elite of a society where those who actually do the work are dismissed as irrelevant.

When Jesus Came to Canada to Lead An Indigenous Rebellion in the Broughton Archipelago

Although the darkness of the fog outside prevailed, it was obvious that Lon Corcoran had a magnificent view of the harbour on a clear day. He did not even bother to get up to greet Aaron, just eased back in his five thousand dollar chair, dismissed his secretary with the wave of a hand and pointed at a thickly upholstered sofa for Aaron to take a seat on. He did not waste any time getting to the point. "So, I understand you want to talk to me about Gilford Island. We have a paper mill there. Keep it going not to make money, but as a convenience to the people who need a job. We are interested in doing a little mining there for some minerals that may prove to be valuable, but who knows. Hey, we take gambles, and sometimes we win. Sometimes we lose."

Aaron was going to enjoy this. He always found great pleasure in sparing with those who thought their money and power made them more exalted. "First, I have learned that the correct name is Kwak'wala. So out of respect for the people who have lived there for thousands of years, I will call it by the name they prefer, not the name their white oppressors gave it. Second, you and I know that this corporation, and most others, don't give a rat's ass about doing anything for anybody. Your only concern is the bottom line, and thanks to the government you have bought, you can even make money when the bottom line shows a loss. So don't play the benevolent corporation with me."

Taken aback by Aaron's lack of respect for him and his position, Corcoran moved forward in his chair and said, "what the hell you want Adams?"

"To tell you the truth, I just wanted to find out something about all the people who run this monument to greed and why all the interest in some small island with only a couple of hundred people on it. The paper mill on one end doesn't even employ any of them. You bring in white people from the mainland to do the work. Yet, suddenly you want to do some mining. Well, I sent a geologist over, and I now know that you have discovered polonium on the island. So, you see, I am just paying a courtesy call now to tell you that I am working for the band of natives there and the man who calls himself Jesus. I am sure you have met him."

Getting a disconcerted look on his face, Corcoran's veins in his neck and temples began to pulsate. "That goddamn guy Jesus is crazy. He thinks he is some kind of penny-anti guru who can manipulate those people and keep them from making millions of dollars. I'll pay you ten times what he is paying you just to go away."

Aaron was really going to enjoy this one. "Asshole, what is 10 times 0?

"What the hell you mean?"

When Jesus Came to Canada to Lead An
Indigenous Rebellion in the Broughton Archipelago

"Just what I said. What is 10 times 0? I'll help you. It is 0. That is what I am being paid. You don't have enough money to buy me. That is why I am an anachronism in a world of people who will sell their souls for a new car, a fancy home or a luxury vacation. Offer me a billion dollars, place it on the table, and I will throw it in your goddamn face. I can't be bought, and my guess is that neither can the people on Kwak'wala."

Corcoran was now on his feet and livid with anger. "Who do you think you are?"

"I'm the man who will, if you take one more step toward me, kick your fucking ass. Go ahead, take a step. Do it asshole."

Corcoran had never been talked to that way by any man, and he stood in silence, not sure what his next move would be. He was scared for one of the few times in his life. Jesus had not scared him with his flowery words, but Aaron had made his pulse rate quicken, not with indignation, but with fear.

Aaron moved toward the door, and as he did, Harold Frommer walked in, almost bumping into him.

Looking at Corcoran and seeing his reddened complexion, Frommer said, "What's going on?"

When Jesus Came to Canada to Lead An
Indigenous Rebellion in the Broughton Archipelago

Somewhat calmer now, Corcoran nodded his head toward Aaron and said, "Meet Aaron Adams. He is here as a representative of that lunatic on the island who is stirring all the people up."

Frommer, erect with a bit of a scowl on his face and a puffed out chest, was definitely a man who was impressed with himself. "So, Mr. Adams, I am sure you don't want to be unreasonable, we can arrange fair compensation, even relocation expenses and nice new homes for all the people on the island. We can even take care of any needs you might have."

Aaron's reply wasn't what Frommer expected, nor was it what he considered respectful for a man in his position. "Frommer, I think Mr. Corcoran will tell you I can't be bought. Neither is Jesus a man who will suckle from the tit of greed. As for the people of Kwak'wala, I have never met them, but my guess is that if my friend is going to bat for them they probably are not going to supplicate themselves to a society that bases everything on dollars and cents. You represent evil of the foulest kind in a country that aggrandizes individuals like you who rape, pillage and plunder the land and use people as chattel in pursuit of wealth, which you think makes you exalted above all others. The truth is that you are a parasite who lives off the labour of those for whom you have nothing but disdain."

Grossly offended by Aaron's manner, Frommer started to interrupt, but Aaron just continued. "Don't interrupt me. You have nothing to say that I want to hear. I am sure that you will have a battery of lawyers filing all kinds of writs over the next few days. If I know Jesus, believe me, you are going to need more than a piece of paper to get those people off the island. You better come with an armada of ships and hands filled with weapons. Yet, you will find his weapons more powerful than any you have, because he fights with words that stir the very souls of those whom you oppress. This will be a fight like you have never had before, because this person is like no one you have ever gone up against. He is mightier than the U.S. government. Talk to them and see. They fear him like no other man on earth. Even the church fears him, because he is a man who knows the only solution to the world's problems is revolution by the very people you, this nation and the church enslave to an idea that is as morally bankrupt as all of you are. The last time I fought by his side, I lost the love of my life, but she died in my arms, safe in the knowledge that she had served him well. People will gladly die for him, because he offers them a life free of the bondage that most of humanity humbly submits to everyday in subservience to people like you who are parasitic capitalists with no compassion or appreciation for those who toil in your sweatshops of misery and despair."

Frommer, jaw dropped from shock, could not utter a word as Aaron turned and boldly walked out the door, his head held high, knowing that he had once again stood tall against a member of the privileged class that sucked the life out of a nation. Aaron was a one man verbal wrecking machine, and if things got really bad, he was also a bashing, battering, bruising, shattering, smashing, splitting weapon of physical destruction.

The reunion with Jesus was an emotional one, the two of them reflecting on the death of Mary Madison, whom they had both loved dearly. Putting his arms around Aaron as they walked to the clinic, Jesus stopped and introduced Aaron to everyone they passed. When the chief met him, he said something that made Aaron swell with pride. "Mr. Adams, you have a great admirer in our mutual friend here. He tells me that he got you into a lot of trouble, but you never wavered in your devotion to him. We have need of a man like you to help us prepare for the coming turmoil we must face in dealing with Trans World Industries. That is, unless our people decide to take the money and turn their backs on this place we have called home for thousands of years."

"From what I have observed," Aaron said as he turned and looked at Jesus, "you have a man on your side who will arouse the instincts of pride and righteous indignation to a fever pitch."

When Jesus Came to Canada to Lead An
Indigenous Rebellion in the Broughton Archipelago

The chief smiled and said, "He has already done that among the people. We still can't figure out who he is. He is a man who never answers a question directly about himself. He seems to relish keeping us guessing about just who he really is. All we know is that he is a man who has reached out with compassion to us all, and made our welfare his chief concern. We have never had a more devoted champion."

Jesus had been both damned and praised over the years. In fact, there had been more ridicule and damnation than praise. Yet, he entertained no delusions as to why he had been damned by so many. Even those poor souls who had been imprisoned by a system of economic and religious servitude often turned their backs on the one man who saw through their enslavement to the masters of deceit. He had been betrayed so often by so many over the years that he never entertained any illusions about the base instincts of most humans. Yet, he was now in a place that was almost completely void of the materialistic obsessions of a world where happiness was defined by how many material possessions one acquired. All Jesus could manage in response to the chief's praise was a modest, "I think you overestimate my effect on people. Had I been that effective over the years, the world would not be a place of constant conflict and compassion would be a commonplace occurrence rather than the rarity it seems to be."

When Jesus Came to Canada to Lead An
Indigenous Rebellion in the Broughton Archipelago

The chief joined them as they walked toward the clinic. Those readers who have read some of the other books about the adventures of Aaron Adams know that he is an aging former Casanova and worshipper of women in all shapes, forms, ages and sizes. His lasciviousness as a younger man kept him in a constant state of arousal, but now, as a man in his early 60's, his libido had diminished like a wilting hydrangea drooping under the mid-day sun. In fact, he often thought that if he were not an atheist that he would drop to his knees and pray for an erection. He was about to have the prayer he never spoke to that celestial entity, in which he did not believe, answered.

Walking into the clinic, Aaron, who had never been one to only judge a woman by her outward beauty, beheld someone who glowed with not only outward attractiveness, but whose very aura shined so brightly that the inner grace and allure overwhelmed that which was obvious to the naked eye.

How does one adequately describe that which is indescribable in the mind of one who was as overwhelmed with awe as Aaron was? Huyana's outward and inner beauty has been alluded to previously, but not from the perspective of the man who was now standing in her presence. Aaron had briefly spoken with her on the phone and discerned that she was, indeed, an attractive woman, as much in the way of understanding a person's makeup can be perceived through the briefest of conversations. Face-to-face encounters are not always the best judge of a person's inner depth. Aaron could not help but longingly survey the physical magnificence of the woman before him. However, she emitted a beauty far beyond the physical manifestation that made Aaron actually, much to his surprise; get an immediate erection that was so quick and so overwhelming that he actually had to put his hand in his pocket to adjust his swelling member. That, which he had thought no longer possible, was actually happening.

Huyana's face was not the perfect, symmetrically plastic edifice that proscribed what was beauty in the modern Madison Avenue version of alluring attractiveness that air-brushed flawless perfection onto models who offered an image that could only be purchased from the capitalists who had made beauty a commodity to be sold by corporations and purchased by those whose brains had been sufficiently massaged into pliable, manipulated mush by mass media that promulgated the idea that women were to be objects of desire. Her nose was a bit prominent. Her cheekbones were high. Her lips were thick, full and ripe. Her chin was a bit rounded and did not jut out to expose a trim, thin neckline, but rather a muscularly toned tautness of dark flesh.

When Jesus Came to Canada to Lead An
Indigenous Rebellion in the Broughton Archipelago

Still, she was as beautiful as a blossoming lotus flower during autumn. Scanning down at her voluptuous, huge, perfectly globular shaped breasts that were obviously braless under her smock top based upon the erect, protruding nipples made Aaron wish he was a baby again, so that he could suckle upon them as she held him in her arms. Damn, he was getting harder, as wild erotic thoughts raced through his mind.

It was obvious to all there what was happening. Aaron even felt a slight ejaculatory movement in his pants, as Huyana let a mischievous smile creep across her lips almost as if she wanted to wrap them around Aaron's member. Hell, he thought to himself, just my imagination. This young woman would want nothing to do with an old, worn-out, useless man who had left his virility behind in the sands of time.

It had only been a few seconds, but seemed like an eternity when Huyana said, "I am so pleased to meet you Mr. Adams. Funny, but you are exactly as I pictured you in our phone conversation."

The intonations of her words were so melodic that they gave pleasure to Aaron's ears. Looking upon her magnificent, long, lustrous, dark black hair shimmering in the dancing sunlight that peeped through the blinds of the nearby window made Aaron want to gently caress it.

When Jesus Came to Canada to Lead An
Indigenous Rebellion in the Broughton Archipelago

Aaron slowly gazed down from her sheltering, shimmering hair, and peered at the warm magnificence of the globular twin peaks of desire. He thought that if he were between them he would let out sobs of satisfaction as if in a trance of contentment where he would forever rest in complete blissfulness in their warmth.

The chief, aware of what was happening, snapped his fingers in front of Aaron's face. "You're embarrassing her, Aaron. We have all gazed at her in the way you are, but, believe me, she has far greater beauty than that which is on the surface."

Huyana, never one to be overtly shy about her sexiness, smiled and playfully admonished the chief. "Chief, let me enjoy it while I can. The day will come when I am old, wrinkled, hereditarily obese and unappealing. I hope that within time, Mr. Adams will realize that I am more than large breasts, pouty lips and a shapely derriere. Besides, he is likely to have a heart attack at his age if he got hold of a wild woman like me."

Aaron, somewhat embarrassed, and feeling his erection wilt, said "I apologize. I am not usually that blatant in my perusal of attractive women. And you are right; I realize that you are much more than just what I see on the surface. I look forward to getting to know you better."

When Jesus Came to Canada to Lead An
Indigenous Rebellion in the Broughton Archipelago

Jesus, one who never passed up an opportunity for some levity, had a sage comment. "I know Aaron, and believe me, he may appear contrite, but watch yourself around him. Like most men, even though his opportunities have diminished with age, he still glorifies in what used to be, rather than what is. His mind is willing, and it is filled with memories of conquests that flutter about like fireflies on a warm night. The trouble is, the mind, like all men's minds, is that of a 15 year old, but the body has not stayed the same age."

They all shared a good laugh, and Huyana, who stayed in the cabin adjacent to the clinic, told Aaron that he could bunk in the four bed ward since there were no patients there. Aaron gladly accepted and the chief reminded him to be at the meeting in the longhouse. Huyana excused herself as a patient came in complaining of a fever. The three men walked back to the do dock, where Aaron had left his suitcase. His two companions mercilessly made fun of him for the way he acted in Huyana's presence and told him that he was far too old a man to handle such a high-spirited woman.

Aaron outwardly agreed with them, but secretly, deep within the recesses of a mind that still longed for frantic fornication; he was asking himself, "what if, what if?"

When Jesus Came to Canada to Lead An
Indigenous Rebellion in the Broughton Archipelago

Huyana showed up at the ward to escort Aaron to the meeting. He had showered, dressed and was ready to see if the people of the community were as committed to fighting TWI as Jesus was. Huyana was dressed in jeans and a loose fitting sweater. Perhaps she thought it best to hide the curvaceous nature of her body from Aaron in order to prevent him from being overly aroused. Maybe she thought, as a medical professional, she was duty bound to try and prevent a heart attack.

Yet, the alluring beauty of some women goes far beyond mere physical attributes. Huyana simply did not understand that, even in old age, she would never be able to mask her magnificent, alluring beauty that was more than just physical in nature. It was the confidence she wore, the defiant sway of her hips, the way her hair softly fluttered about, the intensity of her dark eyes, and above all, the passionate smile that was the doorway to her heart, where all the dreams a man could image dwelled in grandeur that mirrored the soul of inner beauty that glowed like a strong beacon in the darkest of nights, lighting the way to paradise.

The meeting was conducted by the chief, with Jesus meekly sitting by, not saying a word. He was a man who respected the council of all who bore the anxieties of their people like a burden of glory, refusing to consider their own needs before the needs of others.

When Jesus Came to Canada to Lead An Indigenous Rebellion in the Broughton Archipelago

All 205 people of the village were present, several in traditional dress as a matter of pride, and not a one of them, young or old, spoke in favour of accepting money to give up the land where there ancestors were buried. One man, probably in his 80's, stood and declared to much applause, "We should not sell our birthright. However, how do we fight against the modern state that is controlled by corporations that have no reverence for anything but profit? We have a government in Ottawa that kowtows to our southern neighbour like we are the 51st state. Can we expect any justice from a government that wants to turn back the clock of human social progress? I think not. I believe that we will be ignored by those who look upon us as blights upon the land they covet. We cannot afford the lawyers to fight these giants of evil intentions. Nor do we have the weapons to stand against the police, and the military, which are nothing but instruments in service to the forces that surround us with their creeping greed that inflicts mankind like an ancient plague. There is evil among us, and I know not how to fight it. I have lived my life, and have little time left. So, I should not render a decision affecting the young people who are our hope and inspiration for a better tomorrow and a return to ways that we were forced to give up as a result of the government and religious organizations trying to make us white. I carry deep scars from the evil of those who know no restraint.

When Jesus Came to Canada to Lead An
Indigenous Rebellion in the Broughton Archipelago

It is a time of my youth that was mercilessly robbed by those who thought me an incorrigible, heathen savage. However, I very quickly found out who the real savages are, and I shall gladly die battling against the evil intentions of those who want to enslave us to the God of money they all worship."

Then, he turned to the quiet and contemplative Jesus, pointing at him. "This man came among us and became one of us. He bares a name that I had grown to abhor, because as a child in a residential school, I had Jesus beat into me with rock-hard sticks from arbutus trees. Until he showed up, I trembled with rage at the very mention of the name Jesus. Yet, this man claims no divinity and drops to his knees before no man or God. He is someone I have grown proud to call friend, and I say his name, not the name of the one I was beat into worshipping, with pride, for it rings true to the great spirit of the nation to which we belong." He again pointed directly at Jesus. "Give is your wise council Jesus. We appeal to you to guide us through this difficult time. Show us the path, not to heavenly salvation, but to the salvation of our beloved land."

Jesus, confidently smiling, rose from his seat at the table in the centre of the longhouse, where a crackling fire was blazing, and the smoke sweeping upward toward the hole cut in the roof

to allow it to filter out. He touched the old man on
the shoulder as a way of saying thanks for the kind
words he had directed towards him.

"I tell you all that the most holy man is one who
stands against the tyranny of those who oppress
his friends and neighbours. I cannot guarantee you
eternal life anymore than I can promise you that
the moon and the stars will come out every night. I
can promise you that those who do not stand
against tyranny do not live. They only exist. I
come not to meekly bring peace to this small
corner of the world, because peace is not achieved
by turning the other cheek. He who turns the other
cheek only gets slapped on it. I come with a sword
of indignation to sweep away those who laugh in
the face of compassion and fairness."

Jesus walked toward Aaron, who was sitting
next to Huyana and looked down at them as he
continued. "This woman comes to heal the sick
and to uplift the afflicted. She offers relief from
physical pain, because she has a heart of gold that
deplores suffering in all forms. She tries to relieve
the psychological suffering as well, but you all
suffer from deep psychological scars that will not
be healed by medicine, or even the compassion
and knowledge of this good woman. The scars
will only be healed by standing against the evil
manifested by those who have no reverence for the
land and no compassion for their fellow man."

When Jesus Came to Canada to Lead An
Indigenous Rebellion in the Broughton Archipelago

He walked over to Aaron and placed his hand on his shoulder. "This is a man who came to this place simply because I asked for his help. He has paid a great price in his life for helping me and helping others, including the loss of loved ones, because he has always stood against despotism, domination and terror by those who think they are privileged and entitled by virtue of birth, wealth or position to be exalted above all others. He, like me, knows that the most exalted are the least among us in terms of material wealth. The man who ploughs the field, the woman who scrubs the floors, the person who asks you if you want French Fries with your hamburger, or that elderly greeter who welcomes you to Wal-Mart are more valuable than all the corporate CEO's who have ever walked into a board room. They are people who actually work for their sustenance. They do not get rich on the backs of those who toil for minimum wage in the factories, offices and fields of despair. I say to you all that the time has come to stand against the tyranny of the 1%. Do not bend before the wind of greed that is sweeping across the world like a hurricane."

He walked back to the centre of the longhouse, moved toward the large entrance door, so all could see him. "How can you buy or sell the sky, the warmth of the land? The whole idea is abhorrent. You cannot sell the freshness of the air and the sparkle of the water. They are beyond price."

When Jesus Came to Canada to Lead An Indigenous Rebellion in the Broughton Archipelago

Aaron could not help but smile as he looked at Huyana and said, "He is just getting warmed up."

She smiled back and replied, "I have seen him in action. I know."

"Every part of the earth is sacred. Every shining pine needle, every sandy shore, every mist in the dark woods, every clear and humming insect is holy in the memory and experience of people. The sap which courses through the trees carries the memory and experience of your forefathers. The corporations and the people who serve them have no reverence for the earth that you see as your mother who provides you with all you need for survival. They see it as a commodity that must be used for the generation of wealth. But you, you are part of the earth and it is part of you. The perfumed flowers are your sisters, the deer, the horse, the great eagle, these are your brothers. So, when the chief of a corporation sends word that he wishes to buy your land, he asks for that which is beyond a price in dollars and cents. It is a price that tears your heart and soul out and tramples it in the pit of greed. This land is your heaven. You know that the heaven you were told existed in the sweet bye and bye if you would only bow in reverence to Jesus cannot compare to this place you call home. This land is scared. Embrace it with love and take it to your bosom. It has nurtured you, and now it is time for you to protect it from harm like you would a child. The shining water that moves in babbling streams and gentle flowing rivers is not just water but the blood of your beloved ancestors. It is your children's birthright that these greedy people want to buy. Listen to the streams that whisper the sacred names of those loved ones who have gone before you, entrusting this land to your loving care. Do not lose faith with them. They have passed a torch to you. Keep it burning brightly for future generations who should be taught to revere the land."

Jesus strolled back toward the centre of the longhouse as everyone seemed to cling to each word of wisdom that rolled from his lips. "The corporations treat the earth as if it was a garbage dump. They are run by people whose appetite will devour the earth and leave behind only a useless wasteland. In a world that is 2/3rds water, these are the people who want to make you pay for the water you drink. They want to pave the earth with concrete and fill it with belching engines of pollution like the paper mill on the other side of the island that is a plight on this paradise. Most of you have been to the cities, and they are a deplorable sight that pains yours eyes. There is no quiet place in the cities. No place to hear the unfurling of leaves in spring, or the rustle of an insect's wings. And what is there to life if a man cannot hear the lonely cry of a whippoorwill or the arguments of the frogs around a pond at night. I prefer the soft sounds of the rustling wind darting over the ocean, the cleansing of the clear rain and the fresh smell of scented pine to the honking of car horns, the acid rain that poisons the city and the acrid smell of decay that permeates the air in the jungles of concrete and steel that are prisons without walls."

Jesus walked to a group of youngsters who were enthralled by his eloquence. "My dear children, I fear that you will become trapped in bondage to a life in the cities where no notice of the air you breathe is taken, where you step over those who lie upon the pavement, discarded and broken by a system of economic servitude and psychological manipulation by the media that pushes ostentatious consumption as the only path to happiness, where you will become numb to the stench of man-made poverty as a result of a system that protects those at the top at the expense of those at the bottom."

He then walked from the children and with a hand darting through the air; he swirled around with a sweeping motion, taking in the entire congregation that was in the building. "I say to all of you that the ground beneath your feet is the ashes of your fathers, mothers, grandfathers and grandmothers. Respect the land that is rich with the lives of your kin. Know that whatever befalls the earth befalls you. What you sow is what you will reap. If you spit upon the ground, you spit upon your ancestors. This earth under you cannot be bought and sold if you refuse to budge. They may come to physically remove you. You may shed your blood into the rich earth in its defence. But in your perishing, you will shine brightly, fired by the strength of your convictions. I say to each and every one of you that I stand ready to fight the forces of darkness. I say to you once again, I come with a sword of indignation to sweep away those who laugh in the face of compassion and fairness."

In unison, the entire throng arose and shouted, "We fight! We fight! We fight!

CHAPTER 5
JUSTICE OR DEATH

Religion promises rewards in heaven
for the meek who toil in obscurity.
But why must they know the full fury
of hell on earth to reach such a just reward?
Is it not better to stand in hell
than to kneel before tyrants to get to heaven?
Every word of mine shall be fire and action
in defiance of those who laugh at compassion.

With disdain, I throw down my gauntlet
full in the face of the tyrants of despair.
I shall struggle for the collapse
of the giant behemoths of misery.
So, that like a god, I shall walk boldly
through the ruins of their kingdom,
head held high like a god among men,
free from the tyranny of greed.

_____The Son of Thunder

Aaron and Huyana walked home after a brief discussion with Jesus about the next step. It was decided that they would simply wait for the next move by TWI, but Aaron, a man who had seen in combat how preparation was essential to survival, encouraged Jesus to give some thought to how the people should be prepared for any eventuality in the coming battle.

When Jesus Came to Canada to Lead An
Indigenous Rebellion in the Broughton Archipelago

On the way home, Aaron casually asked Huyana why she had decided to come to such an isolated place. Huyana would forever endear herself to him with her answer. "I have been married twice. Once to a man who was a revered figure in the entertainment industry. I mingled, at a young age, with movie stars and the crème de la crème of Hollywood society. It was a life of shallowness that was destroying my soul. I was his possession, not his wife, and all his energy and money went into impressing those who themselves were caught up in the same cycle of ostentatious displays that they thought defined how important they were. I simply woke up one morning and told him that I could no longer function in a world of illusions based on the aggrandizement of self. I walked out of his life just as I came into it, with my self-respect and pride restored and absolutely no money, because he was not only broke in spirit, he was finically bankrupt. I foolishly married again, within a year, to a brute who thought I was a substitute for a punching bag. After a few months, I suggested that he go to a sporting goods store and get a real punching bag. And thus, I decided to abstain from relationships, return to school and do something worthwhile with my life."

Aaron, impressed with her resilience and devotion, could not help asking a question that was actually pretty irrelevant. "So, you have sworn off relationships?"

A devilish grin crept across her lips. "I said I gave up relationships. I didn't say I had given up men. They do serve a useful purpose on occasion."

They both laughed. Aaron took her by the arm in the darkness and led her toward her cabin, feeling a certain pride just being allowed to accompany her home. He felt privileged to just be in her presence. Even though he had experienced erotic arousal when he first met her, he now realized that she would have no sexual interest in a man of his age, but he was so thankful that Jesus had called him, giving him an opportunity to meet an extraordinary woman.

Huyana stood at her door and thanked Aaron for accompanying her home, telling him that the door to the clinic was unlocked as locks simply were not needed on the island. She raised herself up on her tiptoes and gently kissed him on the cheek. He was giddy with excitement as he walked around the cabin toward the clinic. He reached up and felt his cheek where she had kissed him. It was still slightly moist from her succulent lips.

Aaron basked in the simple glory of knowing they were now friends. Aaron's age might have been a barrier to physical love, but the love between two people who had a shared purpose was budding like a tulip springing to life in the spring sun. He found himself over the next few days taking advantage of every opportunity offered to be with her, even just simply watching her at work. Meantime, there was much anxiety among the people as they awaited contact from TWI. During this time, Jesus and Aaron spent a great deal of time just strolling on the beach in silence, but there was a contemplative melancholy manifesting itself in Jesus that finally exploded into a fury one day as he stood in the very spot where he had met Octave Joe and become entwined with the first of those whom he now felt a need to assist in the coming storm that would, no doubt, lead to calamitous consequences as a result of the people refusing to bend to the ill winds of tribulation and despair. As he looked out upon the calm waters of the strait, Jesus turned to his friend and let a torrent of anger pour from deep within his heart. "I deplore vengeance and wrath, but I cannot contain the anger I feel against those who have no compassion for these people and their way of life. I am slow to anger, but there is a great fury building within me to summon a raging storm of retribution against those who want to crush hope and justice under the jack-booted feet of greed. I have a raging whirlwind within me that could destroy everything within its path. Yet, I do not want to see innocents suffer, as they always do, when a war of words and physical conflict rage in an unrestrained clash of opposing ideals. This affair will not end with a faint whimper but with a raging torrent of anguish and misery."

When Jesus Came to Canada to Lead An
Indigenous Rebellion in the Broughton Archipelago

Jesus looked out at the distance where clouds were beginning to form on the horizon. "The billowing clouds are a gathering storm beneath my feet. I know you are a non-believer, and I respect that my friend. However, you can believe this. I am a man who may have no supernatural power within my grasp, but I do have the skill, talent and potential to rain down wrath that will make the oceans and rivers rise, the jungles of concrete and steel tumble into rubble, the green forests of a nation wilt, the mountains sink into the ground, the roads and bridges melt away and the earth tremble in fear. And I have this raging fury within me that says this is it. This is the time when a good and just people will make a final stand against oligarchic despots of despair who refuse to equally share the bounty of the earth. I tell you that I have reached the end of a long road, and I see no more retreat from the inevitability of conflict between those who want to own all within their grasp and those who want a simple life unencumbered by the restraints placed on them by a society where everything has a price tag. Who can stand before my burning fury? My rage is blazing forth like a fire unrestrained as it consumes all before it. These good people will suffer if I lead them into battle against overwhelming forces that oppress them, but is it better to die standing than to live life eternally on your knees grovelling for a mere scrap from those who sit at the table of plenty?"

J. Wayne Frye

Aaron placed his hand on Jesus' arm and said with great conviction, "whatever trouble comes, I shall be by your side, as will all here on this island. I shall shout and wail against the darkness promulgated by those who want to enslave all of humanity to the idea that greed is acceptable in a world where everyone pursues more and more while ignoring the needs of others. I have lived my life in a nation that shouts from the mountaintops how free it is, but binds all but the chosen few in a life of submissive service to an idea that is nothing but words on an ancient piece of paper used to manipulate and control the populace into supporting the evils that keep them on their knees. Let's get ready for the coming storm. I know others who will assist in defending these people, no matter what it takes, no matter what the personal cost, no matter how overwhelming the odds might be. There still are a few who simply are looking for a chance to make a final stand against the tyranny of the 1% who have made the earth their garbage dump and have no respect for it or the people whom they trample over on their way to power and riches."

Jesus turned to Aaron and said, "Let's get to work, my friend. We must prepare for a war that may not be won, but it will be fought to the death in defence of that which is right and just in a world that shows no mercy for those who defy the authority of the privileged."

J. Wayne Frye   109

Late that afternoon, a helicopter carrying Harold Frommer and Lon Corcoran arrived. They immediately went to Chief Marion Harry's home. When he opened the door, the two men insisted on coming in, but Harry said that he had to call the council together to discuss anything to do with mineral extraction. He told them to go in and have a seat, and he would return shortly. Frommer immediately said, "Chief, we can talk privately, and I am sure we can work something out that will be mutually rewarding."

The chief was a bit offended that Frommer would indicate that he might be willing to side with them for remuneration of any kind. He said, "Gentleman, I have nothing to discuss with you in private that I cannot discuss in public. This is not America, where deals are made behind closed doors to benefit the few at the expense of the many. Here, we know real democracy and take no action that would harm our people."

The two white men looked at one another and rolled their eyes, Corcoran pleadingly said, "please chief; at least don't bring that lunatic calling himself Jesus to the meeting. He is detrimental to any chance we have of reaching an equitable agreement."

The chief replied. "he is a member of our community now and a valued councillor."

The chief left and the two men sit contemplating what their next move would be. Things were not looking good, and Corcoran had already scheduled a meeting with a member of the Prime Minister's cabinet just in case things didn't go TWI's way, and it was appearing that these people were not going to compromise.

The meeting was held with Jesus present, and the two men were surprised when Aaron Adams also showed up. They were faced with the dilemma of dealing with two men who simply were not going to give any ground, and it appeared that they had the support of the council.

Frommer was a man who never supplicated himself, but this time he thought meekness might work in his favour. He asked Jesus, "Do you not think freedom is a good thing?"

"Freedom is every man's birthright, but it means more than just words on paper that are ignored by your government that thinks freedom is the right for corporations like TWI to exploit the masses so a few can gain splendorous luxuries and enjoy lives of excess."

Stiffening his back and breathing deeply, Frommer replied, "You may be in Canada, but they are allied with America against the forces of evil, so you are playing with fire here."

When Jesus Came to Canada to Lead An
Indigenous Rebellion in the Broughton Archipelago

Smiling, Jesus walked over to Aaron, who was sitting opposite Frommer. "This is my friend, and he has devoted his life to lifting up the downtrodden and defending those who cannot defend themselves. He has never wavered in his devotion to justice. This is a man who would never entertain the thought of selling his soul for gold. You think he and the people of this island are fools because they do not grab with glee the riches you offer. Nor do they fall for your freedom propaganda. The American people think they are free, because the corporations that dispense the news tell them that they are free. They do not realize that if you depend on a corporation for your job, for your transportation, for the food you put on your table, for the home you live in and for the money you borrow to buy it that you are not free. You are owned by the entities that control your life. Don't come before us and talk of freedom. These island people can live without electricity. They can survive without an automobile. They can hunt game, grow crops and make their own clothes. These people are free. It is people like you who want to own more and more without any core to your being who are the true slaves, and you make slaves out of others to serve your avaricious appetites for material possessions that you don't own yet. It is not you who own the possessions, but it is the possessions that have a mortgage on your soul that own you. Freedom! Americans have no idea what it is!"

When Jesus Came to Canada to Lead An
Indigenous Rebellion in the Broughton Archipelago

Like so many people driven by propagandized patriotism that is dispensed in large doses in a country that has been hijacked of its moral compass, the two Americans heard what was said, but they were not listening. They saw themselves as defenders of a system that they believed was man's salvation, not the bane of his existence.

Corcoran, who had been relatively quiet through the meeting, stood and looked directly at Aaron. "You people don't understand. There is polonium out there. It is necessary for America to defend itself from those who would do her harm. The nation needs that polonium. It is critical to the well-being of the country. Adams, you are an American, surely you have some patriotic fervour left. We ran a check on you. You served your country valiantly in Vietnam. Have you turned your back on all your country stands for?"

Aaron welcomed the opening offered him by Corcoran. "I have not turned my back on my country, just what it represents in a world where it is the chief impediment to peace and tranquility, unwilling, like you gentlemen, to accept the fact that not all people want to live in a world where everything is for sale to the highest bidder. I served my country in a useless, unnecessary war of conquest. I ascribe to the ideal that I support my country always, but I support the government when it deserves it. Gentleman, in my 60 years of life, I have yet to see a government that deserves my support, because they have all incessantly bowed to the interests of the few at the expense of the many. You are the government of America, and you are despicable in your commitment to greed."

Frommer, disgusted with the way events were unfolding, arose and said, "America's nuclear arsenal depends on polonium to trigger its weapons that protect her from harm. Those weapons also protect Canada. The two governments will not allow 200 people to stand between them and the material that is essential for their protection. We will see you in court, and then it will be too late for you to get a just settlement. We will get that mining concession, because we are the only company mining it for American consumption now. Finding a credible, stable source this close to home makes it essential for national security. Make no mistake about it, 200 people will simply not stand between two nations and that polonium."

The two men started toward the door, but Jesus was not through. He very calmly said, "Halt and listen to my final words and heed them well. Share them with your enablers in Ottawa and Washington, for there is much at stake here, much more than any of you are calculating. I am not a man who makes idle threats. I fear no one," he stopped for a second and pointed at Aaron, "and neither does he," he then pointed at those assembled, "nor do these good people."

Moving toward the two men, Jesus was now going to make a lasting impression. "I am preparing these people to face adversity of the cruellest kind. I have made it plain to them what lies ahead when dealing with a merciless corporate entity and governments that serve their interests. But heed what I tell you. This will be no ordinary battle. There are forces at play here that your corporation and the governments of Canada and the USA simply have no comprehension of in a world where they think all the might and all the right lies in their hands. I tell you to share with them what I am telling you. If they back these people into a corner, the hounds of hell will be unleashed like they have never been unleashed before. The American government that was turned into a weapon of torture by Bush and Cheney thought it could torment me into submissive compliance to the will of those who had no moral compass. In a Camden, New Jersey dungeon of evil, I experienced the depravity to which a nation could sink when it turns its back on honour, integrity and justice. Believe me, this may be a battle you ultimately win in the courts, even on a blood splattered battlefield, but the price that will be paid will be so significant that, ultimately, even victory will be hallow."

Corcoran motioned for Frommer to leave. As they opened the door, Jesus had one parting thing to say. "You think you are opening the door into light, but you are about to enter a darkness as black as the pits of hell."

The two men, on their way to the dock, laughed at what they perceived as Jesus' lunacy. Climbing on board, Frommer said to Corcoran, "that guy is delusional. He actually thinks he is some kind of deity who will wreck havoc on those who stand against him and this useless bunch of backward savages. After we extract all the polonium, they should turn this place into an asylum. They already have 200 inmates ready for incarceration."

The two men had another hearty laugh as they headed toward Vancouver to meet with attorney's who were preparing a brief of compliance to file in the provincial court. Then it would be on to Ottawa, where they would file another brief with the Federal Court. They had no idea that on the island they were leaving behind arrangements were already underway to prepare for the worst possible scenario, and it would play out in a way that was far beyond the comprehension of two men who were used to getting what they wanted by simply waving money in front of people. They had seriously underestimated the tenacity of the people of Kwak'wala, and the leadership skills of Jesus and Aaron Adams.

The very idea of freedom presupposes some objective moral law which overarches rulers and ruled alike. On Kwak'wala, they were realizing that the outside world had always played fast and lose with the word freedom, and that those who were trying to destroy their way of life were the very ones who used so-called freedom to enslave others. The ethos of any society is the creation of its rulers, educators and conditioners; and every creator stands above and outside his own creation. So, the people of TWI had created a world where those ruled had to answer to laws that did not apply to the rulers. Frommer and Corcoran had no consent to operate outside simple moral parameters from those they ruled, but they answered to no one, especially not to the people who toiled in obscurity to satisfy the greed of the privileged class. They bought politicians who did not serve the people, but the interests of those with wealth and power. The normal laws never applied to corporations. Mitt Romney, in the 2012 election campaign, had boldly said "corporations are people, my friend" because he genuinely saw them as such. They were people to him, and like those similar to Mr. Romney, who were born into wealth, the corporations were above the laws that applied to normal individuals. Even the few politicians who genuinely felt compassion for the people they were supposed to serve willingly accepted the perks of office without realizing that was in itself showing contempt for the people.

When Jesus Came to Canada to Lead An
Indigenous Rebellion in the Broughton Archipelago

Most people in American society had long ago given up on facilitating a change that would foster equality of opportunity and fairness in the workplace. People were simply too wrapped up in who was going to be the next American Idol, who would win the Super Bowl, what celebrities were getting a divorce and what new electronic gadget would be worth standing in line for so they could be one of the first to possess it. People's brains had been turned into manipulated mush by marketers whose crafty techniques had made consumptive morons out of almost the entire population. In Canada, the long tentacles of the American nightmare of greed were steadily reaching out and wrapping another nation in its insidious grasp. A Canadian government that admired the American model had been in power for years and was aiding and abating the gradual erosion of the wall of protection that had kept the monstrous evil of the culture of greed from spreading northward. However, the valiant people of Kwak'wala Island had, for the most part, led a life that was void of so many things that had made slaves out of others. And they now had Jesus and Aaron Adams on their side in the battle against those who would enslave them. The storm clouds were gathering, and those who thought these people would eventually give up the fight were about to learn that this storm would be like no other that had ever cast its dark shadow over the scared land.

The tribal attorneys skilfully represented the Kwak'wala band in the provincial court in Victoria, but the judge sided with TWI and the government in the decision, casting a pall of gloom over the 205 people who once again saw their way of life threatened by those who looked upon them as anachronisms who were standing in the way of progress. The same thing happened in the federal court on Ottawa, and although appeals were filed in both cases, it appeared that the Canadian government, as a result of pressure from the U.S. government, was determined to give the green light to TWI to begin mining operations as soon as possible.

While all this was going on in Victoria and Ottawa, the people of the island were not complacently preparing to accept their fate. Under the leadership of Jesus and Aaron Adams, they were getting ready to make a stand that would have made Geronimo proud. Jesus stood before a throng and said, "The courts are nothing more than another corporation. They rarely represent the interests of the people. Do you think that an excessively compensated judge can understand or empathize with the man or woman who robs a convenience store to feed hungry children? Can they understand the agony of struggling to make a car payment or a house payment? Do they have any idea what it is like to slave for an oppressive overseer in a factory?"

When Jesus Came to Canada to Lead An
Indigenous Rebellion in the Broughton Archipelago

Jesus, who often strolled among the people as he talked, moved gingerly among the throng and stopped periodically to continue his homily. "I expect no satisfactory results for you from a distant court that has no understanding of what you are fighting for in this place which you and your people have called home for thousands of years. The judges who ride around in Lexus automobiles, dine at expensive restaurants, go to luxurious homes behind locked gates and spend more on one bottle of wine than you spend to feed your family for a week simply have no comprehension of what you are fighting to protect. They think your birthright is for sale to the highest bidder, like everything else in their corrupt society of excess and opulent disregard for those who toil and struggle in lonely desperation to stay afloat in a raging, violent, furious sea of discontented oppression."

Jesus walked toward Aaron, placed his hand on Aaron's shoulder and continued. "This is one man who has fought all his life in defence of those who are crushed by this system of economic servitude. He understands, like I hope you now do, that capitalism is a tool of the privileged class to keep people like you and me in bondage. Prior to the development of capitalism, simple people like you sold the products of their labour, but with the development of capitalism, workers no longer sold the products of their labour, instead they sold their labour itself and the people of TWI and the other corporate thugs think of each one of you as a commodity to be used, abused and then discarded when you are no longer of value to them. They see this land as a commodity, too. They will rape, pillage and plunder this sacred land of your forefathers until it is useless for human habitation. Then, they will discard it and move on to the next place they will destroy with their avaricious appetite for more and more. I say to you, this is the place where one small group of people stand against this evil and shout that they will not submit without a physical fight, to this loathsome, evil malignancy any longer."

The crowd, now in a fiery frenzy of excitement, clapped their hands and stamped their feet as they shouted in unison, "fight, fight, fight!"

Within a few days, a white haired man of about 60 came by boat to the island and was greeted warmly by Aaron. This was no ordinary man. This was an individual who had spent his life in service to a cause which he now saw as a shallow, withering excuse for the enslavement of humanity to a bankrupt economic idea that was literally destroying everything in its path. Tom Morrissey had served in Vietnam with Aaron as an assassin. After the war, he continued to work with the CIA in clandestine operations all over the world, training rebel armies to overthrow legitimately elected governments that were not compliant to America's will. As time passed, he kept telling Aaron that he was no longer able to justify his actions, because he saw who the real impediment to freedom was. It was the very country that shouted the loudest about democracy, the United States.

When the CIA sent him to Guantanamo Bay, where he witnessed the barbaric actions that were promoted by the fascists in the White House and Congress, he simply could take no more and quit, telling his bosses, "you are torturing people, regardless of what benign name you want to call it. Calling torture legitimate use of repetitive force does not mean it isn't still torture. I am not a torturer, nor will I be part of an organization that thinks torture is permissible under any circumstances. You people are becoming worse than those you brand as terrorists. This is just another abomination that will insure that more and more people will fly planes into buildings. I quit. Get me a plane and get me the hell out of this monument to evil."

Tom and Aaron had grown distant over the years because of the work Tom did, but when he quit the CIA, they found one another again. Tom was now working with an anti-colonialism group that trained people to fight against oppressive regimes.

When Jesus Came to Canada to Lead An
Indigenous Rebellion in the Broughton Archipelago

Aaron had called Tom and asked if he wanted to prepare a group of people who would probably die in defending their freedom against overwhelming odds, not the propagandized freedom that was sold by American media and the government, but real freedom that they lived every day of their lives in a way that the average man simply could not comprehend.

Tom had received news a few days before that he was dying of pancreatic cancer, and he saw no reason to sit and wait for the grim reaper to claim him in the year to eighteen months he had left. Aaron was offering him a chance to die for a cause before the cancer made him a physical shell of his former self. He did not tell Aaron about the cancer, because he wanted no pity from anyone. In fact, he was thankful for the opportunity to do one final thing to make amends for all the years he had been on the wrong side of history.

The preparation for a fight would be considered by most knowledgeable people an exercise in absolute futility, but Jesus, Aaron, the people of Kwak'wala, and now, the newest addition to the growing group of anarchists, Tom Morrissey, saw things differently. They did not intend to win a battle, but they thought the willingness to fight and proving it should offer a reason for the forces arrayed against them to reconsider whether it was really worth a fight that would be bad publicity for

TWI, the law enforcement agencies, the military and the American and Canadian governments. Would they be willing to stand against the court of pubic opinion that would hopefully be mostly on the side of people who were considered expendable by the powerful entities arrayed against them? Would the public side with those who wanted to destroy the land and a people's way of life, or would they stand with those who refused to give into the powerful forces that controlled the lives of far too many people? It was the chief who proclaimed in a meeting that the public would be on their side, but Jesus had another take on it, and he shared with all the people gathered in the longhouse what he saw as the likely outcome.

"I want none of you to entertain any illusions about how this situation will play out. I know some of you have come to me and asked if I could not just wave my hand and smite those who want to destroy you. I have never told any of you that I was divine. I am not even sure that I know what divinity is. I do know that Christianity is a religion that the older among you had pounded into you with a stick. I am sure you were all smart enough to ask why you had to believe something that could not be proved. Maybe even some of you, before you learned better by getting a slap across the face, dared to ask why a God you were supposed to love could be so cruel."

When Jesus Came to Canada to Lead An
Indigenous Rebellion in the Broughton Archipelago

"The answers to your questions were more brutality, teaching you that asking questions was simply not acceptable when it came to the faith you were supposed to have. Your old religion was unacceptable, because only the white man had access to the real God, and he was giving you the opportunity to love the true God, not some figment of your imagination, because the white man was always right. I say to you that those people were not of God, but of the devil that dwells in the hearts of those who have no tolerance for anything but blind obedience."

One old man stood and asked Jesus, "but are you saying we shouldn't believe in God, shouldn't believe that his son was born of a virgin and crucified? Are you saying we shouldn't pray to God to help us out of this situation we find ourselves in? Should we not believe in a higher power?"

As was his practice, Jesus began to walk among the people. "I am not telling you what to believe, but I can tell you that in the coming storm, you better not depend on a divinity to come to your rescue, you better depend on yourselves. If you want to believe that the first two people were moulded from clay, go ahead and believe it, but don't expect me to believe it, and don't ridicule me because I don't. Most of you would think a religion that spoke of flying elephants was absurd, but the white man would have you believe in burning bushes and evil snakes that talk, even the stopping of the sun in the sky. I mean, get real. The stopping and reversal of the sun would have been visible worldwide. The idea that people could have witnessed these events without having been amazed by them is, quite simply, ludicrous. Other cultures having witnessed this would certainly have offered their own explanations in keeping with their own cultural and religious beliefs. Surely a society existing at the time would have documented this miraculous event. Yet, nowhere have such works been found. Still, those who pounded your soft flesh expected you to all accept these absurdities without question. I tell you that a questioning mind would be expected by a true and loving God. What kind of God would encourage ignorance among those he professes to love? What kind of deity would condemn a child to the eternal fires of hell because he never had an opportunity to accept Jesus as his saviour? I tell you that kind of God is not worthy of worship. The real and everlasting God is within every one of you, and you have the capacity to use the God within you to rise to the occasion and stand against tyranny."

Jesus strolled over to Aaron and Tom, stood silent for a few seconds and looked up at the opening in the roof, where the sunlight was flickering, almost dancing around his head, giving him what appeared to be a celestial glow behind his long, flowing hair that fell to his shoulders. The people, mesmerized and totally captivated by his soaring rhetoric and his regal bearing, were sitting in abject silence as he continued. "Be not afraid to die on your feet, rather than live on your knees. There will be a vast array of evil assembled against you."

Jesus walked over to Robert Blackwater and said, "I met this young man in the clinic where he feared a needle that was offering him protection from disease." Jesus then pointed at Huyana, who was sitting between Aaron and Tom. "That fine woman over there saw his fear and with the compassion she has shown to you all, reached out with the soothing hand of love to comfort him. I, in my own small way, assisted by distracting him to get his mind off what was happening. Today, this young man comforts others who have fear when they go into the clinic. Never underestimate your power. You don't need some God in the sweet bye and bye to give you strength, because you are all God in your own right, as long as you believe that the good in you can rise to the surface and provide you with a shield of honour that might not prevent death, but it can prevent the deterioration of spirit that kills you just a little bit each day that you do not fight against injustice. I do not want a single person here to think that what lies ahead will end in what most would consider victory, rather it may well end with utter defeat on the field of battle, but when the dust of conflict has cleared and you are bloodied, your body torn and exhausted, your heads will be unbowed, because you will have stood against injustice. Body and cause may suffer defeat, but your spirit will stand triumphant and unyielding to the cause of justice."

Robert Blackwater jumped to his feet, ran over to Jesus, hugged him, turned to the crowd, raised his hand high over his head, pumped it furiously in the air and shouted, "Justice or death!"

In unison, the crowd took up the chant so loudly that the building began to shake. "Justice or death! Justice or death! Justice or death……………….."

CHAPTER 6
DO THE RIGHT THING

If, in the dusk of the coming twilight,
Dimming hopes gather from afar,
Will not the deepening darkness
Need a bright and shining star?

Word came that the court would award fair compensation to the natives who would have to be off the island within six months. No amount was set yet, as the judge would assess what was fair compensation after consultation with authorities and the people of Kwak'wala. The Canadian government would relocate them onto another nearby island where new homes would ne built for all.

People on the island got a good laugh out of the term *fair compensation*. What could be considered fair compensation? No matter how much it was, there was no such thing as fair compensation for losing the home of your ancestors to greed. Thus began preparations for the Armageddon of Kwak'wala. If the people of the island could not continue to live in the place they had called home for thousands of years, they would see to it that no one would rape the land they loved without a fight to the death. Although appeals were filed by the tribal lawyers, the people were now preparing to physically repel any attempt to mine polonium.

When Jesus Came to Canada to Lead An
Indigenous Rebellion in the Broughton Archipelago

Jesus assigned Tom Morrissey the job of preparing a group of people to stop any encroachment on the village, and it was decided that a 360 degree perimeter would be established. Several of the villagers took boats to nearby Campbell River, where they bought supplies from a variety of sources to prepare for a long siege. Salmon were caught, smoked and stored. Firewood was cut, dried and strategically placed where everyone would have easy access to it. A complete building was set aside for kerosene lamps and candles, as cutting the power to the island would be easy. That would probably be one of the first tactics used to force them to leave.

After several weeks of frenzied preparation, the judge, Lorne Hebert, called to set up a meeting to discuss when the people could begin to move. Band members went to Vancouver to meet, but the discussions were fruitless, as the judge seemed to think that offering people money was a solution to the problem. It was obvious that he was uncompromising in his decision to side with TWI.

On the island, preparations were going forward to withstand a long siege. There was talk of killing whales for meat, but Jesus, remembering how the whales had helped him find the island, asked the people to not destroy any, as there was plenty of game in the forest, and the supplies that were pouring in from the constant trips to Campbell

River were already enough to last several months. What they really needed was weapons, but they were not in America, where you could pick up an AK-47 from a local gun dealer. Buying arms in mass would be a problem in Canada, where there were strict controls on guns, but without them, they would not be considered a credible threat against the force of the government that represented the entities that were oppressing them.

This was not a plan for military victory over what would be an overwhelming force, but for issuing a threat that the cost of enforcing an unjust law would just simply be too much to bear. Jesus knew that the governments of the USA and Canada had no real respect for indigenous people whom they looked upon as economic leeches who simply had not joined the modern world and accepted the culture of greed that was the norm.

While the USA had arrogantly disregarded the Geneva Convention and even instituted torture as a part of its defensive strategy against those it deemed evil-doers, Canada, up until the election of a conservative government in 2006, had maintained its status as a peaceful nation that would not blindly follow the USA into its wars of conquest. However, the Canadian government had, in recent years, followed a foreign policy that was increasingly putting it on the side of the USA in its attempt to secure the world for its brand of corporate capitalism that was rapidly enslaving all of humanity to the 1% who wanted complete control over the lives of people who were looked upon as nothing but customers and commodities to be used in the production of products that were marketed to people as necessities for a good life.

Word about the preparations that were going on in Kwak'wala had leaked to Ottawa and Washington. It was decided by both governments to send an emissary to talk to the chief and see if a peaceful solution to the problem could be worked out. A Cabinet Minister named Darryl Robson was sent by the Prime Minister's Office and arrived by float plane on a Saturday afternoon. As the plane was circling to land, Robson was shocked by what he observed. At the dock was a huge flotilla of private boats unloading supplies. The normal population of 205 had seemingly swelled to well over 1,000 as there were throngs of people moving hurriedly about. They seemed to be carrying huge bags on their backs and depositing them in a 360 degree perimeter around the village. Looking at the people, Robson got a sinking feeling in the pit of his stomach. He had no idea what the people were up to, but it couldn't be good. How things got that way is an interesting tale of the solidarity of First Nations people, the determination of Aaron Adams, the skilful military preparations of Tom Morrissey and the incredible charisma of Jesus.

Only a month before Robson arrived, Jesus had asked for a general meeting in the longhouse. He asked that representatives from all the northern bands be present. What occurred at that meeting would be a catalyst for what Robson was observing as his plane prepared to land.

Jesus stood before the overflowing crowd and began what was a plea for the people to seriously consider whether they wanted to go down the path they had chosen or not. "I am here to tell you that the forces arrayed against you are so formidable that a physical victory is impossible. The only hope is for a victory in the theatre of public opinion that will hopefully make the authorities and TWI realize that to continue this thievery of a few people's sacred way of life is simply not worth the cost they will have to pay. I have asked the chiefs or their representatives from the other bands to be present, because this fight is not just the fight of those who call Kwak'wala home. This is a fight for all your rights. This is a stand against the evil of those who want to enslave all of you to their avaricious greed that makes them want to consume everything in their path. I tell you that you can all make a stand against the fascism of corporations and the governments that are enabling them. For when fascism comes, it will not be in brown shirts and jack boots. It will be in $2000 suits, $1000 Italian shoes and a Donald Trump designer necktie. These are the real rulers of this nation and that nation of malfeasant malicious intent south of us. Make no mistake that the elections they foster as representative of the freedom all enjoy are nothing but a charade of the foulest kind, an illusion to keep the masses at bay by manipulating them into falling for an illusion that keeps the few in power at the expense of the many."

Everyone present sat in mesmerized awe, as Jesus continued his spellbinding, captivating oratory. "These are the people who only give you the freedom to make two choices, plastic or paper. Everything in their sick culture is for sale. Money is at the root of everything that drives them to get up and breathe each day. As part of their drive to enslave, they support pontificators of deceit who tell you on Sunday mornings to believe in a book of outrageous fiction that says the meek will receive their reward in the end. These maniacal ministers of mayhem tell you to believe in an invisible man who has a great list of things you shouldn't do. And if you do any of these things, he is going to send you into a place in the bowels of the earth that is belching fire and filled with people who are jamming pitchforks into your flesh as a way of torturing you for all those evil misdeeds." Then he could not resist introducing some levity. "Sounds like a place where Dick Cheney and George Bush have the perfect resumes for employment."

A round of laughter ensued and Jesus continued. "Meantime, they end their sermons by telling you how much this deity that does all this to you actually loves you. After that, they tell you how you can get in his good graces by depositing as much money as possible in the collection plate. One thing about their God, he is good at retribution for any misdeeds, but he sure is not very good when it comes to finances, as he always needs money."

Again, laughter swelled through the longhouse. Huyana and Aaron, who were sitting beside each other as they always did, shared a cheerful nodding acknowledgement of what they both thought about the validity of what Jesus was saying. However, the levity was only a method of Jesus leading into more serious considerations.

"I see all about me in this world that is run by these guardians of virtue things that make my soul rebel in horror that the evils of war, feminine, poverty, envy, disease, destruction and torture are condoned by those who worship this God who is so filled with love. This is not the work of the God I represent. Look in the mirror all of you, and you will see God. The God I represent is in each and every one of you. Let that God of love come forth and stand against the tyranny of those who want to enslave you. I say to you that it is better to pray to someone who can get things done, rather than an illusion sitting on a cloud somewhere. You, your family, your friends and neighbours can get things done, because you all illuminate a heart of sparkling possibilities from the God within each and every one of you. Religion, as it is being used today, is destructive to civilization. You do not need to go to church on Sundays." Then, Jesus' penchant for jocularity came into play again. "Besides, the Bible says that is God's day off. You bother him with a bunch of prayers on his day off, and he is liable to get pissed and wreck havoc in your life. Church is not where the true God resides. The true God resides in your heart," and then Jesus made a sweeping motion and turned 360 degrees as he continued, "and in the lush, green forests of this island. He is in the bright, lucent sun that greets you each day. He is in the foggy mists of possibilities to lend a helping hand to a neighbour in need. God is on the pristine beach that welcomes the waves from the ocean that has provided bounty for your people for thousands of years. The same bounty that corporations now say belongs to them to dole out to those who can afford their price. And those of you here today from other reserves all know the individual beauty of the places you call home. It is a beauty that is under assault by those who think land can be bought and sold. These capitalist con-men look upon you with disdain and contempt. Go to Seattle across the strait. Walk the streets of that affluent city that is home to the richest man in the world. People live in the streets in the dead of winter, with no roof over their heads. People beg for money so they can get sustenance that is denied them, because they cannot afford a plot of land to grow food on, or because they have no job so they can go into a corporate owned grocery store to buy some food. This is the way of the world, a world filled with injustice promulgated by a nation that reaches out with its insidious tentacles of economic enslavement to subjugate all to the evils of a system that is an abomination to the very ideals of the saviour they claim to revere."

"The God in you knows that your heritage is not for sale at any price. I say to each and every one of you assembled here today: man, woman, child, young, middle aged, old, sick in body, sick in spirit to stand with the people of Kwak'wala, because they are not only defending their island, but they are defending your islands, your homes, your families, your way of life that has been under assault for hundreds of years by those who look upon you as savages and consider you leeches in their society of greed. You stand with these people against TWI, the Canadian government and the U.S. government, and you stand with justice. I tell you those who tremble with indignation at injustice of the kind suffered by these people here are our comrades in the cause of fairness in a world where the power structure is in the hands of the devils of despair. I ask you to stand with us in this just fight. The people of this island may suffer ultimate defeat and decimation, but they will not have willingly crawled on their knees pleading for that to which they are entitled as human beings. I appreciate the way you have all looked up to me, but I can not promise victory. I can only promise you that you can take pride in knowing that you took your last breathe wailing against an evil economic system that wants to enslave all to the culture of greed. Join in the fight against injustice!"

A rousing cheer went up, and thus began an alliance of 15,000 dedicated, loyal indigenous people in various bands from Port Hardy in the north to Victoria in the south to the coast communities of the mainland in the east and to the sparsely populated isolated islands to the west of Vancouver Island. They were all determined to help defend **Kwak'wala** against the encroachment of those who had, for far too long, been allowed to reign over a land to which they had no right. By standing up for **Kwak'wala, they were showing they would protect their own lands from encroachment.** This was a defining moment in which the will of these people was fortified and they were determined that this time they would not bow in supplication to any man, to any legislative body, to any court, to any army or to any government.

When Jesus Came to Canada to Lead An
Indigenous Rebellion in the Broughton Archipelago

The flurry of activity in the Johnston Strait went basically unnoticed, until one Canadian naval vessel passing near **Kwak'wala** had a captain who noticed a large number of boats docked on **Kwak'wala and he** asked his first mate in a rather derisive manner, "You think all those savages are preparing to go on the warpath? I guess their navy is getting ready for manoeuvres."

They had a good laugh and continued up the strait and out to sea. No thought was even entertained about informing the authorities of the unusual activity. The first mate replied to the captain, "just a bunch of Injuns probably getting drunk and doing some crazy dance to honour some long dead ancestors. They'll all be sailing back home tomorrow with hangovers. Hell, we should have been to the party. We probably paid for it anyway."

The captain, not realizing at the time, the prophetic nature of his statement, said, "Maybe we should turn around and go to **Kwak'wala** and tangle with a few of them. I'm itching for a little action."

Again laughing, little did they realize that the islanders and their brethren from all across the archipelago, Vancouver Island and the nearby mainland were preparing to give them the action they craved. Tom Morrissey was busy training

some men and women over 16 to defend the
village against encroachment from any side of the
perimeter they had sat up. Meanwhile, all the other
able bodied people were busy digging trenches,
filling sandbags, unloading supplies from the
boats and pouring concrete into a bunker that was
being built for the children and elderly.

That evening, a strategy session was held
between 27 chiefs of the various bands, Tom,
Aaron and Jesus. In order to understand their plan,
it is necessary to realize that no one wanted to
cause any bloodshed, but they had all decided that
if it came to a choice between capitulation and
bloodshed, the later was an alternative they would
willingly accept in order to keep the pristine land
that had already been subjected to the indignity of
a pollution spewing paper mill from falling further
into the pit of capitalistic avarice, greed and
rapacity. This was no longer just a battle for the
sanctity of Kwak'wala, as it was rapidly becoming
a cause célèbre for the indigenous people all up
and down Vancouver Island, the Gulf Islands and
the Broughton Archipelago. This was where the
final, irrevocable line would be drawn as the will
of the indigenous people would not allow another
indignity to be heaped on them without a genuine
fight.

At the meeting, Aaron, a man who had no
delusions about any of the realities of life, made it

plain that the preparations the people were making gave them all a sense of pride, but that when push came to shove, there was no way these people could genuinely defend themselves. In fact, Jesus was simply preparing them all to be slaughtered, and that he (Aaron) would stand by his friend until the bitter end, but that to think this escapade would end in anything but disaster for the people of Kwak'wala and those who were aiding them was delusional. Yet, he understood that there was no real choice other than submission to the will of another corporation and the governments that supported their malfeasant march toward total control over everything and everybody.

However, Aaron felt strongly that those who wanted to leave should be offered that choice with absolutely no recriminations. "After all," he said with deep emotion, "there are people who genuinely feel that it is better to live on your knees than to be dead. They should have the right to make that decision. I personally think it is the wrong decision, but it is not for me to decide who lives and who dies."

Jesus, with deep respect for his friend, replied in his usual calm demeanor. "When the time comes, they will be given that choice. I have never told them that this would be a guaranteed victory for their cause. I have only promised them that they can stand against insurmountable odds with

courage and conviction. Victory is always shallow
when you look at the lives it costs and the broken
minds and bodies that are the result. Yet, there are
times when that price must be paid if you are to
have dignity in your life. These people have been
here thousands of years, and they have had
everything taken by those who have no respect for
the land, its people and their culture. Make no
mistake about it; the incessant march of this evil
called corporations will not be halted here. They
are too entrenched and too powerful, but if they
are made to pay a high enough price, and if people
see that there are those who will stand their
ground against this insidious evil, just maybe
others will begin to see the possibilities and stop
acquiescing to evil and demand governments that
serve them, rather than the corporations.

J. Wayne Frye

When Jesus Came to Canada to Lead An Indigenous Rebellion in the Broughton Archipelago

All nations have individuals who have no loyalty to any cause but their own welfare, and there were a few members of various bands, when getting wind of what was happening, went to TWI, asking for money to supply information on what was occurring in preparation to thwart the company's plan to mine polonium. Lon Corcoran agreed to handsome remuneration for any information that could be supplied. What he, nor the traitors realized, was that false information was being funnelled to the modern day Judases.

The villagers and their helpers from other bands were busy erecting a stockade by the dock. When the fortification was completed, they rendered the water spring accessible in times of stress by means of erecting a stockade on either side of the path leading to it, adding an elevated outer stockade, lest it be cut off by a besieging force.

There was but one entrance to the main way into the village now. Punji sticks at least 6 feet in length were placed all around the village. Construction of two elevated platforms for defenders at the entrance was done in such a way that they could scan the entire 360 degree perimeter.

Where the forest butted up against the village, all the trees were cut down within 100 metres for building the stockade. This was done so that anyone approaching from the rear would be easily visible. Once the outer stockade was built, behind it was a line of two additional stockades, one oblique line bout 20 metres behind the main stockade, leaning outwards and the final stockade lined 10 metres back with pointed sticks extending out about ten feet each.

These fortifications were not meant to stop anyone, because all the defenders knew that a well-equipped assault team would be able to breach the defences in short order. The purpose was simply a show of intentions to defend the village against any encroachment and inflict devastating damage on anyone who tried to force their way in. Any tactician would realize that the nearly one thousand people who had come to defend the island would be no match for even a mildly equipped assault team. However, there were other plans in the works that would make things a bit more difficult for those who dared try and force the people off the land they had called home for thousands of years. Those plans were being formulated in the minds of Chief Harry, Aaron, Tom and Jesus, but it would be Jesus who would foster the ultimate idea for protecting the people and the island from those who thought all things had a price. Jesus was going to see to it that the price that would have to be paid would be so high that TWI and the governments of Canada and the USA would think long and hard before pursuing that which might lead to disastrous consequences.

The fortifications did not stop at the village, as more emplacements were being built toward the interior and the area where the polonium was located.

Morrissey was a master of guerrilla warfare training, and he was teaching the eager people the art of fighting an overwhelming force if the necessity presented itself. The people's lack of skill was obvious, but so was their dedication.

Huge pits were dug in the ground as Morrissey said, "Now, bear in mind that we could all be trapped and the want of food will be sorely felt, for hunger is an effective weapon in war. They well may decide to try and starve us out, rather than attack. Construct as many storage pits as you can and have the boats make as many trips as possible to Wal-Marts in Campbell River, Nanaimo, Duncan and Victoria for canned food. Wipe out every grocery store in every town. Let the greedy corporations think they are reaping a windfall from dumb natives, but the windfall will one day be a whirlwind that will swirl across the Broughton Archipelago and sweep all within its path in a devastating attack on TWI and the governments that are their enablers. Buy pigs, chickens, dry fish and hoard vegetables and grain.

Don't forget fern roots and even tree bark that
may be consumed in emergencies."

Jesus and Aaron visited two nearby islands that
could be used as an outpost to signal the arrival of
any vessels. It was there that a few men were left
to be vigilant and warn of any impending armada
that might be arriving. Ancient methods of
signalling with mirrors would be used, and if it
was night or foggy, flairs would be fired. Then,
the same was done on two islands that could be
used to warn of an attack from the far side of
Kwak'wala. All that was left was the far side of
Kwak'wala itself, and that was a special situation
that Jesus was prepared to tackle when it was the
right time. When Aaron said, "we must defend the
far side of the Kwak'wala near where the paper
mill is located," Jesus smiled and replied, "We
will do something special there. Let us not move
to hastily yet. I still hope that sanity will prevail
among our adversaries."

Aaron merely nodded his head in acquiescence,
and the two men boarded their boat, leaving three
people on each of the islands to keep an eye out
for any suspicious activity. The eyes and ears of a
Native Nation were depending on the men now
manning four islands to warn of any impending
attack. There would be no attempt to bomb the
village from the air. That would be tantamount to
genocide and just would not be acceptable in a

country like Canada; although, in America, genocide had long been practiced against its native population, and indirectly, against blacks, but surely, the Canadian government would never allow American troops on Canadian soil. Of course, the Americans had proved long ago that they needed no one's permission to launch a military strike against any nation it deemed a threat to its march toward total world domination for its economic system. But Jesus even had something in mind to counter that threat.

For many weeks, preparations kept the people busy almost twenty-four hours a day, but old and young alike willingly worked feverously in the common cause. They built a path through the forest to the polonium deposits, and there they constructed another stockade, surrounding the area with fortifications that contained deadly traps all about. While this was going on, weapons were flowing in from all those who had access to them, but there was great need for weapons of a more deadly nature. They could be easily bought in the gun shops of America, where the privilege to be packing was supposedly a right probably handed down by God to Moses with the Ten Commandants. Yet, too many purchases would raise a red flag, and the American Homeland Security Gestapo would be out in force to thwart what might be another attack from those evil-doers who were so jealous of all that freedom the

Americans thought they enjoyed. This need for weapons necessitated contact by Morrissey with two men who might be able to supply a large cache of arms. Gary Gore, an adventurer friend of Tom's and Gary's current employer, the Greek billionaire, Plato Papadopoulos, who used his vast wealth to aid indigenous causes all over the world.

Gary Gore arrived on a huge yacht that anchored in the bay. He took a launch to the dock and was greeted by Tom and Aaron. Gary was a 44 year old man whose small size was not illustrative of his abilities as a soldier. He was so soft spoken that one could almost say he whispered, but Tom told Aaron that he was one of the most deadly men he had ever met, and that he would be a valuable addition to those who were training to defend the village. He usually got $1000 a day as a soldier-of-fortune, but was on the permanent payroll of Plato Papadopoulos, who used him in a variety of capacities all over the world. Obviously, he also had free use of Papadopoulos' yacht.

Gary was taken to meet Jesus, and it was then that he dropped a bombshell. "I've got a load of AK-47's on the boat, several mortars and even a dozen Lars rockets for bringing down planes and helicopters. I have hand grenades and grenade launchers. My employer is providing all this gratis, and will vehemently deny that he did it. In fact, I am sailing the yacht under a different name, and it has been reported as stolen. The crew was recruited in the Philippines, and know me as Robert Rosen. This is a clandestine operation. After the materials are unloaded, the ship will be sailed back to the open sea, the crew transferred to another ship and taken back to their villages in the Philippines. After the crew is off, the yacht will be scuttled, forever letting the sea keep the secret of where it has been and what it left here on this island. I shall take a launch back to the **Kwak'wala** and stay here to assist you in whatever way I can to fight for these people's rights."

So, another fighter for justice joined the group that was determined to stand against tyranny in just one small spot on an earth overrun with corporate barbarism and governments that sanctioned their fiendish heartlessness. Special Cabinet Minister Darryl Robson was supposed to be a representative of the people, but rather, his real purpose in being on **Kwak'wala** was to secure the polonium mining rights for TWI and the American government that was now being coddled by a Canadian administration that had decided to lick the boots of its powerful southern neighbour. Robson, as he got out of the twin engine **Canadair CL-415 Flying Boat** that was luxuriously appointed with all the customary extravagances afforded government representatives, was shocked at what he saw. His heart fluttered incessantly and he turned to his aid and said, "What the hell is going on here? This place is a fortress, an armed camp of goddamn savages who think this is the 18th century. Get back on the plane, contact Ottawa and tell them this situation is out-of-hand. We are going to need some military back-up. I'm going into this fortified monument to stupidity and see if I can talk some sense into these goddamn heathen backward malcontents."

As the aid returned to the plane, Robson was greeted by a smiling Aaron Adams, who said, "welcome to Kwak'wala. I assume you are Darryl Robson?"

Typical of those who carry their titles like royalty who expected subservient awe from those in their presence, Robson replied, "I am Minister Robson."

Aaron, now relishing the opening left by the arrogant response, let Robson know just what he thought about him and others who believed they should be exalted because of their positions. "Listen to me asshole. You are among people who don't give you respect just because of a title that goes before your name. You get respect because of what you accomplish. All you politicians accomplish is figuring out how to screw the taxpayers so you can get your lavish salaries, parsimonious benefits and fancy titles. Robson, get your ass in the compound to discuss our terms

and show some humbleness or get back on that
goddamn flying palace and haul your ass back to
Ottawa where you can play your game of self-
aggrandizement and greed. We have no inclination
and no time to bow before a buffoon of banality
who thinks we are supposed to be in awe of him
because of who he represents and the title he has.
Make up your mind, you want to talk with
humbleness to the most humble man you will ever
meet, or you want to haul your ass back to Ottawa
and tell those who sent you that you have finally
run into some people who do not cower in fear
before you, the government or the corporations
that own you."

Aaron absolutely loved standing firm against
arrogance, and, obviously, Robson had never been
talked to in such a manner previously. "Do you
realize I am a representative of the Prime
Minister?"

"Asshole, we both know exactly who you are
really representing here today on Kwak'wala – a
goddamn life-sucking parasitic corporation and
the American government that enables it and all
the other corporations that have both governments
in their pockets. You are nothing but a lackey, a
boot licker who bows before anyone with
authority over you, so you can hopefully curry
favour and get appointed to a higher position
where you can exercise more power, which is in

close proximity to money as the only thing you
think defines a person's worth."

Now, Robson was well aware that it was
fruitless to try and flaunt authority over a man
who had nothing but disrespect for all he
represented. He hoped that cooler and more
respectful heads would prevail among those he
would meet in the village. He was about to find
out they might be more respectful than Aaron, but
they certainly were not going to cower in fear just
because he represented a government that had for
far to long ignored the plight of those who had
their land stolen and their way of life trampled on
by a distant government that looked upon them as
savages trapped in another century.

Aaron had instructed Tom and Gary to make
sure that Robson saw how well armed they were
by having the residents walk about carrying their
AK-47's and by having the grenade launchers and
Lars Rockets out in plain sight so that he could
report back to Ottawa and Washington that the
island had become an armed camp. It wasn't
meant to indicate that they could repel an
invasion, but that the cost of such an exercise
would be exceedingly high. Illusions are nothing
more than a magicians slight of hand that offer a
false reality, and there can be no way of knowing
what Robson was really thinking, but from his
dilating eyes, Aaron could see that he was

overwhelmed by what he was seeing and that his mind was like a train of moods clinging to the visions before him, and, as he passed through the village, the illusions created by Aaron, Gary and Tom proved to be many-coloured lenses which painted the world their own hue of a coming cataclysm. You could see the awe, fright and concern in Robson's eyes as he silently walked toward a meeting with the chief and his council of advisors.

Watching Robson's reaction to what he saw created a euphoric sensation for Aaron. He thought to himself that the plans they had formulated to show a fortress of discontent and rebellion proved that it was indeed possible to turn an illusion into reality. The greatest ally against discovery is ignorance. Robson was fooled because he only had an illusion of knowledge. He was only observing that which was on the surface, without bothering to look beneath the superficial to understand that what might lie below belied a much different truth. He was like so many people who looked on the surface, without seeing what was beneath the facade.

The chief's house was, no doubt, the very opposite of the places where Robson conducted most of his negotiations. It was an austere and relatively bare place, free of all the trinkets and baubles that adorned most homes. There was no

52 inch flat screen television. There were no luxuriously upholstered chairs and sofas, but old, cheaply made utilitarian furniture that had obviously been used for many decades. Even the large table behind which the council sat showed the wear of many years of use by those who had no need for the ostentatious displays that only indicated a lack of respect for those who paid the salaries of the servants of the people. They all looked upon themselves as stewards of their people's money and welfare. Spending money foolishly on superficial extravagant décor would be an insult to those whom they were supposed to serve. These people represented true democracy, where those who served, feared the people who elected them, rather than the people fearing those they elected. Robson was about to get a lesson in how elected officials should act, how they should spend the people's money, and how they should respect those who elected them by defending the people rather than corporations, the wealthy and powerful.

After a round of introductions, which included Huyana, who had been asked to join the group, and had, as one might expect, attracted the eye of Robson, who could not understand why a woman of such obvious good looks and breeding would associate herself with people he considered barbaric savages. He could tell she was Aboriginal, but she was not what he considered a typical Aboriginal. Obviously, she was just someone who had decided to immerse herself in an outdated culture as part of a self-awareness quest. Ah, he thought, if only I could get her alone, I would dazzle her with my power and prestige and have her in my bed in short order.

As Robson was scanning, with erotic delight, the generous curves of Huyana, the door to the kitchen was quietly opened and Jesus, unnoticed by Robson, quietly walked end, standing in the doorway to the living room as Robson began to speak to the chief and council. "Gentleman and ladies, I am appalled at what I have seen here today. You are violating any number of Canadian laws in putting up this fortification and brazenly carrying about weapons that are forbidden to be in the hands of ordinary citizens. You are playing with fire here, and you are going to get burned."

Robson puffed out his chest and continued. "I represent the government that is expected to enforce the laws of the land. The court has ruled that this island is vital to the national interests of Canada and the United States. You are going to receive adequate compensation, one and all. In fact, I am prepared to offer you even more than the judge will probably award you. I can arrange for every one of you to have a new home, fully furnished with the latest appliances, lavish furniture, an automobile for each household and as much as $100,000 deposited in each person's bank account. Think what that can mean to each one of you. That is more money, more material possessions than you would ever be able to accumulate in your lifetime. TWI is offering this to you without any strings attached, and the governments of Canada and the USA are prepared to do even more. We have selected a nearby uninhabited island that you can turn into a paradise, a place that will sparkle with all the wonderful things that will improve the lives of your people. This is an incredible opportunity for you do something positive for your people. They will be able to afford trips, new clothes, dine in fine restaurants, have all the latest electronic gadgets like other people and show your children and grandchildren that they, too, can have all these things that will lift them up from this scrap-heap existence that has you trapped in a place that binds you to a life of want."

Chief Harry pointed at the kitchen archway where Jesus was nonchalantly leaning. He calmly told Robson as he pointed toward Jesus, "we would like you to meet our friend and spokesman, Jesus."

Robson, shocked at the mention of the name, was momentarily stunned as he stared at a tall, thin man with a chestnut beard and scraggily, long flowing hair that cascaded over his shoulders. All he could do was murmur almost incoherently, "you mean Hey Soos?"

The chief, very sternly replied, "No, his name is Jesus.

At that moment, Jesus stepped into the room. Huyana and Aaron, as usual, stared at one another, expecting the typical Jesus homily that would disarm the arrogance of another representative of those he deemed as interlopers into the lives of the genuine people whom he loved with all his heart. "First, what you call me is of no concern. My name is of absolutely no importance. What is important is the ideal that I represent, an ideal that these people cherish. It is not something a man like you can understand, because you view everything in dollars and cents. You have no idea of the true value of this land that you, the governments of the USA and Canada and TWI covet. This land cannot be bought and sold, because it has no one owner. It is equally shared by all generations, held in trust for those who follow. That concept is beyond your meagre ability to understand that there are societies in this world that have no use for your avaricious ideas of ownership. These people share everything. If one hungers, they all hunger. If one is ill, they are all ill. If one grieves, they all grieve. If one is rich, they are all rich. You, Mr. Robson, represent a bankrupt idea that has ravaged culture after culture with an evil that plagues mankind and destroys his inner worth. You lost your ability to hold yourself up as an example of fairness when you stopped using your eyes to see the damage you were doing, but rather looked at what your material gain would be. You stopped feeling with your heart and only felt the size of your wallet. Choice has become but one illusionary fascination with you – the fascination with money. You are all playing a great masquerade, hiding behind masks of indifference where the mind is engaged in fornication with possessions. You are part of a horror that only leads to emptiness. You surround yourselves with riches, but you are poorer than the beggar who crawls on his knees asking for a measly crumb from your table of plenty. You are poor of spirit and soul. A man poor in soul and spirit may have material wealth, but he has no inner wealth. He is bankrupt in his heart, because the constant pursuit of wealth destroys the soul and hardens the heart. You, and those you represent have a malignancy that is contagious and spreads like an ancient plague."

Robson had never been talked to in this manner and he took great offence to it. "Who the hell do you think you are to point the finger of condemnation at me?"

That was a tailor made response for Jesus, as he interjected. "I do not point my finger at you. You point it at yourself with your deeds and actions. Who am I? I am the son of thunder in a land that needs a cleansing rain to wash away the filth and decay from a society based on greed. I am the lightning that strikes the tree of greed and burns it all the way to the ground, exposing it for having no depth to its root system. Make no mistake about it; I am not the meek son-of-man who turns the other cheek. I am the son-of-thunder who rains down a storm that will wash away the slime of a system that binds one man to another in monetary slavery so that a few can stand atop a mountain of riches while ignoring those lift in the valleys of despair. I speak to you as one who knows these people have had enough, and they are prepared to do all it takes to die on the rich soil of this land they will protect and nourish with their last breath. You come to take this land,but first you must take the lives of the people who are prepared to defend it to the last man, woman and child."

Robson, now fuming with anger, blurted out, "you are fucking nuts. You can't stand against two governments like this. You are insane!"

Jesus smiled and replied in his usual calm demeanour. "Mr. Robson, go back to Ottawa, and join the rest of your asylum inmates in the world of insanity you call civilization. And tell the Prime Minister, who can relay the information to the USA President, who can then relay it to the real leader of both countries, the Trans World Industries CEO, that to mine the polonium on this island will cause an explosion bigger than any that has ever been triggered by a nuclear device. You may not believe it, but you are about to unleash Armageddon, and I am going to be riding the horse down from Apocalypse, leading the troops of righteous indignation, wielding the sword of retribution."

Robson, cursing, ranting and raving, turned and walked out of the chief's house, shrugging off Aaron's attempt to escort him. Even Aaron was taken aback by the harshness of Jesus' rhetoric. He sounded like he was ready to sacrifice these people in a cause that simply was un-winnable. Yet, Aaron knew that he must stand by him. He was committed to a man he had grown to love. He had never believed in him as a deity, because that was as ridiculous as believing in Mother Goose, but there was something about the man that simply gave you confidence in him. There was something that made you feel an aura in his presence, something that seemed to say that he was a bright and shining star who would do the right thing.

CHAPTER 7
THE DARK WATERS OF DECEPTION

I have looked upon the dark waters of despair and
have watched a nation look upon me with disgust.
I am swimming upstream against a mighty tide,
looking afar to the open sky of expectation.
Let the cold winds blow and swirling waves beat.
I stand unbowed in the courtyard of hope.
The one with great knowledge assures me
that thus do all things flow gently away.

I move with the wind as the deer and bear are still.
Great plans are afoot in defence of wilful dreams.
A bridge of endurance will span all aspirations,
turning a deep chasm into a thoroughfare of hope.
Mighty walls of promise will hold back the foe.
Narrow gorges of defence guard against anguish.
The God of confidence shall reign supreme, as the
world marvels at how things will be changed.

Aaron and Huyana had been spending a great
deal of time together, but Aaron was careful to
avoid any impropriety, as he knew their great age
difference and his lack of libido precluded that
which he wished to be capable of once again. He
often lay in bed fantasizing about what it would be
like to just gaze upon her naked body and bask in
the magnificence of a woman who was as near
physically and psychologically perfect as the three
other loves of his life who were now gone forever.

When Jesus Came to Canada to Lead An
Indigenous Rebellion in the Broughton Archipelago

The day that Robson stormed out of the village, Aaron and Huyana walked back to the clinic together. Aaron had continued to sleep in the clinic and had grown accustomed to spending every evening chatting with Huyana. This evening, Huyana, who had not felt the warmth of a man for the many months she had been on Kwak'wala, was taking a leisurely bath, thinking that afterwards, she would walk over for her usual evening conversation with Aaron. Reclining so that the water could flutter over her huge breasts, she reached up to slowly massage them with her left hand. At the same time, she traced gently over her right thigh with her right hand and let her fingers make their way between her legs. She eased back and sighed deeply, letting her mind float away in the blissfulness of the erotic pleasure she was deriving from gently manipulating the root of her passion. Her knees begin to rise out of the water as she explored deeper and deeper.

While this was going on, in the cabin that abutted the clinic, Aaron, for some reason, found himself walking toward the back of the empty ward where there was a door connecting the cabin to the clinic. Huyana's bathroom was adjacent to the back wall. Aaron stood by the door to the cabin and just touched the knob. The door was never locked, so all he had to do was turn it and he could walk in. He started breathing heavily and wondered what it would be like to walk into her cabin and find her naked. How he wanted to gaze upon her nakedness just once.

As he stood there with his hand on the door knob, he could hear the bathwater sloshing about through the walls. Oh, she was in the tub!

He visualized what she must look like lying there in the tub, and he found himself reaching down to fondle his slightly hardening member. Then, he heard Huyana's sighs though the walls. He immediately realized what she must be doing in the tub. How he longed to barge in on her and offer his assistance in bringing her the erotic relief she was seeking, but he knew that he had long ago lost the kind of libido that it took to satisfy a young woman, particularly one as obviously erotic as Huyana. He unbuttoned his pants and began to pull back and forth on his swelling semi-erection. Damn, he had not done that in ages, and it did feel so good. He could tell by her sighs that Huyana was also in a frenzy of excitement and when she let out a moan of blessed relief, he knew that she had reached a climax. He looked down at his crotch and saw that in all the excitement, he had squirted his seed all over the wall. He grabbed a Kleenex and wiped it up. Oh, how good he felt. In fact, he was immensely proud of himself for squirting so hard that it seemed to have indented the wall with its intensity. Now that, he thought, is something to be proud of for a man in his sixties.

When Jesus Came to Canada to Lead An
Indigenous Rebellion in the Broughton Archipelago

He zipped up his pants and took a shower to cool down from his frenzied masturbating that had made him feel like a teenager again.

That night, when Huyana walked into the clinic, Aaron could not help but look at her differently than he normally did. There was always lust there. Huyana was used to that from men, but this night she noticed that Aaron seemed to be concentrating his gaze between her legs, constantly staring down at her tight fitting jeans that formed a bit of an indention that is often referred to as "camel toe." How he wanted to dive between those legs and taste her nectar.

There appeared immense discomfort between them, so Huyana said that she was going to bed. She got up and walked toward the back of the clinic to her cabin door. She stopped at the door and looked to her left at the wall. She instantly knew what the stains on the wall were, and she realized that Aaron had been listening to her through the wall. Aaron, standing about ten feet from her, was immensely embarrassed, because he knew what she had discovered. Huyana turned toward him, and took a deep breath, as Aaron hung his head a bit in shame. She smiled and moved toward him, stopping about two feet away. She stood there smiling. "My dear Aaron, you are a naughty boy." She kissed him on the cheek, turned and walked toward the door again.

Aaron was simply speechless as he watched her walk away. Then, he was amazed when she stopped at the door, pulled her sweater up over her head, exposing smooth, dark shoulders that seemed to cry out for a soft touch. She was obviously braless, but she did not turn around. She just reached down and turned the knob, walked through the door, leaving it open. She stopped about five feet inside the door, stepped out of her slippers with a flick that sent them flying precariously down the hallway and pulled her jeans off, revealing that she had no underwear on under them. Aaron stood there in amazement at what was happening. She tightened the cheeks of her magnificent ass, turned to the left and walked into her bedroom. She was waiting for him. Yes, she was waiting for him.

Aaron bounded down the hallway, turned to his left at her open bedroom door and gazed upon the most magnificent sight his eyes had ever beheld. With her legs spread wide, exposing an incredibly hairy mound of desire, she was lying there waiting for him.

He removed his clothes and told her as he moved toward the bed, "you will be disappointed. I am not a young man. My virility is in the trash can of yesterday, disposed of like old refuse, but I am yours to command. I shall give you whatever pleasure I can."

When Jesus Came to Canada to Lead An
Indigenous Rebellion in the Broughton Archipelago

She smiled up at him, raised her arms into the air and said, "Just being in your arms is a pleasure that will bring me untold delight."

They swept into each others arms and the two of them felt the warmth of genuine passion, rather than pure lust. Affection flowed between them like a babbling brook of serenity. A rapturous intensity overwhelmed them where the sex act itself was secondary to the intensity of devotion they felt for one another. They did not need sex. They needed each other. Embracing, they fell asleep in complete peace and tranquility.

The next morning the two lovers, lying in bed with the bedroom door open, were surprised to wake up, and there standing in the doorway was Jesus. Aaron quickly covered his naked body, but Huyana, who knew no shame, just smiled, got up and unselfconsciously put her gown on and sit up on the bed.

Jesus, like Huyana, saw no shame in people being naked. "I tried to get you this morning Aaron, but couldn't find you in your usual place. I can see why? Sorry I walked in on you but the door from the clinic was open. If you want to hide your rendezvous, it might be a good idea to close the clinic door; although, there is no reason to hide it. There is nothing to be ashamed of." He winked at Huyana as he continued, "I am glad he survived an evening with you, Huyana. At his age, that is a major accomplishment. I have an important task to ask of him this morning. I will let the two of you get dressed while I make some coffee."

The two dressed and joined Jesus for coffee. It was Aaron who appeared the most contrite about being caught in bed with Huyana. On the other hand, she seemed totally unashamed of what had occurred.

As they sat at the table, Jesus, who always enjoyed seeing two people find mutual compatibility said, "Aaron, if you can tear yourself away from Huyana for a few days, I would like for you to go somewhere for me."

Aaron turned to Huyana as he said, "That will be difficult, but I suppose I can manage it."

"Good. I want you to visit your friend Eric Hindle in Vancouver and then go to Seattle to find out just why TWI and the American government is so intent on making sure that the natives are off the island. It is more than the polonium. There is something suspicious going on at that mill. I think I know what it is, but I need confirmation."

Huyana, sensing that she could be of no value to the conversation, got up and said, "I'll take my bath while you two talk." She looked down at

Jesus and continued, "Your friend here caused some trouble the last time I took a bath. With you here, I think he may be able to control himself." She laughed, turned and headed down the hallway.

Jesus, putting his hands together and resting his chin on them seemed to be in deep thought. "Aaron, I am about to unleash hell in defence of these people. You know that I do not want you to do anything that you consider against your principles of fair play. I am a man who is supposed to be the prince of peace, but peace with honour sometimes can only be achieved if you are willing to resort to violence. I have said many times that I come not with meekness but with a sword. Meekness simply does not work in a world where there are evil, self-indulgent forces arrayed against justice. The people of Kwak'wala have put their faith in me. I know that you are a non-believer, and I respect that immensely, because what most people believe is an abomination to all that this person they worship stands for, anyway. I usually have more respect for non-believers than believers, because believing in the absurdities most people swallow as truth is an affront to an inquiring mind. A mind that does not question the existence of God is a mind that is nothing but useless mush and can be massaged and manipulated by a skilled orator or interpreter of God's so-called word. Just because you question God's existence does not mean that you are not doing his works. You, Aaron, have a great tally in the book of life, because you have always stood against injustice of any kind."

Aaron, knowing Jesus' ability to sway people, smiled and said, "Cut out the bullshit. I have never questioned your integrity, only your methods on occasion. What the hell you want me to do?"

"Sleeping with a beautiful woman makes you kind of testy in the morning," Jesus said with a sheepish grin on his face.

Aaron grinned back as Jesus continued. "O.K., you know there is a paper mill on the other side of the island. My suspicions are that it is more than a paper mill. A Cree from Saskatchewan named Harrison Black Elk worked for TWI at the paper mill. The men who work at the paper mill are brought in by boat from the mainland daily and they are totally unaware of what is going on in the area designated as the Chemical Research Division. They work from 7 until 3 and take a boat back to the mainland. Those in the Chemical Research Division are Americans, all employees of TWI, and they stay on the island three months at a time, living at the plant. There is a dormitory where they all sleep during the day, but at 3:00 PM they can be seen going into the Chemical Research Division. There is a strict count done on the boat each day to make sure all the paper mill workers are off the island, but one day about four months ago the boat had engine trouble and the men were forced to stay at the dock, waiting for a relief boat to arrive. Around 5:00 PM, when darkness set in, Harrison noticed something strange when he looked up at the plant toward the area where the Chemical Research Division was housed."

Aaron, his curiosity now aroused, interjected, "he saw what?"

Jesus replied, "The detective in you is aroused. I hope you are as aroused about this as you were aroused by Huyana last night."

Aaron let out a slight laugh and shook his head. "You are an asshole."

Jesus, smiling, continued. "There was a pale blue light glowing in one of the windows. It was something that Harrison just couldn't get out of his mind, so he sat about to clandestinely find out more about what went on in the Chemical Research Division. He utilized every means at his disposal to get access to the area. One day he managed, while walking through a corridor to deliver a message to the main office, to get a glimpse into the lab when the door was opened by someone. He saw, just for an instance, white chemical containment suits hanging on racks. The man who came out the door immediately asked him what he was doing in the hallway. When he said that he was delivering a written message to the main office, he was unceremoniously shooed down the hallway."

Jesus got a stern look on his face. "Aaron, find out what is going on there. It is vital to the well-being of the people on Kwak'wala. If you want, you can wait until Wednesday and take the Medi-Plane back to Campbell River with Huyana. Her Supervisor, Jane Drummond is taking over for her, so she can have a few days off in Campbell River. A sly, suave, ladies man like you might even convince her to go to Vancouver and Seattle with you."

Aaron snickered. "Yeah, I might just do that."

As Aaron and Huyana were preparing for the trip to Vancouver and Seattle, in the Privy Council Office on Parliament Hill in Ottawa, Darryl Robson was meeting with the council to decide what steps had to be taken to get the situation on Kwak'wala under control without creating a public furor. Robson was adamant that something had to be done post-haste. "Gentlemen, I tell you that if word gets out that we are allowing a U.S. company to utilize this facility for the purposes you all are familiar with, Canadians will be so outraged that this government will fall. We must be very careful. Yet, it is imperative that we get these people off that island. We absolutely have no choice in this matter. The PM has been advised of the situation, and he wants something done as quickly as possible with no publicity. This cannot get out. If it does we are all screwed, and we may not only be booted from office, but prosecuted for violating a variety of laws."

A member of the council asked about rumours of this guy named Jesus. Robson shook his head in disgust and replied, "A nut case and those idiot Injuns are falling for his rap. They actually think he is some kind of messiah sent to deliver them from their self-imposed stupidity. What they all need is to get the hell away from Gilford, get a job and start earning their keep. This government is sick of coddling a bunch of backwards malcontents who don't want to join the 21st century."

Another council member interjected, "I also hear that nuisance of a private eye, Aaron Adams, the one who got the story released about this guy calling himself Jesus when he was down in New Jersey, is on the goddamn island stirring up trouble, too."

Robson replied, "He is there, but believe me, the real problem is this guy calling himself Jesus."

When Jesus Came to Canada to Lead An
Indigenous Rebellion in the Broughton Archipelago

The seven council members voted unanimously to ask the PM to send in troops if necessary to thwart what was seemingly becoming an open rebellion. Robson planned to fly to Seattle the next day to meet with TWI CEO, Harold Frommer, to see how they might coordinate a joint statement about how the company was offering the residents an incredible financial package for moving along with firm support from the Canadian government for removal assistance.

Meanwhile, Aaron and Huyana were already in Seattle. Aaron set out to do some background checking on TWI and Harold Frommer. He had learned long ago that it was critical to thoroughly know your enemy. Only then could you genuinely understand how to effectively combat him.

The two checked into a small hotel in downtown Seattle. The desk clerk stared long and hard at the two, probably wondering what such a young woman wanted with an old man. Huyana flippantly said, "he's bought me for the week," as they strolled toward the elevator laughing.

"You have no shame do you," Aaron said as they entered the elevator.

"Those with shame rarely have any fun. They are too busy worrying about what people will think. I say let them think the worst. Most of them are just jealous because they want the same things I do. They are just too timid and too hung-up with religion to realize that sex is nothing but a game, played by most people their entire lives." Then she reached down between Aaron legs and gently grasped his manhood. "If we had more time on the elevator, I'd give you something I know you are craving."

She reminded Aaron of a few other women he had met, women who were not ashamed of their sexuality. In a world where proscribed rules of behaviour kept people from freely expressing themselves, it was gratifying to be with someone who looked upon conventionality as a prison of the mind.

They got off the elevator and walked arm-in-arm to the room. Aaron slid the key in into the door and swung it open. He stood there waiting for her to walk in. She smiled at him and said, "You can't wait can you?"

As she wrapped herself in his arms and their lips meet in feverous longing that overwhelmed them with passion, he managed to reach behind his back and gently close the door. The kiss was long, deep, wet, sensual and passionate as their tongues danced a tango of delight in each others mouths. Aaron ran his hand down her back, resting on her shapely, soft ass, kneading it gently.

When Jesus Came to Canada to Lead An
Indigenous Rebellion in the Broughton Archipelago

Huyana led him toward the bed as she was removing her top. Her fabulous breasts bounced as they stood high and firm on her chest. She kicked off her shoes, then unbuttoned her jeans and stood there in naked splendour. She reached down and unzipped Aaron's pants. She slowly pulled them to the floor around his ankles. She untied his shoes while on her knees, and he stepped out of them while he was removing his coat and shirt. Still on her knees, Huyana gently pulled down his briefs and watched as his half-erect member seem to beckon her forward. He thought that she deserved a more virile man, but as he was doing so, in one sweeping motion, she took him into her mouth and Aaron's mind sailed into the oblivion of blissfulness that he had been denied for far too long. She had not done this to him the previous night. They had only fondled and kissed, but she wanted much more this time. Aaron thought to himself that he probably could not deliver what she really needed, but as she enthusiastically devoured him, he floated in complete, total and harmonious surrender to her wantonness.

She eased up and motioned for Aaron to lie on the bed. She crawled between his legs and looked up at him with a sheepish grin. "This thing has been well-used over the years you naughty boy. It looks like it has been into a war zone. No doubt it has been a piston of pleasure."

Aaron, gasping for breath as he was still breathing heavily from the excitement, muttered "you are making fun of an old man. It has indeed been well-used when it functioned at a higher level."

Still looking up at him as she gently played with it and blew on it, she said, "you are still enough man for me. I am not looking for sex with you. I want to make love."

Her last words trailed off as she began to swirl her tongue and seemingly worship the only partially erect dangling demon of delight between his legs. He was now the man who had captured her heart, when she thought that it was forever sealed from those who might break it once again. He might not have the virility of the men Huyana was used to having sex with, but he had something none of them had. He had her heart.

Aaron could feel the tingling sensation signalling that he was about to erupt like a volcano getting ready to spurt its ash into the heavens. Huyana, enjoying her immense power, slowed her rapturously enchanting worship of Aaron's member and crawled on top of him. Even though it was not as stiff as that to which she was accustomed, her opening of desire ravenously swallowed it up as she bent forward and placed her mouth on Aaron's, moaning softly.

When Jesus Came to Canada to Lead An
Indigenous Rebellion in the Broughton Archipelago

She whispered, "this is going to feel good for both of us," as she kept raising and lowering her hips, making sure that she kept Aaron's semi-erect member firmly within her.

She gradually slowed down and just sit on it, working her love muscles without moving the rest of her body, all the time smiling with delicious delight that she had such power over Aaron. Then she begin to gentle move her hips back and forth, then side to side, making sure that she never let the object of her desire slip from the grasp of her love muscle. Her incredibly huge, globular breasts jiggled with each downward thrust and sway of her hips from side to side. Her lustrous, dark hair flayed all about and her sighs became almost guttural as if some wild animal was astride Aaron, wanting to devour him. She had broken into a sweat from the feverous intensity of her lovemaking and a thin bead of perspiration settled on her brow.

Aaron put his hands on her soft shapely ass as she rhythmically swayed from side to side, then up and down. She was breathing heavily and whimpering as the intensity of her pumping became more earnest. Suddenly, she let out a loud wail and gripped Aaron's upper arms tightly as her orgasm exploded. Aaron could not contain himself. He gripped her undulating hips and saw stars fluttering across the ceiling and then his eyes rolled back into his head, as he exploded into her warm opening. The intensity was like a bat coming into contact with a ball. The euphoric delight raced through their bodies and a sense of complete contentment overwhelmed them both. Completely spent, Huyana collapsed onto Aaron, burying her head in his left shoulder. He could feel her heart beating furiously.

They lay there, holding each other gently as Aaron went flaccid and fell out of her. She turned her head and put her chin in the middle of his chest, smiled and said, "I am full of you my love. I have your essence inside me. I cherish it."

While Aaron and Huyana were enjoying the ecstasy of the moment, in the board room of TWI, Darryl Robson had arrived to meet with Corcoran and Frommer, who had, through a reliable source, heard that Aaron Adams was in town. Also at the meeting was Damon Matthews, a CIA operative sent to coordinate with TWI and the Canadian government how to effectively neutralize those on Gilford Island who were interfering with the plans of the U.S. government to guarantee a steady supply of polonium. What follows is partly conjecture and partly supported by what occurred after the meeting. In all likelihood, it is fairly accurate, but the conversation between the four men is reconstructive in nature, and its accuracy can only be summarily assumed.

When Jesus Came to Canada to Lead An Indigenous Rebellion in the Broughton Archipelago

Frommer

"This situation is rapidly getting out of hand. This idiot calling himself Jesus and this private eye from New York are fomenting rebellion among people whom we have been leading around like sheep for years. All of a sudden this guy Jesus shows up and then he brings in this rebel-rouser from New York and the damn Injuns all of a sudden get a back-bone and decide to defy us."

Corcoran

"Boss, you've met Adams. You know what an arrogant son-of-bitch he is, but you ain't seen anything until you meet this guy calling himself Jesus. That bastard actually believes he is some divine being."

Matthews

"Gentlemen, we have dealt with this Jesus character once before in New Jersey. He stirred up a whole lot of trouble there, but we managed to neutralize him. Then, this Adams shows up, and he breaks him out of a secure facility where he had been interrogated. We assumed he was dead, but the doc must have been mistaken. Adams shows up, kills several agents and gets him out of a cold storage unit in Camden. Then Adams goes back to New York, where he kills four more agents while getting his girlfriend killed and manages to get some lie-filled notebook about the whole affair in a shopping cart pushed by a homeless bum who was apprehended by us before he could get it to the *New York Times*."

When Jesus Came to Canada to Lead An
Indigenous Rebellion in the Broughton Archipelago

We've been looking for this Jesus character for years. We could never prosecute Adams, because it was a deep-cover operation in New Jersey; consequently, we had to let him walk for fear of exposure. Now, we are so fed up with both these characters that we are prepared to eliminate them with extreme prejudice. The only thing standing in our way is approval from the Canadian government to go onto this god-forsaken place called Gilford Island and take this rebel-rousing son-of-bitch out once and for all. We'll take Adams out at the same time."

Robson

"Mr. Matthews, the Canadian government for far too long, while that great defender of freedom, George Bush was in office, turned its back on our greatest ally, but I am extremely proud to say that now there is a Canadian government that will stand by the USA in its endeavours to go after the evil-doers. I am authorized to give you permission to do whatever is necessary to take care of this threat to the nuclear arsenal of America as long as discretion is assured. This government is also tired of coddling these Indians who think they have a right to stand in the way of progress."

Frommer

"Mr. Matthews, I have it from a good source that Aaron Adams, with some island whore he brought with him, is in Seattle right now.

Matthews

"That problem is taken care of then.   I will get a

our very best men on it right away. Mr. Adams will have a serious accident while in Seattle."

This was the crux of the meeting, although there were further discussions of the logistics of landing a team on the island to take care of the threat to mining the polonium. Meanwhile, back at their hotel, Aaron and Huyana were dressed and ready to explore the depths of deception being practiced by TWI. They were about to encounter much more evil than they had anticipated in the dark waters of deception

Chapter 8
THE FIGHT AGAINST TYRANNY

The chill of their lies
keeps the masses in bondage.
They fend off the truth.
They steal the day,
and they own the night.

The falsifications of the oppressors,
who are corrupt in their power,
pile indignities upon the people
who are crying out for freedom
in a land that lives a lie.

The government is silent
and complicit in the deception,
giving a stage for the madness
that enslaves the masses
with hypocrisy and betrayal.

Aaron and Huyana spent the morning at the
law firm of Heath, Coggins, Phillips and Merrill.
They met Mr. Heath, a man who had spent years
in litigation against TWI. Aaron had researched
the history of TWI, and found that there was a
multitude of law suits filed against them, but all
had been dismissed on one technicality or another.
Several had been simply dismissed when the
government intervened with that notorious caveat:
prosecution deemed inappropriate due to national

security concerns. In other words, the corporation was immune from the law, because the government simply said they were. In eleven of those cases, the firm of Heath, Coggins, Phillips and Merrill had represented various litigants. One such litigant was the Navajo Nation in the Four Corners region of Colorado, New Mexico, Arizona and Utah. They had tried to prove that people on the reservation were suffering from uranium poisoning as a result of mining operations under a government licence granted to TWI. The case had dragged on for almost 40 years, as the Navajos living near Monument Valley had an unusually high rate of cancer, and a life expectancy of nearly 20 years less than average. High levels of radiation had been found in the soil since 1957, but still, the mining operation continued unabated.

The 82 year old Marvin Heath was a tenacious, dedicated, litigating dynamo who saw the United States government as an oppressor of the very people it was supposed to represent. So, he and Aaron immediately hit it off. He also was enamoured with Huyana to the point where he asked her, "You want to dump this old man and go out with a man who can really make you feel like a woman?"

Although Huyana got a good laugh out of it, Heath adamantly interjected, "don't laugh young lady. One night with me, and you'll never sleep with a man under 80 again."

After discussing all the cases that had been brought against TWI, the two were invited to review the case files which numbered well over one million pages. Trying to get a handle on exactly what they needed, Aaron asked, "have there been any cases where they have mined polonium in the USA?"

Heath, who was tall, white haired, robust and hardy replied in his gravely voice, "No categorical proof that there are any deposits in America, but there have been suspicions of surreptitious activities in the Four Corners region. You know where that is?"

"I do Mr. Heath."

"And I assume you know what polonium is used for?

Aaron, with a melancholy tone, replied, "Yes, I am afraid I do."

"Then you are very unusual. Most people have never heard of it, or confuse it with plutonium. It is vital to this country's nuclear arsenal. Without it, this nation could not trigger its nuclear weapons."

"I know this country has enough weapons of mass destruction to destroy the world several times over, and that the power to do that is more important to those who run this country than the power to eliminate hunger, disease, poverty and injustice. This is an arrogant nation that thinks it has the right to tell other countries they cannot have these weapons to defend themselves against us, while we continued to stockpile more and more of them. TWI is just one of the many corporations that depend on war to make profits. Like all corporations, they see people as nothing more than expendable commodities."

Smiling, Heath said, "Mr. Adams, if you had a law degree, I'd offer you a job. That is the kind of thinking that has kept me fighting those behemoths of evil and the U.S. government that enables them all these years. I will battle the bastards until they close the lid on my coffin, and even then I might just kick the lid off to go at them one last time. I hate the bastards!"

Aaron asked if there was anything at all in the files about the paper mills that TWI ran all over the world. Heath replied, "sure," as he walked over to a large filing cabinet, pulled out the top drawer and removed three files, tossing them down on the large conference table. "Here you go, help yourself. These are files on the paper mills in this country, Canada and Columbia."

When Jesus Came to Canada to Lead An Indigenous Rebellion in the Broughton Archipelago

Aaron and Huyana didn't even know what they were looking for, but they judiciously poured over the files and three ring binders, seeking anything out of the ordinary. Just as he was about to put a binder away, Aaron's right thumb felt an unusual thickness to the last page of the binder. Two pages had stuck together. He meticulously tried to pull them apart to no avail. Huyana reached over and took the binder. Her long index finger nail managed to separate the pages and she gently began to peel them apart. At the top of the page, in hand written capital letters was: *UNUSUAL OCCURANCES AT FOUR CORNERS AREA*. What follows is the exact handwritten, cryptic notations on the page:

1. In March 1993, Old Navajo man was out illegally hunting red foxes one night near Page, Arizona. Was hunting near a paper mill and power plant, notorious for polluting Colorado River and fouling the air of the nearby town. The owner of the paper mill and the power plant is Trans World Industries. The old man trailed a fox through a restricted area outside paper mill, and after catching the fox, on the way out of area heard strange noise which made him turn around and look back toward the paper mill. In the darkness, he saw a blue glow in one of paper mill windows. The blue glow lasted about five seconds and then the room went dark except for a faint overhead light.

2. Curious, old man went toward building for a better look. When he got near the inner gate, he saw four men wearing what were probably chemical containment suits, carrying a large cylindrical container about six feet long and maybe with a circumference of possibly three feet. The container was giving off an intense bluish glow that glittered in the darkness. He hid behind a bramble bush, lying flat on the ground. The men loaded container on what appeared to be a steel reinforced van, closed the door, walked back to the building and the truck drove off toward the power plant.

3. Man was taken to hospital next day by daughter. Diagnosed with severe polonium poisoning, similar to what killed Alexander Litvinenko and may have possibly killed Yasser Arafat. Government showed up to investigate, but nothing ever came of it. Family of man was brushed off and told diagnosis by doctor had been wrong. Man was cremated by county and ashes never returned to family. Paper mill was closed.
4. Suggest further checking to see if any unusual death rates from cancer in area.

"Harrison Black Elk saw the same thing on Kwak'wala. You and I both have a pretty good idea what this is, but I need to be sure. Let's copy this and share it with Heath," an indignant Aaron said.

Thrilled at what they found, Heath seemed ready to once again go up against TWI and the U.S. government. As he handed the paper to his secretary to copy, he told her, "Get me the chief of the Navajo Nation on the horn, too. We are about to blow the lid off TWI and the government that lets them get away with murder!"

Watching Aaron and Huyana leave the building were two CIA assassins, Bob Wingate and Dick Malloy, who had been given the assignment to tie up any loose ends with extreme prejudice. However, they were about to go up against a man like no other they had faced in their combined 44 years of service to the dark forces evil.

Getting in a taxi, Aaron immediately noticed they were being tailed. Turning to Huyana, he said, "Somebody is tailing us. Could be TWI, but is more likely the CIA. They aren't supposed to be doing domestic spying, but they have infiltrated every nook and cranny in this country that is now a monument to oppression to supposedly keep people safe. The only trouble is we need to be kept safe from them, not some outside enemy."

"What are you going to do," asked Huyana.

Aaron very quietly whispered into Huyana's left ear. "Well, I was in Canada, so I have no gun, but we are in America now. This is a place where people can walk into an elementary school packing and blow away little kids. Courtesy of the NRA, this is a nation with more firearms than people. Only Bibles outnumber guns. Frankly, I don't know which is deadlier, a gun or a Bible. More likely, it's the Bible. This state does have some regulation, but not much. However, I may have to go up against the CIA, so I want an untraceable gun."

Aaron leaned forward and tapped the driver on the shoulder. "Got any idea where a man could pick up a firearm in a hurry?"

The driver vehemently replied, "Wrong guy buddy. Don't know nothing about no guns, nothing but trouble, big time trouble. I've had cops try and pull this on me before."

Aaron reached in his pocket, took out a $100 bill and, still keeping his hand on it, laid it on the top edge of the front seat. The driver said, "I know the law. You gotta tell me if you are a cop if I ask. So, I am asking, are you a cop."

"I am no cop."

"I'll drop you off at a place called Lloyd's Taxidermy. Tell him Fred sent you. He will give you whatever you want. Will cost a minimum of $500 though for a small calibre."

When Jesus Came to Canada to Lead An
Indigenous Rebellion in the Broughton Archipelago

Aaron let the $100 float down onto the front seat, leaned back beside Huyana and smiled at her. "More expensive than Wal-Mart, but I never shop at Wal-Mart, anyway. Hate those low-paying, slave-driving bastards who destroyed free-enterprise."

They stopped at Lloyd's and it only took a few minutes for Aaron to have a big bastard of a 45 in his hands, a box of ammunition and a shoulder holster thrown in for free. He felt dressed now, dressed to do battle with any body that stood in the way of the truth.

They got another taxi and the tail was still there. Why were they tailing him? Were they just there to see what he was up to, or were they sent to eliminate someone who was daring to stand against injustice? He didn't want to take a chance with Huyana's life, but asked himself if it was safer for her to stay with him? He eased closer to her and whispered in her ear. "You afraid?"

Smiling up at him, she replied, "What is there to be afraid of? I've got my knight in shining armour by my side."

The taxi went down Alaskan Way to the waterfront, where they got out and headed up to Pike Place Market and then over to Pike Street. One of the men had gotten out of the car tailing

them and was trying to inconspicuously follow
Aaron. He wasn't doing a very good job.

Aaron and Jasmine meandered over to 4th
Avenue and went into the main branch of the
library. Their tail was on his cell-phone, no doubt,
telling his compatriot where they were. Going
over to the reference section, Aaron started going
through old files on the history of people who had
been fired or left TWI under mysterious
circumstances. Nothing out of the ordinary
appeared until Aaron found an innocuous story of
no more than a few lines in the 1992 May edition
of a Seattle Community College newspaper:

*Trans World Industries Linked to Toxic Poisoning
By Fired Employee in Law Suit*

*Chemical engineer, Gerald E. Rainey claimed in
a lawsuit filed in the Superior Court of King
County that he was unjustly terminated by Trans
World Industries because he became aware of
their involvement with a CIA front company that
was secretly processing polonium and dumping
toxic wastes in an area of the south-western USA.
The case is on the docket for January of 1993 in
the court of the honourable Benjamin Fuller.*

After looking though various other sources,
there was no further mention of the case or the
claims made by Rainey in any other documents.

Next step would be the Hall of Records to review the files on the court case. The King County Courthouse was on nearby 3rd Avenue. They would walk over there to see what they could find out about the case, and if it might lead to a credible explanation on just what TWI was up to on Kwak'wala.

Their tail was now joined by his comrade. Aaron smiled at how crafty the two thought they were. How grown men loved to play he thought. As a child, Aaron and his cousin had loved to play spies. The two tailing them were probably $150,000 a year employees who genuinely believed they were protecting their country, rather than the oligarchy that was the real power that controlled everything. The two were pawns in the grand game of economic servitude, but they were too steeped in patriotic babble to realize that they were being used just like everyone else. They were in service to their own oppressors and didn't even realize it. Of course, they were better off than most. They had great salaries, benefits and free healthcare while most others lived lives of deprivation in a nation of abundance. That was the price the rulers were willing to pay in order to assure the loyalty of those whose job it was to keep the masses in line.

At the Superior Court Hall of Records, the two men tailing them stationed themselves outside, one at the front and one at the back. The clerk was a rather gregarious man who was too busy ogling Huyana to hear a thing Aaron said. Finally, Aaron motioned for Huyana to talk to him, assuming that was the only way to get his attention.

She flashed that provocative, come-hither smile. "We are looking for the records from a 1993 case in which Trans World Industries was sued by a Gerald Rainey for unlawful termination. Think you could help us? I would be really appreciative. It is very important."

The man, about forty with thick glasses that magnified his brown eyes that were twinkling with delight that Huyana had addressed him, replied, "you bet little lady."

He made an abrupt turn and went to his desk where he started pounding computer keys like he was hammering nails. A quizzical look stretched across his face and he looked up and said, "Sorry lady, but that is a case that has been sealed by order of the court. Curious though, never heard of a civil suit being sealed by the court. Sometimes they seal the settlement, but not the whole proceedings."

Aaron leaned forward, placing his hands on the counter. "Any idea where the judge in the case could be found?"

Almost ignoring Aaron, the man addressed Huyana with the answer. "Ben Fuller is a pretty tough judge, a real hard-ass, if you know what I mean. His office is on the fourth floor, 407."

As Huyana said thanks and they turned to leave, the clerk shouted out, "Wait a minute."

They stopped, turned back and waited. The man got up, moved to the counter and said, "There's a notice on the file. Says sealed for national security reasons and that I'm supposed to get the names of anyone requesting information on the case."

Aaron smiled, took Huyana by the arm and as they turned to leave, said, "Mr. and Mrs. Barrack Hussein Obama of 1600 Pennsylvania Avenue, Washington, DC."

The man didn't look too pleased but did nothing, just stood there trance-like staring at Huyana's gorgeous, shapely ass as she looked back over her left shoulder and smiled at him. He took a deep breath and sighed, thinking what a lucky man Aaron was.

The judge's secretary was a stern looking woman who sat behind her desk like it was a barrier that separated the righteous from the heathens. She reminded Aaron of the wicked witch of the west from *The Wizard of Oz*.

Aaron very politely said, "We would like to see the judge to discuss a case he handled back in 1993."

The woman, barely parting her lips, replied, "the judge is a very busy man. You need an appointment. You can't just walk in and expect to see him."

Aaron detested arrogance from those who were on the people's payroll. He held his anger in check but only barely. "I am really sorry to bother him, but we are only in town for a today, and it is imperative that I see him about a highly important matter."

The woman puffed out her chest, sighed and got up. "I'll see if he can spare you just a few minutes."

She went into the judge's office, and Aaron looked around at the elaborate furnishings that obviously weren't bought at a discount furniture store. He thought to himself that there was no limit to extravagance from those at the top of the public payroll. Judges like Fuller were always siding with the corporations and the wealthy, because they were part of that class. Most judges were like the politicians who kept telling the public to tighten their belts for the good of the country, while they never applied that caveat to themselves.

When Jesus Came to Canada to Lead An
Indigenous Rebellion in the Broughton Archipelago

The wicked witch of the west returned and curtly said, "The judge needs to know what case it is about."

So, thought Aaron, the judge is too busy to give me five minutes, but he will waste five minutes with a back-and-forth between his surrogate and me. The arrogance of people simply knew no end, and Aaron had enough of it. He blew! "Listen; tell the arrogant asshole sitting behind his $3,000 desk that one of the taxpayers wants to converse with him."

The judge's office door, which was partly ajar, suddenly sprang open and the judge stood in the doorway. "I'll dare you come into my office and use that kind of language. You don't talk to a judge that way."

Now, an enraged Aaron was ready to let loose with both barrels. "Judge, you are a fucking employee of the people. I am people, and I need a couple of minutes of your time. You going to give it to me or not? If not, I'll head down to the newspaper and take out a full-page ad attacking you for your arrogance and sanctimonious attitude."

Fuller stood defiantly but seemed to realize that he was not dealing with the usual defendant who cowered before him in the courtroom. He stepped to one side of the doorway and gestured with his hand for Aaron and Huyana to enter.

He left the door open, probably out of fear, so, if the secretary heard anything outlandish going on, she could call security. As they sat down, he said, "So, what can I do for you?"

"I am Aaron Adams, a private investigator from New York, and this is my friend, Huyana Patrick from Canada. We are looking for any information you might be able to provide in regards to the case that was sealed almost twenty-years ago. It dealt with a man named Gerald Rainy who was suing for unjustified termination from Trans World Industries."

The judge sat up straighter and got a quizzical look on his stern, cold face. "I am not at liberty to discuss any details of that particular case. There was a settlement between the parties, and the records were sealed at the request of the government due to national security concerns. You want any more information, I suggest you go to Washington, DC and talk to someone there. We have nothing else to discuss Mr. Adams. Good day."

Aaron sighed and replied, "Sure, I'll go, but could you at least tell me if Rainey is still in Seattle?"

Shaking his head, the judge was adamant in his reply. "Don't know anything about him. Last time I saw him was when he was handed a check."

Aaron got up and said, "So, TWI did give him a financial settlement."

"I suppose that is no secret. Rainey accepted a settlement that included an agreement not to discuss the case. If he does, the agreement would be null and void. He would be hauled back into court and forced to make restitution to TWI for violating the orders of the court. That is all I can say. Again, good day, Mr. Adams."

Looking over at Jasmine, Aaron directed his parting remarks at her, but they were meant for the judge. "You know Huyana, most people hide behind a mask of respectability and self-aggrandizement. There are many people in this world who fool the masses, but the truth is that some of us see through their charade of self-importance. The people who think they should be exalted don't realize just how insignificant they really are. You cannot hide your shallowness from those who see through the mask."

Huyana proudly took Aaron's arm and they strolled out together. They both looked at the wicked witch of the west and smiled, defiantly waving good-bye, both of them with a smile of smug, self satisfaction. As he opened the door to leave, Aaron glanced back though the judge's open office door and saw the judge speaking frantically on the phone. Someone important was being informed of their visit with the judge.

As they walked to the elevator, Jasmine tilted her head onto Aaron's shoulder and whispered, "You're my hero."

Aaron asked Huyana to call Heath on her cell phone and tell him that they needed to meet with him again to discuss what he knew about Judge Benjamin Fuller. An appointment for 4:00 PM was arranged, and Aaron and Huyana decided since it was 2:00 PM maybe lunch was in order. Afterwards, they decided to try and locate Gerald Rainey. Hopefully, he was still in Seattle.

One of the men tailing them had disappeared, but the other one was still doggedly on the job. As long as they were in public, Aaron assumed they were safe, but that was a dire misconception that was actually being proved by what was going on near the offices of Heath, Coggins, Phillips and Merrill.

Marvin Heath was, as usual, taking an afternoon stroll. It had been a rigor he judiciously followed ever since having a light heart attack ten years before. This day, his devotion to an afternoon

stroll would prove fatal. As he stood at the corner
of Madison Street and 8th Avenue, waiting for the
light to change, a tall slightly balding man walked
up beside him. When Heath turned to look at him,
the man smiled and cordially nodded, as if to say
"good day." In the man's left hand was a syringe
filled with what the CIA agent holding it
considered an elixir of justice. As the two walked
across the street, Heath felt a slight stinging
sensation in his left side. He managed to get to the
other side of the street and collapsed. The man
who had nodded at Heath eased the syringe into
the left coat pocket. He took out his cell phone
with his right hand and asked his partner where
Aaron and Huyana were. He strolled back toward
Pike Place Market where Aaron and Huyana were
having lunch as Marion Heath lay on the
pavement in the throes of pain from the polonium
that had been injected into him.

Like most of those who serve the hypocritical
idea that all is justified in the defence of liberty,
Agent Dick Malloy had no remorse about
dispatching an 82 year old man whom he
considered a detriment to his beloved country's
destiny to preserve the capitalistic system that had
made it so great. To him, Heath was an
impediment to true progress. His death was just
one of many that could be justified in the on-going
battle to keep those who wanted a more
equalitarian economic system from destroying

capitalism. Heath was anachronism in the modern global economy that had no place for sentimentality or fairness.

Aaron and Huyana finished their meal and noticed the missing man had joined his partner. As they got up, Aaron observed the man take something out of his coat pocket that looked like a syringe and toss it into a trash can. That's strange thought Aaron.

The two spent a little time wandering through Pike Place Market, visiting a few of the shops, even stopping at Daily Dozen Donuts for some sugary desert to top of their lunch. As they were enjoying their sack of miniature donuts, Aaron looked up at the clock and noticed it was 3:30. It was a good 15 minutes walk back to Heath's office, so they left, heading up Pike Street with their tails close behind.

Arriving at Heath, Coggins, Phillips and Merrill, there was a sombreness pervading the office as they walked in. Heath's secretary looked up at them and said, "He's in the hospital. He's in the hospital."

Aaron asked, "How? What happened?"

"No one knows, he just dropped to the pavement after going across the street. He was on his daily stroll and just collapsed. Probably another heart attack."

Aaron, instantly realizing that it was more than a coincidence that Heath would collapse the very day he showed up asking about TWI, reflected on what he saw outside Daily Dozen Donuts. This was no accident. The government was concerned about what Heath knew.

Obviously, Aaron and Huyana were also on the hit list. He asked what hospital he was in, but before he and Huyana went to the hospital they headed over to Daily Dozen Donuts at Pike Place. Strangely, their tail was gone, but it didn't take Aaron long to figure out why. When they arrived at the donut stand, the trash can outside had been turned over. The tall, slightly balding guy had realized his mistake and gone back to retrieve the syringe.

Huyana, hurriedly asked, "what is it Aaron? What is going on?"

"Heath, and now you and I, are on the government hit list. My guess is that Heath got the same deadly dose of polonium that was surreptitiously administered awhile back to Alexander Litvinenko in London, and very possibly was the cause of Yasser Arafat's death. This whole affair is getting out of hand. I'm not going the hospital, because I don't want to deal with any government agents, but we'll call and see how he is."

Aaron's quick call to the hospital from a nearby phone booth brought the news he had feared. Heath had died, but it was just more confirmation that Aaron's suspicions about what was going on at the paper mill were correct. He asked to be connected to the doctor in charge and just said, "check Heath for Polonium poisoning," and then hung up. The doctor would find it, but the government would, in all likelihood, cover it up under that abominable phrase, "national security." That phrase kept the people from learning the truth about the evil under which they lived their lives of quiet desperation in a society steeped in government and corporate propaganda that was used to keep the masses bound in patriotic servitude to an idea that had long ago been tossed into the dust bin of history. They needed to do one more thing and then they would return to Canada. They needed to confirm some things with Gerald Rainey, if they could locate him.

Investigative work can often be gruelling and tedious, with many hours spent pouring over old documents and antiquated materials in search of that ever elusive link that will lead to solving a case. Then, often, the answer is right there in front of you. Before exiting the phone booth, Aaron picked up the torn and dilapidated phone directory that was so tightly bound to the chain that tied it to the bottom of the phone that he could hardly open it. The cover was dated 1999. So, no one had bothered to replace it for almost 15 years. Anyway, the phone company wanted you to pay a dollar now to call information, so no phone book was just another way to extort money from the poor who couldn't afford a cell-phone. Delicately pressing the pages that were tightly bound, he scanned through the R's and there it was, Gerald Rainey. He put fifty cents in and dialled the number. An answering machine came on and a voice said, "Gerald is not home. Please leave a message."

So, it was that easy. Just look in the phone directory and there he was. Looking at the address, Aaron quickly exited the booth and turned to Huyana. "My superior detecting skills have done it again. I found Gerald Rainey's name in the phone booth. Damn, I am smart."

Huyana, smiling sheepishly at Aaron, said in a matter-of-fact manner, "of course you are smart. You've got me don't you?"

They hailed a cab and headed for Gerald Rainey's. They would wait until he got home. Then, Aaron would get the confirmation for which he was searching. He was sure of it.

When Jesus Came to Canada to Lead An
Indigenous Rebellion in the Broughton Archipelago

Rainey lived in the affluent area of Seattle known as Magnolia. It was an eclectic mix of stately homes, townhouses and condos, many with breathtaking views of the Puget Sound. It was just another example of the great social and economic divide in a nation that proclaimed equality but did not know the meaning of the word. There was no equality of opportunity in a country that allowed the few to enjoy lives of excess while their neighbours, a short distance away, lived in squalor- all because the nation refused to address the inequality of opportunity. Those at the top insulated themselves from those at the bottom, and those at the bottom were too complacent to demand that the obscenity of excess be addressed. It was just as much the fault of the poor as the rich. The 99% had the power of numbers, but they had been propagandized into believing that they actually had the chance to be among the 1% some day. How delusional, yeah, if they won the lottery, maybe.

Obviously, the settlement Rainey received must have been an extremely handsome one. His palatial home was a sprawling two story monstrosity of excess that backed right onto the Puget Sound. The steps up to the door were polished Italian marble and the doorbell was encrusted with what appeared to be sparking jade. The ring was answered by an immaculately attired platinum blond woman who looked as if she had just stepped off the cover of *Playboy*. Her perfectly formed breasts were, no doubt, primarily plastic, but it was some damn fine looking plastic thought Aaron.

Smiling through perfectly straight white teeth, she said, with an incredible air of sophistication that did not give any hint of arrogance, "Yes, may I help you?"

"We would like to see Gerald Rainey, please," said Aaron.

Extremely polite, the woman replied, "of course, he is in the kitchen, may I tell him who is calling?"

"Well, he won't know us, but I am Aaron Adams from New York City and this is Huyana Patrick from Vancouver Island in BC."

Ushering them in and pointing in an almost provocative manner to a lavishly furnished den on the right with a fireplace the size of most bedrooms, she, in her articulate and precise manner said, "Have a seat in the den. He will be with you in a moment."

Aaron and Huyana looked at one another and shook their heads in disgust at the ostentatious display of wealth.

J. Wayne Frye

When Jesus Came to Canada to Lead An
Indigenous Rebellion in the Broughton Archipelago

As they sit waiting for Rainey, Huyana, who was sitting on a Queen Anne chair opposite Aaron, said, "I'm going to get up, come over there and grab your crotch, and if you have a hard-on, I'll rip your eyes out."

Aaron smiled and replied, "If I have a hard-on, you can do something worthwhile with it while you are ripping my eyes out. Believe me; if I can't get a good erection with you, nobody else is going to do it for me."

Rainy walked in with the blond by his side. "Mr. Adams, you are wrong, I do know you. Aaron Adams is a name known by most people who have read about your escapades in the biography written by Wayne Frye. It is a pleasure to meet you."

As he reached out to shake the rising Aaron's hand, he turned to the blond and said, "this is the famous private detective who nearly got a whole city blown up a few decades ago and recently was credited with fabricating a story about a modern day Jesus." He then motioned with his right hand toward the woman and continued. "This is my very good friend, Denise Dolman."

"A pleasure Ms. Dolman," replied Aaron as he nodded toward Huyana and said, "This is my associate Huyana Patrick."

When Jesus Came to Canada to Lead An
Indigenous Rebellion in the Broughton Archipelago

After the pleasantries were over, Rainey asked if he could get them a drink. Aaron and Huyana declined and then Rainey, direct and to the point, said, "I assume a man in your line of work could only be here for one reason, TWI."

"Pretty astute Mr. Rainey. I would like to ask you a few questions about their integrity and penchant for skirting the law."

"Mr. Adams, like 99% of the large corporations, they have no integrity. I can say that and be safe in honouring my settlement agreement, but beyond that I must avoid any discussion of them or what they were up to when I worked for them. As you can see, the agreement has led to me being able to live an extremely affluent lifestyle. I would not want to jeopardize that."

Aaron, sighing, replied in a quizzical manner, "So, could I still ask you a few questions? You are free to simply say that you can't answer it. I would not want to jeopardize your well-being in any away."

"Ask away, but I can assure you that it will probably be an exercise in futility"

"I appreciate your candour, but any amount of information would be of great assistance, believe me."

When Jesus Came to Canada to Lead An
Indigenous Rebellion in the Broughton Archipelago

Rainey and Denise took a seat on the Eastlake antique settee to the left of Aaron, and Aaron thought that for a rich bastard, Rainey wasn't all that bad a guy.

Denise, as she crossed her legs and smiled at Aaron, was not, Aaron deduced, just an air-headed hot-bodied broad. The woman had some class, but she didn't exude the arrogance that so many women like her did. Aaron figured he would start with the most direct question in regards to what Rainey had found out. "You discovered that TWI was operating a CIA front company that was processing polonium?"

"That is a matter of public record. Yes, I did, but I cannot divulge the company's name or location, other than it is in the southwest."

Aaron probed a bit deeper. "And they were processing polonium. I assume for nuclear triggers?"

"Again, it is public record that it dealt with polonium. You are, obviously Mr. Adams, an intelligent man, so you can draw your own conclusions about the uses of polonium, but I would be violating my agreement if I confirmed it. I can tell you, without violating the agreement, that TWI is the biggest miner of polonium in the world, however."

Aaron, gaining respect for Rainey, continued, "And this company in the southwest, my guess being in the Four Corners region, was dumping toxic materials that were fouling the drinking water and land around the nearby Navajo Reservation?"

Rainey, seeing Aaron as a man of integrity, replied, "your geography is good, but, again, I cannot confirm that it was in the Four Corners area."

In a nod to the accuracy of Aaron's suggestion of the location, Rainey reiterated, "As I said, your geography is excellent. As for dumping toxic materials, again, that is public record only as far as what the newspaper stated about the case. There has never been any proof that toxic materials were dumped there. However, an intelligent person could look up records to see if there were any dramatic increases in death rates from cancer, birth defects, etc. in that area of the country. I, due to the agreement, cannot confirm that is the case from what I learned, because I cannot even confirm the location you mentioned. However, I have read accounts of unusually high cancer death rates and a multitude of birth defects among the Navajos who live in that area. That is public record. Of course, that is assuming your geographical placement of the polonium problem is accurate, and I am not confirming it is."

Aaron was now ready for the big one. "Did Lon Corcoran and Harold Frommer ever mention anything about Gilford Island and its relation to polonium trigger mechanisms?"

Rainey sit up more erect, seemed to be contemplating and slightly scratched his head. "Interesting question, Mr. Adams, interesting."

Aaron waited. There was an intense silence before Rainey decided to ask a question. "You representing someone from Gilford Island?"

"I am, Mr. Rainey, but if I told you whom, you would just laugh. Let's just say I am representing all the Aboriginals who live there and are threatened with being evacuated because of the discovery of polonium on the island, but that discovery is only a part of the problem. I believe there is something sinister going on in the so-called paper mill on the far side of the island. What you discovered was going on in the Four Corners area, and yes, I know you have not confirmed that location, I believe will confirm my suspicions about the Gilford Island paper mill."

Rainey got up, turned to Denise and said, "for your own good, it is better if you are not privy to what I am about to tell Mr. Adams." He then looked at Aaron and continued, "letting Ms. Patrick hear what I am about to say might also be detrimental to her welfare. I suggest you ask her to leave, too."

Aaron looked at Huyana and very seriously said, "That's her call. In all frankness, I will probably share it with her anyway once we leave. She is a respected member of the Kwak'wala community and privy to everything I have discovered up to this point."

As Denise walked out the door, Rainey replied, "very well Mr. Adams, I signed no agreement in regards to Gilford or as the natives call it, Kwak'wala; consequently, I am violating no agreement in regards to that place."

Just as Rainey was getting ready to continue, a loud scream could be heard from outside the room. That muffled sound that signified a firing gun with a silencer on it made Aaron instinctively reach inside his coat pocket and pull the 45 out. He looked toward Huyana and motioned with his head for her to find cover, which she did behind the sofa. As Rainey walked through the archway, he came to an abrupt halt and stood there two or three seconds, unable to move as bullets riddled his body until he finally dropped into a lifeless heap on the floor. The assassins were professionals, so they made no attempt to enter the room for fear they might unduly expose themselves. Not a word, not a sound of any kind was uttered by any of the combatants. Any sound, no matter how faint, might expose the combatants to a fusillade of hot lead.

Aaron did not move, just stood perfectly still and looked over at an obviously frightened Huyana, and he very deliberately and slowly put his index finger to his lips as a signal for her to keep completely quiet. He wasn't sure how many assassins there were, but his guess was two - the two who had been tailing them.

Aaron dropped to his knees, gun hand extended toward the archway to the den. He could hear a faint rustle in the hall to the inside right of the archway. He stretched out and rolled across the floor to the opposite side, as he knew the two were to his right and he could get a better shot from that side. Damn, they were patient.

Aaron could hear himself breathing. He glanced back at Huyana, who was still in the same spot. He gave her a faint smile of reassurance. He had been up against pros before, and always came out on top, but he was old now, and even though the instincts die hard, he knew that he was not the man he used to be. Age not only adds wrinkles on the skin, it puts wrinkles in the mind. He simply wasn't as quick as he once was. If it were just him, he might walk through the door gun blazing and take his chances on getting them before they got him, but he had Huyana to think about. If they took him out, she was next.

He looked into the hallway and saw a shadow on the wall opposite the archway. From the looks of the shadow, the guy was probably about a foot to the right of the archway. Aaron figured a well angled shot might hit him, but unless the bullet hit somewhere besides the chest or back it would have no affect. They were wearing bullet proof vests for sure. They would not go into battle unprepared.

The stalemate continued for what seemed hours but was only a few minutes. Aaron figured time was on the assassins' side. He had to make a move. Looking at the shadow, he pivoted his gun toward the area by the archway where the head appeared to be. Stretching out on the floor and extending his gun, he tilted it upward and took careful aim at the wall. The wall was thick, but not thick enough to stop a bullet. He gently squeezed the trigger and the sound reverberated throughout the silent house like symbols clanging in a rousing symphony crescendo. The shadow dropped from the wall and someone screamed, "Dick, Dick."

The only answer Bob Wingate would get from Dick Malloy would be in the afterlife. So, Aaron knew he was dealing with just one man now. The odds were a little better. Wingate figured out how

Aaron had been able to get Malloy, so he was careful to make sure he cast no shadow on the far wall. He was in the hallway, sitting beside Denise's body, gun hand extended and elbows resting on his knees, ready for Aaron to come bolting through the door. Then, Aaron heard the faint sound made by a cell-phone. He was calling someone. He was obviously sending a one word text message so his confederates could get a fix on him and send help. Aaron would have to make a move before the cavalry arrived and all avenues of escape were cut off. He had maybe five to ten minutes tops.

Aaron assumed that Wingate was in a crouch, as most professionals would be. So, if he could come through the door high, he might have a chance to get him first. He rolled back across the room to an oak table that was next to the right side of the archway. He carefully removed the lamp from it. No doubt, Wingate could hear the commotion and was wondering what was going on, but he figured time was on his side. Just wait Aaron out and help would arrive. The table was about three feet high. That was just enough to give Aaron the trajectory he needed to make a leap into the hallway about five or six feet off the ground. He figured Wingate would be looking to shoot low, and that split second before he reacted to an airborne Aaron would be just enough to finish him off. Aaron slowly pulled the table back from the wall, pushed it forward nearer the archway and got on top of the table as quietly as possible, while Huyana looked on perplexed, but with complete confidence in Aaron. Standing on the table, Aaron leaped forward through the archway and trained his gun downward, and sure enough, Wingate was in a crouch. Before Wingate could adjust and raise his gun barrel upward, Aaron squeezed off two rounds that split Wingate's skull like a hot knife cutting butter. Aaron banged against the wall and flopped to the floor, as Huyana gingerly came out from behind the sofa and cautiously approached the archway. Aaron, in great pain from banging the wall looked up at her and said, "It's O.K."

She ran to him and tried to comfort him. He said, "No time for that, more of the bastards are on the way. Let's get out of here."

They stepped over the bodies of the two agents in the hallway and felt no sympathy, but as they looked down at Denise, a wave of emotion overcame them both, as they realized she was just another innocent victim in the ongoing war of aggression by the government against its own citizens. She was one of many who had to pay a high price for the so-called freedom that no one actually had.

They scampered out the back and down to the beach. They headed north toward the towering buildings, finally turning up a street and finding a cab. They had what they needed, now. Aaron was sure what was in the paper mill, and he was sure that the U.S. government and the Canadian governments were conspiring to bring an end to the mini-rebellion that was taking place on Kwak'wala. He would not risk the life of his good friend Eric Hindle by going to Vancouver to get any further confirmation on what he was now sure was on the island. He told Huyana that they could not risk crossing into Canada from the normal routes, because the word would be out to detain them, and the next stop might well be one of the American gulags of torture that had become the norm since Bush and Cheney decided if you called torture by another name it wasn't really torture.

They made their way to Bellingham, Washington where they rented a four wheel drive vehicle from Hertz and headed into the wilderness in search of a place where they could slip across the border undetected. They followed an old logging road until they came to the BC border, where they crossed through a dried up creek-bed and made their way to Abbotsford, British Columbia. Aaron drove the car to the airport and turned it in. They boarded a plane for Victoria where they chartered a float plane and went to directly to Kwak'wala where preparations for the defence of the island had progressed to the point that it had swelled to nearly 1500 indigenous

people who had come to help the brave souls
make a stand against the tyranny of greed.

Throwing his arms around Aaron, Jesus said,
"and what news have you my friend?"

Aaron whispered, "We need to talk in private."

"And we shall. Follow me."

As Aaron left with Jesus, Huyana headed toward
the clinic. Upon arrival, she found it empty and a
note for her: *Be advised that you have been
ordered out. Call to arrange transportation. It is
no longer safe on the island.*   *Jane*

Huyana tossed the note into the trash can and put
the open sign on the window. The people of the
island were her patients and her friends. They
could cut-off her pay. They could demand her
resignation. She was going nowhere, regardless of
orders. Kwak'wala was her home.

She took a seat at her desk and looked out the
window at the bevy of activity from people who
were finally making a stand against the corruptive
influence of the society of greed. The outsiders
would call it anarchy. She thought to herself that
none are more hopelessly enslaved than those who
falsely believe they are free. Those people did not
know the difference between dissent and anarchy.

Meanwhile, Jesus and Aaron went to the chief's home where they sit down with him to go over what Aaron had learned.

Aaron glanced over to the far corner and saw 10 or 12 wooden boxes stacked up all the way to the ceiling. Chief Harry winked and said, "A gift of 432 Kalashnikov rifles from our benefactor Plato Papadopoulos"

Aaron, concerned about the continuing stockpiling of weapons, looked in a concerned manner at Jesus. "You may need a lot more than that when I tell you what is going on at the paper mill; although, I think you have known what was going on there all along. You just wanted confirmation before acting on some scheme you, no doubt, have been hatching for some time."

Jesus' eyes twinkled a bit in that mischievous way that Aaron was familiar with when dealing with a man who always seemed to know what was going to happen before it occurred. Aaron had no belief in him as a divinity, but he had to admit that there was something almost god-like about his ability to seemingly know what was going to happen. However, he was a man who never claimed any divinity, and he always made it plain that people's fate was always in their own hands, not in the hands of some omnipotent celestial being. Still, Jesus did not utter a word.

Aaron saw it as a cue for him to continue. "That it is no paper mill. Oh, they make some paper there, yes. However, that is just a cover. It is a plant where they produce polonium nuclear triggers for all the missiles in the USA, now that the main plant in the Four Corners region of the USA has been closed. That is why the polonium discovery on the island is so important. It is right next to the source they need to make the triggers for atom bombs. They would no longer have to sneak the polonium in, as the source is right here on the island."

Jesus, not stunned by what he was hearing, but seemingly elated at the confirmation of his suspicions, said "you know this for sure? You are getting this from a verifiable source?"

"Jesus, my profession is investigating. I have no written proof, only a series of circumstances that indicate to me that my assumption is absolutely, beyond a doubt, fact. This island is on its way to being a toxic hazard, and as long as that mill continues to operate, it will eventually be completely uninhabitable. In 2006, the government of Canada secretly agreed to allow this mill to operate as a cover for a plant where nuclear triggers are manufactured. The people working there are not Canadians, they are Americans employed by TWI. They are rotated in and out at three month intervals."

When Jesus Came to Canada to Lead An
Indigenous Rebellion in the Broughton Archipelago

Chief Harry was shocked that a usually independent Canadian government, apparently with the election of an apologist for America, had become an accomplice in a malfeasant clandestine operation. This explained the immense pressure to get the people off the island before the truth was discovered. It was not just about polonium, although that was the biggest factor. It was also about Canadian connivance with a U.S. company and the American government. The chief, with deadly earnest leaned forward and asked Jesus, "What do you we do?"

Jesus, now convinced of his suspicions, said, "first, we must meet with the people and lay out what is happening to this sacred land, and get final acclamation on whether they really want to go forward with what may well be a catastrophic course of action in defence of their way of life. Many of the Aboriginals here now do not call this home. They are only here to defend the honour of the few people who are expected to bend to the will of the United States. I think they will believe, as I do, that the USA will have to make other arrangements for triggering its obscene weapons of mass destruction. These people are true patriots of indigenous rights, because they are defending another band's freedom, but I believe they see it as a defence of all Aboriginal rights, because somewhere, somehow, someway a stand against this abominable abrogation of rights must be made or the hundreds of years of oppression will continue unabated by both the U.S. and Canadian governments. Send word that we will have a mass meeting at 4:00 PM at the dock of all the people on the island. Then, if they all are in agreement that we should move forward against the forces of darkness, I shall reveal to you my plan that might well advoid any real bloodshed."

Aaron and Huyana stood in awe of the man they had both grown to deeply love. It was like no affection they had ever felt for someone before. Neither believed he possessed any divinity whatsoever, as they were both committed non-believers, but there was no denying that there was something special about him that just simply wasn't found in an ordinary person, or for that matter, even in an extraordinary person. If there was such a thing as divinity, this man was as close as anyone could get.

He looked over at Huyana and Aaron. They could always tell that he was pleased that they had found each other. He seemed to relish the binding of two souls. It was as if he saw in them and others who shared romantic love that which he denied himself. His love was not just for one individual, but for all those who toiled in the misery of day-to-day survival in a world that had no compassion and no justice for the marginalized. He was a man who gave so much love that it almost seemed to drain him of life. You could see the hurt he felt for those who suffered indignities, but he was no complacent, turn the other cheek purveyor of wisdom who said you would receive your reward in the end. No, he carried an anarchist sword of unwavering retribution against those who oppressed and imprisoned people who were caught on the periphery of a greed-based world where all the wealth and power flowed to the few at the top. He saw great possibilities for a paradise on earth if the disenfranchised and forgotten of the world banded together to fight against injustice. And now, he was about to offer nearly 1500 people, who looked upon him for words of wisdom, the opportunity to take a bold, determined stand against injustice.

Jesus stood on a picnic table and motioned with both hands for everyone to take a seat on the grass and the dock. "I am here to not tell you people what to do, but I am here to tell you that your way of life is threatened, not just those who live here on this magnificent place called Kwak'wala, but all of you who subscribe to a simple life not based on the white man's obsessive drive to own more and more. He does not understand that the pursuit to own comes at an incredibly high price that even the billionaire should not be willing to pay. The price is not in dollars and cents, but is a price that is paid in the loss of one's soul. The depravity of greed is all consuming."

J. Wayne Frye   223

When Jesus Came to Canada to Lead An
Indigenous Rebellion in the Broughton Archipelago

Jesus paced back and forth on the picnic table, seemingly in deep thought and then continued. "One day a wealthy father took his son on a trip to the country so that the son could see how the poor lived. They spent a day and a night at the farm of a very poor family. When they got back from their trip, the father asked his son, 'How was the trip?' 'Very good, Dad!' replied the son." Then Jesus paused a bit and looked up at the clearing sky. The rays of the sun seemed to dance about his head, almost forming a halo behind it.

Jesus continued. "Did you see how poor people can be? The father asked. 'Yeah, he replied. And what did you learn?' the father then asked." Again Jesus paused and Aaron and Huyana smiled at each other in anticipation of the lesson he was about to teach.

"The son answered, 'I saw that we have a dog at home, and they have four. We have a pool that reaches to the middle of the garden; they have a creek that has no end. We have imported lamps in the house; they have the stars. Our patio reaches to the front yard; they have the whole horizon.' When the little boy was finished, the father was speechless. His son then added, 'Thanks dad for showing me how poor we are!' So, you see, the boy saw what real poverty is – poverty of the soul." Then a collective hush fell over the crowd as they digested the depth of what Jesus told them.

J. Wayne Frye

When Jesus Came to Canada to Lead An Indigenous Rebellion in the Broughton Archipelago

"The people in the outside world have no idea what real success is. For example, a young and successful executive was traveling down a neighbourhood street, going a bit too fast in his new Mercedes. He was watching for kids darting out from between parked cars and slowed down when he thought he saw something. As his car passed, no children appeared. Instead, a brick smashed into the Mercedes' passenger side door. He slammed on the brakes and backed the car to the spot where the brick had been thrown. The angry driver then jumped out of the car, grabbed the nearest kid and pushed him up against a parked car shouting, 'What was that all about and who are you? Just what the hell are you doing? That's a new car and that brick you threw is going to cost a lot of money. Why did you do it?' The young boy was extremely apologetic. 'Please, mister, please, I'm sorry. But I didn't know what else to do,' he pleaded. 'I threw the brick because no one else would stop!' With tears dripping down his face and off his chin, the youth pointed to a spot just around a parked car. 'It's my brother who has leukemia,' he said. 'He rolled off the curb and fell out of his wheelchair, and I can't lift him up.' Now sobbing, the boy asked the stunned executive, 'would you please help me get him back into his wheelchair? He's hurt and he's too heavy for me.' That brick damaged a car, but the dent it made was a small price to pay for the executive to learn what was really valuable."

When Jesus Came to Canada to Lead An
Indigenous Rebellion in the Broughton Archipelago

As usual, all were in awe of this remarkable man, and he continued his spellbinding oratory. "I am telling you that each and everyone of you are far richer than anyone" and then he pointed toward Vancouver hundreds of kilometres south, "living in the most affluent section of Vancouver," and then he pointed toward Vancouver Island, "and richer than anyone on the big island that has 30 million dollar mansions that sit on the ocean in Victoria behind gates that keep the poor out. But the residents in those estates do not realize that they also have a gate that keeps them trapped in poverty of the soul." He paused, and as he did. A dark cloud covered the sun.

"They are truly bankrupt in heart and spirit but think it is those who toil to keep them in their palatial estates who are the poor ones. The rich live a life of material excess, but they also live a life devoid of that which truly has meaning. All of you do not know fabulous riches. You have had your birthrights stolen by those who wanted to displace you from your ancestral homes that were shared for the benefit of all. This evil has grown and incubated for hundreds of years, and today you can continue to accept your fate as determined by others, or you can stand against tyranny. I offer you no panacea of hope. You may well be defeated by the great forces of greed and power that will be arrayed against you. Standing against this evil of mind, body and spirit may lead to catastrophic circumstances for the First Nations people of this area. You must all ask yourselves if you want to stand against overwhelming odds and fight or do you want to once again, as you have done for so many years, submit to tyranny of the vilest form?"

The crowd, unified in purpose, shouted "fight, fight, fight!" Jesus managed a slight grin and said, "I tell you that win or lose, there is no life that can be better than a life where you cherish every second and use it for the benefit of all your fellow sojourners who must battle for a scrap from the table of plenty set for those who oppress you. Imagine there is a bank that credits your account each morning with $86,400. It carries over no balance from day to day. Every evening the bank deletes whatever part of the balance you failed to use during the day. What would you do? Draw out every cent? Of course you would! Each of us has such a bank. Its name is the Bank of Time. Every morning, it credits you with 86,400 seconds for that day. Every night it writes off, as lost, whatever of this you have failed to invest to good purpose. It carries over no balance. It allows no overdraft. Each day it opens a new account for you. Each night it burns the remains of the day. If you fail to use the day's deposits, the loss is yours. There is no going back. There is no drawing against tomorrow. You must live in the present on today's deposits. Invest it so as to get from it the utmost in life. Do not use those seconds just for yourself, but reach out with the hand of compassion to those who, like you, are victims of a system that steals from the poor to give to the rich. Use every cent of your time to right wrong and injustice. The clock is incessantly running. Make the most of every minute you have. To realize the value of one year, ask a soldier who has been in battle for that time carrying out the evil policies of a morally bankrupt and spiritually corrupt nation. To realize the value of one month, ask a mother who gives birth to a premature baby that struggles for life in an incubator. To realize the value of one week, ask the prisoner who is scheduled for execution in 7 days by a society that proclaims murder the highest form of evil and then sanctions it when carried out by the state. To realize the value of one hour, ask the lovers who are spending their last hour together before parting. To realize the value of one minute, ask a person who missed the train home to his family. To realize the value of one second, ask a person who just avoided an accident. Treasure every moment because you shared it with someone special, special enough to spend your time with. Remember that time is your mortal enemy. The second lost is never recoverable. It is gone forever. Your time is now. It is time to get off your knees and never again bow before inequity. Stand up against hypocrisy and betrayal. Join me in the fight against tyranny."

CHAPTER 9
MAGIC ELIXIR OF HOPE
THAT WILL END THE PAIN

Science flies you to the moon.
Religion flies you into buildings.
Love has nothing to do with religion.
Religion destroys more than it builds.
Love anything and your heart will be
wrung, twisted and possibly broken.
If you want to make sure of keeping it intact,
you must give it to no one, not even an animal.
Wrap it carefully around meaningless things
that are transitory and temporal in nature,
lavish yourself with luxuries and baubles,
avoid all difficulties and entanglements.
Lock your heart up safe in the casket or coffin
of your greed, self-indulgence and selfishness.
But in that casket - safe, dark, motionless, airless,
it will irrevocably change and harden.
It will become as cast-iron.
It will not be broken; it will become unbreakable,
impervious, impenetrable and irredeemable.
To love is to be naked, exposed and vulnerable.

The people, after hearing Jesus, were roused to a
fever pitch. They were all committed to the cause
of justice, but an old person in the front of the
crowd raised his hand, almost like a child in a
classroom. Jesus indicated that everyone should be
silent, so the old man could be heard. Jesus smiled

down at him. It was Octave Joe. Jesus said, "Yes, Octave Joe, what is your question?"

"I am an old man, Jesus. My time is near, and I have no fear of death. So, for me to stand and fight is of little consequence. A bullet in my head may well be preferable to the suffering I will probably go through before my existence terminates. But, I have lived an often wanton life, and I have never believed in that black book that I think is filled with the vengeance of a fierce and unforgiving God. Yet, since the first day I saw you on the beach, I have wanted to ask you a question that no one dares ask you. Is there a God, and are you his son?"

A great hush fell over the crowd, as that was the one question all present had avoided asking, because, as Aboriginals, most saw the white man's God as an aberration of the Great Spirit their forefathers had been taught to venerate, and this man, whom they had all deified, seemed perturbed that anyone would consider him a god. Jesus smiled and said, "You were the first person here to reach out to me with love, Octave. You are just one of many who have shown me what genuine affection is. Am I the son of God? I have already told you all that I may be better deemed the son of thunder, because I have a rage inside me that boils with indignation at every injustice I see in a world that has no genuine empathy for the majority who are left on the periphery of abundance, begging for sustenance from those who sequester all that abundance for themselves."

The clouds in the sky were dissipating, seemingly gobbled up by the brightening of the sun. The sun's rays were twinkling with a celestial glow that appeared to filter down in long strands toward the thick forest on the hillside. Jesus, bathed in the bright glow of the sun, seemed to sparkle himself, almost glow with the warmth that he felt for those to whom he spoke.

"Man makes religion, religion does not make man. Religion is the self-consciousness and self-esteem of a man who has either not yet found himself or is truly lost. Man is no abstract being encamped outside the world. Man is the world. This world produced religion as a mechanism of control. Tell people that they will receive their reward by doing as told by the religious hierarchy that is part of the privileged class, and those who represent God feather their own cap, not the caps of the oppressed. Listen not to the pontificator in an edifice of intolerance called the church, listen to your heart. You do not need somebody else to lead you to God, you are God. Each one of you is capable of being God, but you let yourself be manipulated and controlled by those who see you as chattel. That is why science flies man to the moon, but religion encourages man to fly into buildings, to bomb innocent women and children in some distant land, to fight terrorism with terrorism, to set-up a gulag of prisons to lock away those who defy authority."

All present seemed to be hanging on every word, as he continued. "Religion is the general theory that enslaves the poor to the rich. The Bible makes Osama Bin Laden seem like a Boy Scout. It is filled with a God who is a cold-bloodied murderer who goes about killing after he issued the Ten Commands that stated 'Thou shall not kill.' That makes God seem a lot like the hypocritical politicians who run the world today." There was quiet laughter at that comment among the crowd and a nodding of heads in affirmation.

"What kind of god kills 70,000 innocent people because David ordered a census be taken? What kind of god orders the destruction of 60 cities so that the Israelites can live there? He ordered the killing of all the men, women and children of each city, and the looting of all of things of value. Was he just another capitalist in pursuit of plunder? He ordered attacks and the killing of all the living creatures of the cities: men and women, young and old, as well as oxen, sheep, and asses. Even animals are not spared his voracious appetite for blood. He orders the murder of all the people of Jabesh-gilead, except for the virgin girls who were taken to be forcibly raped and married. When they wanted more virgins, God told them to hide alongside the road and when they saw a girl they liked, kidnap her and forcibly rape her and make her a wife! Just about every other page in the Old Testament has God killing somebody!"

Jesus now began to pace back and forth on the table. "It tells you that a father can sell his daughter to the highest bidder. It says a parent can kill a rebellious son. In fact, God even encouraged the bashing of babies on rocks. God condones slavery. The God I see in that book is not one who loves, but one who hates. If God loves you so much, why would he let so many suffer the indignity of begging for sustenance when so few are given so much? Am I the son of the God you have been told to worship and venerate? No, I am not the son of that God. I am, like all of you, the son of the God I carry within me. I am God, as are all of you."

As always, Jesus never addressed the question of his divinity directly. Yet, it was apparent that this was no ordinary man born of woman. He was a man like no other who had trod on the earth under his feet. His disdain for main-stream religion was the most endearing element to his persona. As the enthralled crowd sat spellbound, he was still not through. "The struggle against religion is therefore indirectly a fight against the world of which religion is the spiritual aroma. Religious distress is an expression of the distress people fill in a world where their only hope is some pie-in-the-sky, because there is no hope in this life, so all hope must be reserved for the after-life that is reserved for the faithful. I tell you that if you wait until the after-life, you have missed life. Religion is the sigh of the oppressed creature, the heart of a heartless world, just as it is the spirit of spiritless conditions. As Karl Marx said, it is the opium of the people, and I tell you that it is the drug that keeps people high on after-life tripe to bind them in invisible chains during this life."

He then looked down at Octave and said, "So, I am whatever you believe in your heart I am, but remember that God is in you, and you need no supernatural being to guide you down the path of a righteous life. You have that power within you, and let no pontificators in the pulpits of judgmental arrogance define what is righteous. I tell you that all those who hunger for fairness where there is none, all those who stand against hatred when it abounds all about, all those who rail against poverty in the midst of plenty, all those who shed blood, sweat and tears in defence of those who suffer injustice are gods. What I am is insignificant. What you are is what counts. For those who fear the coming calamity that may befall those of us who stand against tyranny, put your invisible chains back on and submit. For those who, like me, believe it is better to die on your feet than live on your knees, join me in raging against the machinery of oppression."

All stood and vociferously shouted support for what they were about to do in defence of the liberty to which all men are entitled. No one was afraid, and they all embraced in love and devotion to the cause.

What follows next is an unofficial account of a momentous decision that was made by American authorities, with the acquiescence of a conservative Canadian government, to bring what was seen as miscreant anarchists to their knees. There are no official records of the meeting as all parties wanted to be able to deny that any such meeting ever took place. Had the authorities in both countries been more amenable to compromise, much consternation and bloodshed could have been avoided. But this meeting that was held in Ottawa between CIA representative, Damon Matthews, Canadian Cabinet Minister Darryl Robson, American General Maxwell Bridgman and Canadian General Robert McCabe and several high ranking officials from the Prime Minister's office was nothing more than a prelude to effectively declaring war on a tiny island in the Broughton Archipelago. The decision had been made by higher ups in both governments that the polonium was more important than the people and the land they revered.

When Jesus Came to Canada to Lead An
Indigenous Rebellion in the Broughton Archipelago

Robson

"You have all read the files and been thoroughly briefed. There is no doubt that what is happening on Gilford Island is rapidly escalating toward what could be a confrontation involving armed conflict. I have no doubt who would prevail in a conflict, but the public reaction is our primary concern."

General Bridgman

"Well, if this was the good old USA, all we would have to do is call them terrorists and the people would support any action we wanted to take. Canadians are a different breed. How you people can get anything accomplished in this country with all the bleeding hearts you have here is beyond me."

Damon Matthews

"General, name-calling is not going to ameliorate the problem we are facing. Mr. Robson is a politician representing a political party that is very supportive of the American cause. I am sure you will find that this particular Canadian government is amenable to assisting the USA in any way it can to continue to make our two countries partners in the battle against the forces that support anarchy and the destruction of capitalism."

When Jesus Came to Canada to Lead An
Indigenous Rebellion in the Broughton Archipelago

Robson

"Thank you, Mr. Matthews, I do believe that it is extremely well-documented that this government has wilfully repudiated the policies of the former liberal government that often refused to side with America. Had we been in power during the Iraqi invasion, we would have stood shoulder-to-shoulder with you in that righteous cause. We are not a government that sees the rich and corporations as the enemies of the people.

General McCabe

"We have a team ready to go in and institute a forced evacuation at any time. All we need is the green light. These Indians are nothing but a pack of malcontents who want to be coddled and mollified for what happened to their ancestors. It's high time this nation and the American nation stopped trying to make up for what happened hundreds of years ago. They need to get over it and join the modern world."

General Bridgman

"If the Canadian government will give us the go-ahead, I have a couple of seal teams that can have the people neutralized in less than an hour. This anarchist calling himself Jesus can be taken out and all resistance will wilt almost immediately.

One of the Representatives from the PM's Office

General, this is Canada, this government would fall within a few hours if word got out that we were sanctioning the murder of anyone. I know your country had no problem with the murder of a man blamed for over 3,000 deaths, but our people demand justice not revenge, and this man calling himself Jesus is not Osama Bin Laden. As far as I know, no one has died as a result of any of his actions. We want to keep it that way."

General Bridgman

"Don't question the integrity of the United States of America. We are the vanguard against the evil doers of this world."

Robson

"General Bridgman I don't question in any way the integrity of your country, but we are devoted to our country, and we have a parliamentary democracy here. That means one inappropriate action can end the government in a matter of days or even hours. We have to tread very lightly on the Charter of Rights, which is often an impediment to this government taking the kinds of actions it would like to take. The courts here too often side with the people, rather than the government or business interests which our party sees as a detriment to the economic and social future of the nation. If we are in power long enough, we can tilt the balance our way through appointments to the Supreme Court and eliminate the liberal actions that have led to a far too permissive society, but we must maintain our power base to do so, and that requires very delicate measures in situations like we are facing on Gilford Island. I assure you that this government is going to do all it can, and that we will get those people off that island, because your nuclear capabilities are not only in your national interests but ours as well."

Damon Matthews

"Could I suggest that it might be prudent to dress the seal team in Canadian uniforms? If the government of Canada would agree to do that, we could take care of this man Jesus, the same way we took care of Osama bin Laden. We have the manpower and the know-how to make a surgical strike, take this reprehensible anarchist out and then the whole group would simply collapse in disarray. This can be done with minimal, and probably no loss of life. If any of our men are killed or injured, we have the means to cover it up with absolutely no questions asked. The families of any killed or injured will be kept in the dark, so nothing about the operation would ever see the light of day. Our people are dedicated and loyal to the cause for which they fight.

When Jesus Came to Canada to Lead An Indigenous Rebellion in the Broughton Archipelago

Robson

"General McCabe?"

General McCabe

"I don't like the idea of American soldiers doing what Canadian soldiers should be doing, but I must admit that the bin Laden raid was a success, and we have not had the training Americans have. I say going with the experts is a smart move. You can categorically depend on our military to back you up if needed. This stand against authority cannot go unchecked."

Robson

"I agree, but this will have to be reviewed by the PM, and I can assure you that there will be at least one more attempt to get this man and those who follow him to do the sensible thing. If all here are in agreement, I say we move forward to deal with the eventuality that these anarchists will not accede to our demands."

All in the room nodded or verbally agreed, so the die had been cast. There would be one more attempt at negotiation and then the forces of repression would be unleashed to secure the island for exploitation by TWI and the American government.

When Jesus Came to Canada to Lead An
Indigenous Rebellion in the Broughton Archipelago

Meanwhile, on Kwak'wala, Jesus was having a meeting with Eric, Gary, and the chief. They were the inner circle upon whom Jesus placed his unwavering faith and confidence. "I am asking you Aaron, along with Eric, Gary, the chief and as many men as you need, to go to the west side of the island to a place called Harmony Cay about ten kilometres from the mill, where you will meet a man named Harrison Black Elk tomorrow night at 9:00 PM. We all know now that what Harrison saw in the mill was the processing of polonium. Although I suspected that all along, I needed confirmation from you Aaron, and now that we have it, I think it is incumbent upon us to take action."

Jesus was as serious as Aaron had ever seen him. In a stern, determined voice, he continued. "Polonium is being fused to make nuclear triggers at the paper mill, as it gives off a pale blue glow when that happens. So, it doesn't take too smart a person to figure what is going on there. Pretty good for a long-haired, parable-quoting, rebel-rousing misfit don't you think?"

Aaron, now intrigued about just what he was expected to do, looked up and saw Huyana standing in the doorway, glowing with a radiance that lit up the room. She looked down at Jesus and said, "So, you through with your secret discussion?"

When Jesus Came to Canada to Lead An
Indigenous Rebellion in the Broughton Archipelago

Jesus, looking up at her, realized there would never be any secrets between her and Aaron. "Sit Huyana, there will be no secrets Aaron will keep from you now. I have a feeling the two of you are fused to explode on occasion just like polonium."

All enjoyed a good laugh, and Aaron was secretly thinking to himself just how much he wanted to fuse with Huyana and blow a mountain of his radioactive essence deep inside her. He could feel a little tingle in that former instrument of destruction that lay between his legs as Jesus continued with his plan details. "We are going to take over the plant Aaron, and use it for leverage to show the whole world what is going on here.

Jesus got up and walked about the room. "Many people laugh at me. The chronic believers think I am an impostor, because I don't adhere to their ideal of the son-of-man who has been manufactured by the manipulators to keep them in bondage all these years. The ones who truly believe, but think independently, unencumbered by the pontificators of deceit, still can't figure out whether I am the real deal or not. Then there are the non-believers, like all of you here. They don't care whether I am a fake or not, because they have no faith anyway. It is they who are the most dependable, because they expect no divine revelations from me. They look at me as I want to be looked at, just a man who fights against injustice everywhere he sees it. I know that I can depend on all of you."

He walked over to the easel that was set-up against a far wall, unfurled a large diagram and began to discuss how they were going to take-over the paper mill and remove the polonium to use as a barrier against encroachment of the village. All present were shocked at what was now coming to fruition. This was no longer just an exercise in pseudo, mock preparations to put up a front that would give the illusion that the people would fight. It was now looking as if this man was genuinely preparing to wage a war that he absolutely could not win. The forces arrayed against the people were simply too powerful and overwhelming.

Smiling Jesus said, "Did you all think I was playing a game? Did you not believe that I was prepared to use all the methods at our disposal to protect this island? Chief, your people have never wavered in their confidence. You have seen their determination to finally get off their knees and stand against tyranny of the vilest form?"

Chief Harry, at first, stuttered a bit, but finally got his composure. "But I never dreamed that we would actually take aggressive action. I believed you were preparing us for victory without having to shed blood.

When Jesus Came to Canada to Lead An Indigenous Rebellion in the Broughton Archipelago

"I do not want to shed blood. However, sometimes without the shedding of blood, your adversary looks upon you as weak. Do you think that if North Vietnam had not shed the blood of American soldiers in the rice paddies of Southeast Asia that they would have won that abominable war of American aggression? Do you think that if the Blacks had not burned down the cities of America that the government would have finally passed the civil rights bill? It was not Martin Luther King's non-violence that won the day, but government fear of people like Huey Newton and the Black Panthers, who were shouting 'burn baby burn.' Do you think that if the African National Congress had not blown up buildings, trains and bridges that the architects of Apartheid would have ever yielded their power? Meekness is weakness."

Jesus pensively looked at his dependable friend, Aaron. "My dear friend Aaron, I will not ask how many men you have killed in your life, but I ask you if many of the deaths led to a victory against tyranny."

Aaron did not answer verbally, but he did nod his head in affirmation. Then Jesus turned to Huyana and said, "My dear angel of mercy; how many times have you seen people writhing in agony, pleading for the relief of pain only a shot of morphine can give them?"

When Jesus Came to Canada to Lead An
Indigenous Rebellion in the Broughton Archipelago

Huyana, thinking back on the times she had witnessed those who pleaded for relief, replied, "Far too many times."

"I tell you that the people," Jesus then pointed toward the compound, "here are pleading for a shot of morphine to end the pain they have suffered for far too long. I am prepared to give them the magic elixir of hope that will end the agony."

CHAPTER 10
PREPARING THEIR OWN TOMB

So they have snatched from them all,
In the curse and rack of destiny,
All sane worlds that are gone beyond recall!
Nothing but revenge is left to them.
They shall build thrones high overhead.
Tremendous shall the summit be.
For its bulwark - superstitious dread.
For its Marshal - blackest agony.
Who looks on it with a healthy eye,
Shall turn back, deathly pale and dumb,
Clutched by blind and chill mortality.
May the enemy prepare its tomb.

Jesus was very careful to make sure that no one had any doubts about what was to be done. If there was any timidity on the part of anyone, the plan would not be carried out. He put up a diagram.

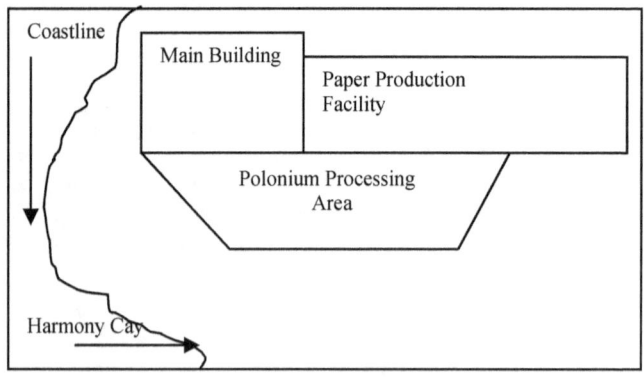

When Jesus Came to Canada to Lead An
Indigenous Rebellion in the Broughton Archipelago

Jesus sighed and said, "From the birth of civilization, mankind has used its gift of intelligence for some progress, but that progress has come at a great cost, because it is always oriented toward monetary profit, not the esoteric profit of soul. Now, today, we have either reached or gone over the tipping point. There is no where but down this time. The few who control wealth work mechanically in a clockwork fashion, consume everything in their path, and leave the waste behind for others to scavenge. The people of this island are tired of being scavengers in the land that made their forefathers kings and queens one and all." Then he pointed at the mill in the illustration. "This place is a cancer that must be cut out."

Continuing to point at the illustration, Jesus pensively said, "Harrison Black Elk is ready to do his part in bringing this abominable blight on the sanctity of this island crumbling into a pile of rubble. If you can pull off the capture of this building and hold it for a few days, Plato Papadopoulos has a vessel that is entering the Queen Charlotte Strait as we are talking. He has three nuclear devices that were picked up in North Korea, and all they need to be prepared for detonation is a polonium trigger. With those devices, he has three short range missiles capable of reaching Seattle, Portland and San Francisco. I have no intention of firing them, but their

presence will be insurance against an attack on
the island. They are our trump card in a game of
chicken."

Aaron, a man who deplored the fact that the
USA had made itself the decider of what nations
were to be allowed nuclear weapons, felt a deep
sinking sensation and a tightness in his chest. He
always believed that other nations should have
the right to those deterrents until the USA agreed
to destroy all its own nuclear weapons. What
made the USA the righteous decider of who
should have instruments of mass destruction?
Aaron could not resist asking, "You are telling us
that nuclear weapons have been on the high seas,
coming to Kwak'wala and the US satellites have
not detected anything at all?"

Jesus let a slow grin creep across his lips.
"Plato Papadopoulos assures me that his
engineers have the ability to completely mask any
radiation from being detected by satellites. He is
a 77 year old man who has inoperable cancer, and
has decided that his last days will be spent
defying a nation that he sees as the chief
impediment to a world where there can be an
abundance for all if only sanity, rather than greed
were allowed to prevail. He intends to die on this
island. He is on the ship, himself, with other
aging volunteers who are engineers, chemists and
propellant specialists who are dedicated to seeing

that the indigenous people of the planet are finally protected from the onslaught of avaricious greed that has destroyed their far superior way of life. This will be his last opportunity to truly assist those who need a champion in the on-going battle against the evils of a consumptive society that knows no end to its voracious appetite for more and more."

Aaron and the rest were mesmerized. Even Papadopoulos' friend Gary Gore had no idea that Jesus had been plotting with him to bring nuclear devices to the island.

Jesus, looking at the dropped jaws and the looks of absolute astonishment seemed to be relishing the effect his revelation was having on all who were present. "I realize this is a shock, and I wish that we could have put this decision to a vote of all the people, but, my friends, there are spies among us. As much as I hate to admit it, there are a hand full of people here who would sell us out for thirty pieces of silver. I have been sold out for much less many times in many places. This decision for secrecy was not taken lightly, because I believe people have a right to decide their own destiny, but for now, it must be kept secret, so that no one knows but those on the ship and those in this room. When the time comes, I will again give people the choice of staying or leaving. I am not here to dictate, I am here to serve and try to end once and for all time the acrimonious arrogance of a nation that destroys the very soul of humanity."

Jesus had dumfounded all present, and he was now ready to deliver a homily of righteous justification for his actions. "I want this island and its wonderful people to be metaphoric justification for the dismantling of the society of greed – a place that continues its repudiation of the evils of corporate capitalism that destroys all compassion beneath its jack-booted crushing of hope, charity, fairness, humanity, honour and truth. We are on the cusp of an incredible awakening for the First Nations of Canada. This island can be the first tiny ripple in a wave of indignation that will sweep across this land and the USA, and in the process, light the first of many fires across indigenous communities that will turn into a raging blaze of fury against those who have oppressed them for far too long. In the process, the non-indigenous communities will begin to feel the heat of the fires of outrage and light their own fires of indignation that will bring down the system that has kept almost the entire human race in bondage since its inception."

Huyana, overwhelmed that she was now part of what she saw as an escalation beyond what she envisioned, could not help but ask if this was truly the only alternative to save the island and the people's way of life. She quietly said, "Is all this necessary? Is there no way to negotiate with the two governments and TWI without the threat of a cataclysmic calamity?"

Jesus, his eyes seemingly filled with pain, replied in his usual calm manner. "Huyana, you are a healer. So, you know that the mind can actually cause sicknesses of the body. For too long these wonderful people have had a sickness of the mind, and many times that has manifested itself into a sickness of the body that has withered on the vine of indifference. The arrogant, sadistic Christians mocked Aboriginal religion. Then, took their children and tried to make them white by making them speak English and learn the ways of a society they did not understand. They beat Jesus into them with a rod and staff, not with love. They taught them to covet. They taught them to lie and steal. They taught them jealousy and thievery. They tried to teach them the idea of possessions as the judge of a person's worth. Yet, the people on this island have repudiated all that makes life in the outside world an abomination of selfishness and self-indulgence. Just as the body cannot exist without blood, the real soul of an individual cannot exist without substance. Without substance one does not live, one only survives."

Jesus then waved his hand to the right and pointed toward the east. "There is no substance to that world out there. It is an abomination of all that man should and can be. I tell you that the man who will not use every avenue available to fight those who perpetrate injustice and to confront every indignity is not a man. He is a slave!"

Aaron placed his hand on Huyana's arm as she defiantly proclaimed, "I shall stand with you and fight for these people's right to live free from the culture of greed. We must do whatever it takes to protect this last vestige of freedom from those who want to destroy the foundations of a far superior society to the one that puts a price tag on everything."

Jesus smiled and Aaron squeezed Huyana's arm with an acknowledgment of support. The others nodded in agreement, and Jesus now was ready to forge ahead with his plan to combat those who were determined to enslave one more island of sanity in a world of corporate, religious and economic madness.

Jesus said, as he looked at Huyana, "criticism may not be agreeable, but it is necessary. It fulfills the same function as pain in the human body. It calls attention to an unhealthy state of things. Never hesitate to question. That is why we are here today. For too long these people on Kwak'wala simply never questioned authority in regards to that abomination on the other side of the island. Consequently, they are once again considered expendable in a world where profits come before people. They should have questioned authority. Huyana and the rest of you must never acquiesce to my pleas when you feel they are morally repugnant. Bow before no man."

Moving toward the illustration, Jesus began to lay out a plan to commandeer the paper mill and the polonium necessary to prepare the nuclear triggers for the weapons being brought in by Papadopoulos. He turned toward Gary and Tom. "You two are the professionals when it comes to this type of operation. As I said, you will meet Harrison Black Elk at Harmony Cay. He has all the information on where the guards are. Strangely, it seems that in order to keep suspicion of what is going on there to a minimum, very little security is maintained; consequently, it should be easy to take over the facility. Papadopoulos will anchor at the harbour and his team will immediately place the launchers at the dock, while his engineers begin the task of activating the triggers for the missiles. Gentleman, this is the key to avoiding bloodshed. I leave it in your capable hands to figure out how to facilitate the takeover." Jesus turned and walked toward the door, looked back and said, "I now prepare for the final meeting with Mr. Robson, who will, tomorrow, no doubt deliver an ultimatum from the Canadian government to acquiesce to their demands or suffer dire consequences. This will be a time of great trial and tribulation. I offer no easy solution. I only offer a faint hope that perhaps sanity will prevail, but sanity when dealing with those whose eyes are blinded by sparkling riches at the end of their rainbow of self-indulgence and greed gives me little comfort."

You could see the agony in his face as he left. This was a man carrying the weight of not just those on Kwak'wala on his shoulders, but the weight of all who cried for compassion.

Aaron stared at the door as it closed and almost wept. Son-of-God? No, Aaron could not believe that, because to believe that you would have to believe in God. Yet, this was the closest thing to God there was in a world that was filled with people who proclaimed their love for God, but whose actions were counter to anything a loving deity would accept.

Plans were made to take 20 well-armed men to the mill and overpower the 12 guards who were always on duty. The 20 were chosen and the training began in earnest that day. Not a man asked why they were doing it. They all simply were committed to Jesus, who had sanctioned the action as a necessary step to protect the island from those who refused to allow the people to live in peace. However, Jesus adamantly exacted promises that all efforts would be made to avoid bloodshed.

When Jesus Came to Canada to Lead An
Indigenous Rebellion in the Broughton Archipelago

A mass assemblage was called for that afternoon, and all gathered to hear Jesus once again plead for those who had doubts to seek safety by leaving the island. A flotilla of boats was assembled to evacuate all who wanted to leave. At this meeting, an elderly Aboriginal woman, who was one of the few practicing Christians in the village, asked, "are we do believe that what we are about to undertake is Christian in nature?"

Jesus mounted the picnic table, so all could see him as he addressed the woman. "My dear Sybil, what is a Christian? Do not those whom we are making a stand against profess to be Christians? Is not the nation that covets the mineral deep in the interior of this island a Christian nation? Does not that so-called Christian nation that kills innocents in its monstrous march toward domination of the world by its diabolically aberrant arrogance practice torture and harsh imprisonment for all who stand against it? Does not that Christian nation, and even your beloved Canada, allow the exploitation of the very land under your feet for profit. While people beg for a crumb from the table of plenty set for those at the top, does not that fallacious and illusionary democracy that calls itself a bastion of freedom and Christian love south of this island turn its back on the poor and disenfranchised to support a system of economic thievery that robs from the poor to give to the rich? Is that Christian? I say to you that the word Christian has grown to be an abomination to my ears. It no longer represents love, it represents intolerance, hatred and indifference."

As usual, Jesus began to pace back and forth as he continued. "I say to the people of this island old enough to remember the residential schools: was it not good Christians who took you from your mothers and fathers and forced you to repudiate your culture through intimidation and beatings? Was it not Christians who stole your homeland? I can call a bird an airplane, but does that make it so? Be very careful of any word used by those who want to enslave you. Enslavement of people can be attributed to the Christian religion that always promises a better life in the hereafter. The hereafter is used to keep you in bondage, to keep you from demanding your fare share here and now. That promise of pie-in-the-sky is the work of charlatans who see you as sheep to be fleeced."

Then, looking down at Sybil, with deep affection, Jesus said. "You have lived your whole life here Sybil, except when you were a child. You were whisked away to a residential school when you were six by whom? By Christians, who told you that the fires of hell awaited you if you did not submit and worship their God, the only true God, the God you should fear and cringe before in supplication."

When Jesus Came to Canada to Lead An
Indigenous Rebellion in the Broughton Archipelago

Sybil shook her head in knowing affirmation, and one could see the intense pain she felt in reflecting upon the time she was forced into submission to the white man's way and the white man's religion. Jesus, now with the rapt attention of all present then began to recite a poem.

Immaculately attired preachers come out at night,
Try to tell you what's wrong and what's right.
But when asked how about something to eat,
They will answer in voices so sweet.

You will eat, bye and bye
In that glorious land above the sky.
Work and pray, live on hay.
You'll get pie in the sky, when you die.

Christians with their musical instruments play,
And they sing and they clap and they pray,
Till they get all your coin in the collection plate,
By telling you that is the way to avoid hell's fate.

Holy Rollers and Jumpers come out.
And they holler, they jump and they shout,
Give your money to Jesus, they say,
He will cure all diseases today.

If you fight hard for children and wife,
Try to get justice in this life,
You're a sinner and bad man, they tell,
And you're headed straight to hell.

J. Wayne Frye   257

When Jesus Came to Canada to Lead An
Indigenous Rebellion in the Broughton Archipelago

The poor all about must unite,
Side by side, for freedom, they must fight.
When the world and its wealth they have gained,
To the grafters you can all sing this refrain:

You will eat, bye and bye
When you've learned how to cook and how to fry.
Chop some wood, will do you good.
Then you'll eat in the sweet bye and bye.

Sybil stood, turned to the crowd and shouted, "I shall not be moved from my home. I was born here, and I shall die a peaceful death here, or I will die a violent death defending my right to be in this scared land bequeathed to me by my ancestors."

The crowd began to shout, "justice, justice, justice………….."

Jesus stepped down from the table and three men, far in the back of the crowd, started to leave, heading for their boat in the harbour. They were the betrayers, those who had sold their souls for a few pieces of shiny silver. Gary, Tom and Aaron looked at Jesus, as if pleading to stop them. Jesus shook his head left to right and said, "Let the Judases go. They will be able to tell the authorities nothing that they will not know as of tomorrow anyway. The three traitors do not know it, but they only go to assist the enemy in preparing their own tomb."

CHAPTER 11
IN THE COLDEST OF HEARTS

My will is easy to decide,
For there is nothing to divide,
My kin don't need to fuss and moan-
Moss does not cling to a rolling stone.
My body? Ah, If I could choose,
I would to ashes it reduce,
And let the merry breezes blow
My dust to where some flowers grow.
Perhaps some fading flower then
Would come to life and bloom again.

Life is transitory at best, and all the leaders of the rebellion were prepared to make whatever sacrifices necessary to complete the mission. The following day, Darryl Robson arrived to discuss the situation. He met with Jesus, the council and the chief. As they sat at the conference table, Robson seemed, for the first time, actually intimidated, but he was determined to let all know that there would be no more negotiating. The decision had been made, and he categorically stated that the people had 48 hours to get off the island. If they did not beginning the evacuation of the island by then, a contingent of armed soldiers would forcibly remove them. The Canadian government's patience had simply run out. There was no mention of the U.S. government and its participation in the whole nefarious affair.

When Jesus Came to Canada to Lead An
Indigenous Rebellion in the Broughton Archipelago

Jesus had sat quietly through the discussion, not even uttering a word, but as Robson made the statement about the government's patience running out, he rose from his seat and walked over to the same side of the table Robson was on and sat beside him. His intensity was apparent as he reached out and placed his hand on Robson's left arm. "Your patience is at an end? Is that not an affront to the patience of these people? Do you not understand that these people have been patient for hundreds of years, waiting for this nation to do the right thing? Now, you will not even negotiate with them, because the United States thirsts for yet another place where it can subject good people to the wrath of its corporate theocracy and crass military machine that knows no restraint. Make no mistake Mr. Robson. You may be here, but the real power behind you and the Canadian government is the United States, which refuses to let any opportunity to exploit a nation for its wealth escape from the grasp of its capitalistic carnivorous machine of subjugation. Go back to Ottawa and plead with the government to stand up to the USA, and not be one of the many that bow before tyranny. Do as these people here on Kwak'wala are doing. Do not submit to the coercion of capitalistic totalitarianism that looks upon people as commodities that can be bought and sold. The people of Kwak'wala will not sell their birthright for a few pieces of silver. They have had enough and are ready to fight."

When Jesus Came to Canada to Lead An
Indigenous Rebellion in the Broughton Archipelago

Robson's arrogance had become less apparent.
You could see that Jesus had touched a soft spot in
his psyche. Almost pleading, Robson said, "You
don't understand. We have no choice. The United
States is a nation that lives in mortal fear. They are
a nation frightened by perceptions that everyone is
out to get them. The entire populace has been
propagandized into believing their way of life is
superior to all others. They cannot see that other
nations do not envy them; they only fear them. We
fear them, too. Don't you see that they will use
any excuse to wreck havoc here. I warn you that
the Canadian government can only restrain them
for so long until they will use the terrorism card to
demand this place be obliterated."

Jesus, now sensing that Robson was an
honourable man who had been put into a bad
situation by his government, removed his hand
from Robson left arm and said, "A scientific
convention was held at a lakeside resort. After the
first day's proceedings, a mathematician, a
physicist, an astronomer and a molecular biologist
hired a boatman to row them around on the lake.
As they sat in the boat, they discussed string
theory, bubble universes, the Gaea Hypothesis and
other abstruse topics. The biologist noticed the
boatman looking at them from the corner of his
eyes. He asked him, 'What do you think of these
ideas?' The boatman replied, 'I didn't understand
any of it. The astronomer asked him how far he

had gone in school. He told them he couldn't even read. 'I hate to say it,' said the physicist, 'but you seem to have wasted a good part of your life.' The boatman remained silent. By now they were out in the middle of the lake, far from shore. A sudden storm whipped up. The waves started churning and heaving. All of a sudden, the boat flipped over. The boatman started swimming for shore. The scientists cried out, help! We can't swim!' The boatman called back, 'I hate to say it, but you seem to have wasted your whole lives.' You see Mr. Robson, you are a smart man. The Canadian government is filled with smart men and women, but you are all going to find out one day that you have wasted your whole lives by worshipping at the altar of greed. The government looks upon the people of Kwak'wala as heathen savages simply because they do not ascribe to the culture of greed that has all of you in its grasp."

You could actually see the wilting of Robson's resolve. Jesus continued. "You are all in service to a bankrupt idea that only serves the needs of the few while the many are cast adrift in a sea of sharks. I must admit to misjudging you based upon first impressions. I believe you are an honourable man who is carrying out a task in which you do not believe. I think for all your bluster and arrogance, you are, at your core, wrestling with the idea that you may well be on the wrong side of history. I think that you have much less disdain for Aboriginals than you probably profess. I believe you are a victim of circumstances like so many who find themselves with mortgages to pay, car payments to make, children to educate and a host of other a burdens that condemn you to psychological and economic slavery to meet your obligations. These people here know they are considered the dregs of society, but they are truly the kings and queens of society, because they do not covet. They are all richer than you will ever be, because they have peace of mind and contentment that you will never know in your world of greed. Think about these people Mr. Robson. Please consider their importance in a world that judges everything in dollars and cents. In America, when the victims of 9/11 were compensated, the janitor's wife received much less than the stockbroker's wife, because their worth was based upon their earning power, not their contributions to society. Let me share a story with you."

Aaron could see Robson's arrogance dissipating as Jesus started another parable. "A nurse is someone who is supposed to care about people. There once was a nursing professor who gave his 4th year students a one question test. The question was 'what is the name of the janitor in this building whom you see cleaning the halls every day?' Everyone in the class had passed the man hundreds of times. Yet, none of the 75 students could answer the question. One student blurted out 'this is ridiculous. What does this have to do with nursing?' The professor very calmly replied, 'this is one of the most relevant questions you have had in the four years you have been here. In your career, you will meet many people. They should all be significant to you. The person who cleans the operating room is an important part of the healthcare process. The person who prepares the meals for patients is critical to the recovery process. The person who delivers flowers to a room is improving the aesthetics that facilitate well-being. All are significant. They deserve your attention and care, even if all you do is smile and let them know you recognize their presence. You do not heal just with medicine and know how. You heal with the heart. You, Mr. Robson, are at a crossroads. Are you going to help heal injustice here on Kwak'wala with your heart or are you going to continue to serve the master of discontent, arrogance and deceit that destroys all compassion in its path?"

Aaron and the others could not believe it. Robson had not been defeated by any physical weapon, but had been literally destroyed by words that flowed out of Jesus' mouth like fresh, soothing water from a babbling stream. The words Jesus used were not just heard by Robson. He had seen them, seen the beauty of a possible world that was painted by Jesus with words.

J. Wayne Frye

When Jesus Came to Canada to Lead An
Indigenous Rebellion in the Broughton Archipelago

Awe-struck, Robson's reply was not what anyone, except maybe Jesus, expected. "You people are in trouble here. They are going to give the green light to an American Seal team to come in and secure this compound. I will be dismissed from the cabinet for telling you this, but I will not be a party to this abomination any longer. When I get back to Ottawa, I will plead for the government to acquiesce to your demands, but I can assure you that the influence of the Americans is just too strong. I will only be a voice crying in the wilderness."

Jesus reached over and placed his hand on Robson's right arm again. "You do what you can Mr. Robson. That is all we can ask. We will do what we must, and thank you for your candour. Do not resign, because no one will ever know what you have shared with us. Maybe a man of your character can make a difference among the indifferent in the government of Canada; and thereby, have a residual effect on the U.S.A."

Robson looked into Jesus' eyes and it was as if he was really seeing the celestial magnificence of him for the first time. "Thank you for today. Thank all of you for showing a man who has been lost how to once again find his way. Regardless of what occurs, you have, in me, someone who will do all he can to procure justice, not only for Aboriginals, but for all Canadians."

When Jesus Came to Canada to Lead An
Indigenous Rebellion in the Broughton Archipelago

As Robson walked back to the float plane, Jesus walked with him, arm around his shoulder, and the people all stared in bewilderment. There seemed genuine affection between the two and gone was Robson's arrogant swagger. They shook hands, Robson boarded the plane, and as the plane soared skyward, he looked down upon Kwak'wala. A sinking feeling overwhelmed him. How could he protect them and the man he now loved with all his heart from harm?

That evening, as Aaron, Gary and Tom prepared for the rendezvous with Harrison Black Elk and the assault on the paper mill, Huyana sat quietly in the clinic. Around 5:30 PM Tom Morrissey came by to pick up some first aid kits, and it was then that Huyana's suspicions from the first time she saw him were confirmed. His skin had a yellowish tint and the lymph nodes in his neck were extremely swollen. She smiled as she handed him the kits and said, "Is you back pain severe?"

Tom, surprised by the question, said, "what do you mean?"

Slightly smiling, Huyana very tenderly, said, "I notice you are losing a lot of weight, too. I am a medical professional, you know."

Almost relieved, Gary asked, "you know don't you?"

Sympathetically, Huyana said, "yes, you have pancreatic cancer. How long did the doctor say you had?"

Tom, without a tinge of self-pity replied in a matter-of-fact manner. "Six months, maybe as long as a year. I hope you won't tell anyone about it. I have lived an exciting life, and I am pleased to be ending it here among these people, and I do not want pity from anyone."

"Of course, no one will know, not even Aaron. But you will let me know if there is anything I can do for your pain."

"I have plenty of pain-killers. Thank you so much though Huyana. Aaron is lucky to have you."

She reached out and touched his arm, "Tom, you have me, too. I am here to help you anyway I can. Don't hesitate to come to me."

He nodded affirmatively, turned and walked out with the kits. Huyana thought to herself that so many men who seemed tough on the exterior were actually, like Tom, soft as cotton on the inside. Tom was right, it was a privilege to end your life in a place like Kwak'wala, where serenity and contentment brought an inner peace that simply could not be found anywhere else. It was a place where there was a magic elixir of gratifying comfort and happiness.

While Tom, Gary and Aaron prepared to lead 20 men to the rendezvous with Harrison Black Elk, a seemingly obsessed Darryl Robson, eschewing normal protocol, ignored the chain of command and made a frantic call to the Prime Minister's appointments secretary pleading for an immediate audience with the PM. Told that the Prime Minister was busy meeting with an American trade delegation, but that he could speak with his Administrative Assistant, Robson got a sinking feeling that the wheels for catastrophe had already been set in motion, and that the whole operation had been turned over to the Americans who had worked so hard to get a conservative government in power in Canada, so they could manipulate it more readily. It appeared that yet another country had sold out its sovereignty to the USA. As he pleaded with the Administrative Assistant to allow an immediate meeting with the PM, he was abruptly rebuked and told that the PM had turned the decision over to his military advisors and that if there was anything to discuss, it should be discussed with them.

The despondent Robson was supposed to be in charge, not the military. There was something nefarious afoot, and the hope of avoiding catastrophe was rapidly disappearing.

J. Wayne Frye

When Jesus Came to Canada to Lead An
Indigenous Rebellion in the Broughton Archipelago

A call to General McCabe facilitated an immediate meeting, and Robson got a sinking feeling as he walked into the general's office. Sitting on the sofa was American general, Max Bridgman.

Robson took a seat and said, "General McCabe, I think we should talk in private."

McCabe, seemingly more arrogant than usual, said, "Darryl, the whole operation has been turned over to the American Seal team. The PM has personally decided that they will be given Canadian uniforms and make the assault. We simply don't have the resources to carry off an operation of this type. We appreciate how hard you have worked to facilitate a settlement, but we have been informed by sources that you have apparently been seduced by the machinations of this fellow calling himself Jesus. You may contact the PM's Office if you wish, but you have been relieved of all responsibilities in reference to this operation."

Robson lowered his head and felt a sinking feeling in his chest. As he was wondering which member of his staff had betrayed him, he said, "You can't do this general. This is nothing but genocide against people who just want to be left alone. I tell you that there is something about this man there – something that sets him apart from any man I have ever met. I beg you; don't go ahead with this operation."

Throwing up his hands, McCabe said, "it is out of my control now. The PM's Office has made the decision – no more negotiation. That's it. General Bridgman has been given the green light. He will get all the support he needs from us, but this thing will be over in a less than an hour, and this miscreant anarchist calling himself Jesus will either be dead or under arrest. He has already escaped from American justice once. It won't happen again. "

General Bridgman got up, walked over to Robson and placed his hand on Robson's shoulder. "Mr, Robson, I know how these charlatan's work. He has managed to beguile you. America is a Christian nation, and believe me, this man is no Christ-like figure. Any real Christian could see that. He is the very reverse of what a good Christian is. He encourages people to question authority. Why that would lead to anarchy. Surely, you can see through the façade of this obvious fake. Don't be beguiled by his homilies of brotherhood, love and compassion while encouraging open rebellion against the capitalistic system that ensures all people the opportunity to succeed if they are willing to put forth an effort and lift themselves from poverty to abundance."

When Jesus Came to Canada to Lead An
Indigenous Rebellion in the Broughton Archipelago

The hypocrisy had become too much for the newly sensitive Robson to bear. "General, that is bullshit and you know it. That system you revere is great for people like you and me, but it permanently relegates the majority of humanity to a life of want. That man and those people he loves on the island are the hope of a world that has absolutely surrendered compassion to the corporations and the powerful who have no sympathy for those begging for their sustenance. You represent the very apex of the evil that has captured humanity and made all slaves to the bottom line of the corporate ledger."

Taken aback by the outburst, the general quickly backed away as Robson got up from the chair. General McCabe was also on his feet, as Robson said, "I'll fight you every way I can. What you are about to do is insanity. It is a crime of monumental proportions!"

The general hit a red buzzer on his desk. Robson knew what it was. He dropped his briefcase and started running for the door. Just as he got there, it opened and two armed guards stood in his way. General McCabe said, "Mr. Robson is to be detained until further notice."

Robson looked back over his shoulder as he was being escorted out and said, "McCabe, you are a disgrace to your country and all it stands for. I am ashamed to have served a government that is bowing before an America that has no heart and no soul. The Canadian government has never before been so complacent in aiding the evil of corporations that know no boundaries in the pursuit of profits. You have surrendered Canadian sovereignty to a pack of thugs!"

His voice trailed off as he was led down the hallway. The two generals shook their heads in disbelief that anyone who had once been so dedicated to the cause could make such an abrupt change. They simply did not have the compassion in them that Robson had, or maybe they did, but it was kept hidden deep within, because they had never met Jesus who could reach the deepest recesses of a man's soul to extract that spark of compassion and understanding that lay dormant in all but a few. Yes, Jesus was, by the power of the spoken word, able to make the deaf hear, to make the blind see and to make the heartless feel compassion. He had done that to Robson. The two generals simply could not understand the power of a man who had no material wealth and no sanctioned power from a government or corporation. It was beyond their comprehension that a man like Jesus was able to make breezes of freedom blow across the land, and through the power of love and compassion sow the mighty seeds that would let flowers bloom in the coldest of hearts.

. CHAPTER 12
SENSE OF VICTORY EVEN
IN THE BITTERNESS OF DEFEAT

First, the powerful ignore you.
Then they ridicule and belittle you.
Then they defile you with words.
Then they threaten you.
Then they send in their goons
to suppress, maim and kill you.
Then, one day they think they have won.
But the true winners are those
who know the exhilaration of fighting
a just cause against overwhelming odds.
Lying bloodied, defiled and exhausted
on the field of battle with head unbowed,
there is a glorious sense of victory,
even in the bitterness of defeat.

On the Whidbey Island Naval base, near Seattle, the U.S. Seal team was assembling for the assault on the island. Although only 18 in number, the satellite images made it possible for them to pinpoint a perfect area for a night landing. The three spies had supplied them with the exact location of Jesus' cabin. That would be their main objective. Once he was taken out, it was assumed that all resistance would desist and the signal would be given for Canadian troops to land and round-up the residents and escort them off the island. They had decided that, like the Osama bin

Laden assassination, this was not an operation to bring Jesus to justice before a military tribunal where the outcome would be predetermined, but to eliminate him for once and all.

Back in Washington, DC, the decision was made to, if necessary, totally ignore Canadian sovereignty. After all, the Canadian Prime Minister was a great admirer of America and its ability to impose its will all across the world. He would never stand up to a nation that he wanted to emulate. With the Conservative Party in power in Ottawa, Canada's reputation as a peace-maker had already suffered irreparable damage, as it now consistently sided with the USA in its militaristic approach to solving problems. If there was too much resistance on Kwak'wala, there was an additional force of troops sitting on alert at the Whidbey Island Naval base. It would take less than 30 minutes to have them at Kwak'wala. Fifteen hundred men, with experience in Iraq and Afghanistan, were ready to embark from giant flying boats and initiate a reign of terror to subdue those who dared stand against the USA. These were no ordinary troops. They were the soldiers who had callously subdued foe and friend alike in two Middle Eastern countries that had dared stand up against the greatest military power in the world. They were embittered and hardened by years of repressive actions against people who were, like those on Kwak'wala, determined not to submit to the will of America and its corporate agenda of economic enslavement of the masses.

Thus, the stage was set for a clash of wills between those who were seeking the bright light of justice and those who answered to the dark forces of suppression that trampled fairness beneath jack-booted soldiers of anguished repression. It was these soldiers who Jesus said had been brainwashed into serving the needs of those at the top of the economic ladder while they, themselves, were instruments of their own repression. Patriotism, according to Jesus, was the last refuge of scoundrels who manipulated others into doing the fighting and dying. These scoundrels used patriotism to get the poor youths to sign up for service in an army of volunteers who were just like conscripts. They had little or no choice in a system that offered meagre job opportunities to the uneducated and poor. While these patriots were fighting and dying, the sons and daughters of the wealthy got a pass on defending the system that kept them in the lap of luxury. The stupidity of the masses could never be underestimated. Jesus had told a crowd that he hoped for the time that the poor, manipulated soldiers who were told to go to some far-off land to fight for the freedom that was nothing but an illusion, would simply hand their guns to the politicians and the wealthy and say, "if it is such a damn noble cause, here is my gun. You go and fight." That would be the end of American wars of conquest, as the wealthy would never permit their children to die for an unjust cause.

The human heart is capable of a sentiment that can turn dirt into diamonds, or darkness to light. Under its influence the peasant's hut becomes transformed into a princely palace; and the lowest of humans on the economic scale become titans of wealth. Jesus had seen the hearts of the people of Kwak'wala, and they were the wealthiest people he had ever known. Their small, clapboard houses were palaces of love, the dirt on Kwak'wala was rich with diamonds of forest creatures that provided sustenance and the crops to feed the entire band, so that no one knew hunger. The billionaires in their gated estates had material wealth, but the people of Kwak'wala had wealth of the heart and soul. One type of wealth could buy material things; the other could buy peace of mind. Jesus was there to defend a way of life that was far superior to that of the outside world, and he told Aaron, Gary and Tom as they started out to meet Harrison Black Elk that the success of their stand against tyranny might well lie in their ability to take and hold the paper mill. It was a bargaining chip that could stave-off an invasion.

The group took a boat up the coast and rendezvoused with Black Elk. He slowly led them toward the mill. While the group was making its way through the thick forest, Plato Papadopoulos' ship was just entering the strait, headed for the harbour at the paper mill, where the stage was being set for a monumental clash of wills.

As they approached the building, all but Gary, Tom and Aaron became a bit nervous. Up until this time, they had never faced the realities of what they were going to do. Aaron could see the consternation in their faces. He squatted down and whispered, "Gentlemen, this is not a game. It is no longer talk of doing something. It is the actual performance of the act. Jesus told me the story of three frogs on a log in a pond. He said that one frog made a decision to jump in and get some food from the pond. Then Jesus asked me how many frogs were left. I replied that there were two, but he said no, there were still three, because the frog had just made a decision to jump in, but making a decision and carrying out the act are two different things. This is the time you must decide whether you follow through with your decision or not. No one is going to ridicule anyone who goes back, but once we move into the building, it will be too late."

No one left. In fact, all of them got a determined look on their faces. Robert James Blackwater, the young boy who had been so vocally fearful of Huyana's needle, now a young man, simply said, "let's go!"

Gaining entrance to the main mill building was easy. There was only one guard at the door, and Gary quietly crept up behind him, subdued him with a headlock and tied and gagged him. They entered the building and made their way upstairs, where they halted at the doorway to the laboratory.

Gary reached down and flipped the lock off his rifle and signalled for everyone else to do the same. He quietly said, "If there is any shooting, aim at the legs. We don't want to kill anyone unless we have to. Only aim for the head if you have no alternative. According to Black Elk, there are only four guards. Too many guards would call attention to the place. We have numerical superiority, but that is no guarantee they won't put up a fight. Remember, all these people are indoctrinated to believe they are the vanguards of freedom. Those without weapons are dangerous, too. They must be immediately herded up and held in abeyance."

Aaron reached for the door, and then very gently, quietly and deliberately turned the knob. Tom slammed his shoulder into it and the raiders stormed into the room. Rather than pandemonium, everyone, including the guards, stood in bewilderment and shock. Aaron shouted, "Any son-of-a-bitch move, you're dead. Drop the guns, now."

The four guards were so dumbfounded that they immediately dropped their guns. A group of four men in chemical suits stood by the door to what was obviously a containment room, as a bright blue glow could be seen through the small window in the thick, iron door. They, like all the others, were mesmerized with astonishment. They simply could not fathom anyone attacking the mill.

One man blurted out, "What the hell are you doing? You have no idea how much trouble you are in."

Aaron smiled and said, "We have the guns, we are taking over the building, and we are in trouble? Think about it fellow. Think who is really in trouble. Everyone over against the far wall and turn all your pockets inside out." He pointed to Black Elk and continued, "take out your cell phones and hand them to this gentleman. Move. Move."

What a completely flawless operation thought Aaron. Then they heard the fog horn of a ship. Plato Papadopoulos was entering the harbour. It would only be a matter of time until the engineers were in the building, getting ready to remove that for which they came, the polonium triggers. The portable missile launchers would be taken off and placed in strategic location and targeted for the American cities of Seattle, Portland and San

Francisco. Aaron could tell that one guy, obviously the head engineer, was rapidly figuring things out. He said, "You people are playing with fire. This is a dangerous place, and if these materials aren't handled properly, massive amounts of radiation can be released. We can all die. Those lucky ones will die instantly. Others will suffer radiation poisoning and die the most horrible death possible."

Aaron let his death smile creep across his lips just for effect. "Yeah, we all know what polonium poisoning can do. It's the favourite weapon to eliminate spies these days. I am sure the USA is using it all over the world to go after the evil-doers. Too damn bad they aren't using it on some American politicians, who are the real evil-doers. Now shut up and sit down, all of you, and this operation will be as painless as possible. Do anything foolish, and we are prepared to do what we must."

The men eased down onto the concrete floor. Gary told Aaron to keep them under guard while he led a team to meet the engineers and fire off a flare to signal the village that the mill had been taken. Aaron gave him a thumbs up, and felt that old exhilaration from days long past.

Seeing the flare, a collective sigh of exhilaration went up throughout the village. Huyana looked skyward as she heard a muffled humming sound overhead like the flapping of a bat's wings in the darkness. Suddenly, a huge spot light shown down on Jesus' cottage, bathing it in an intense shimmering light that seemed to almost sparkle. Grappling ropes were extended from three dark black objects that hovered overhead as men in dark combat fatigues that blended into the night leaped onto the ground and started spitting hot lead in all directions as people frantically ran toward Jesus' cottage. The killing was indiscriminate and no attempt was made to ask for surrender. As scores of people lay wreathing in agony on the ground, Huyana rushed to the aid of as many as possible, braving bullets that whizzed overhead, leaving bright orange tracers in their wake. America had brought war to the peaceful island of Kwak'wala, like it had brought war to so many other places that dared question its authority.

The commander of the Seal Team was Major John Donnelly, who immediately radioed for troops to land and pacify the village, despite the fact that the residents of Kwak'wala had not fired one shot. It was apparent that there weapons had been for intimidation, not actual use, but the Seal Team was not concerned with the lack of aggressiveness. They intended to destroy everything in sight and secure the cottage that they assumed housed Jesus.

When Jesus Came to Canada to Lead An
Indigenous Rebellion in the Broughton Archipelago

From the other world, I come back to you.
My locks are uncurled with drenching dew.
You know the old, while I know the new.
But tomorrow, you shall know this, too.
The unfurling of your flag of despair
turns against all that is just and fair.
But from the ashes of your
murders on this distant shore,
a great awakening will be born.
And your presence is but a mist
in a world that you think cannot exist.

Like a terminally ill patient, Jesus knew that
death was around the corner. He had mapped out a
path and written a ticket reading *end of another
earthly life*. Mortality is a frightening thing but
Jesus faced it by doing what he always did. He
walked among the people and cried for them to
stand against tyranny, and to fight until their last
breath for the hope of victory over those who were
possessed of that devilish demon, greed. Jesus
walked stoically about into his valley of the
shadow of death, seemingly a glowing beacon
who cried, "Do not give into despair. Death is
preferable to a life on your knees. Stand against
these representatives of the evils of the outside
world. I say to you that all is not lost. Some of
your loved ones are already dead, but that is the
way of a world where the strong prey upon the
weak. Justice may not win the day, but pride and
conviction refuse to bend before tyranny."

J. Wayne Frye

When Jesus Came to Canada to Lead An Indigenous Rebellion in the Broughton Archipelago

Suddenly, the entire village was now aroused and a burst of gunfire was aimed toward the invaders, but they had no night vision goggles, so they were easy targets for the invaders. Villager after villager, men, women and children fell to the devastating firepower of the invaders, but one group of men made their way behind the invaders and with a fusillade of deadly fired aimed at the heads and lower torsos, which were not covered by bullet proof armour, dispatched six members of the 18 men team to rolling on the ground screaming in agony.

Unlike most who face death, Jesus was not angry, nor was he stoic. He was not withdrawn. Refusing to pick up arms, he rallied the people with the shout, "fight for your homeland, fight for justice, fight against greed, fight to resurrect that which has been killed within you. These invaders are the vanguard of a coming armada of savages who know no restraint in pursuit of the evil which they serve."

As more and more people rallied, Jesus shouted, "your will be done. It is your time to stand against evil. If that means suffering, so be it. If that means death, so be it. Face your darkest hour as a shining light of hope."

Donnelly and his men retreated from the onslaught of firepower that they had not expected, as he realized they could not reach the injured men. They backed toward the long house, and suddenly the doors and windows sprang open and a voice shouted, "Drop the guns and put your hands up. We will cut all of you down with shots to the head. Drop them, now!"

Donnelley, realizing help was only about twenty minutes away in an armada of flying boats, ordered his men to drop their guns. For the first time in his 16 year career he was faced with defeat by a rag-tag bunch of people he considered heathen savages.

The soldiers were herded into the long house, and the injured ones were taken to the clinic, where Huyana worked valiantly to save as many of them and the villagers as she could. Despite her abhorrence of those who had rained devastation down on the village, she categorized their wounds and assisted those whose injuries were so severe that they needed immediate attention. Eight villagers were dead, three of them children, two elderly men and three women. Not a single shot had been fired by the soldiers at an armed individual; only innocents had been gunned down.

There was a flurry of activity around the village as preparations were made for what they assumed would be a larger assault. The pits outside the gates were quickly doused with gasoline and everyone assumed their assigned posts. The children and elderly were herded into the underground shelters and mass amounts of arms and ammunition were moved toward the ramparts.

Careful preparation had been made to repel an invasion from the shore and the forest, but they had not assumed an assault from above would be instituted. It was deeply troubling to Jesus that he had let the people down, and as he apologized to those who had lost love ones, an outpouring of love overwhelmed him. People were not afraid. They were exhilarated by what they had accomplished. "Those who died, died honourably" was the refrain of the many who tried to comfort the emotionally distraught Jesus.

There was no time for grieving. As Jesus prepared the people for the coming assault, he looked in the direction of the paper mill and wondered if all the preparations had been made to equalize things and perhaps ward off more bloodshed. His plans were to use the missiles as a bargaining chip to get concessions for those whom he loved. He thought that indeed he had promised to bring a sword, and this time, the sword would be three deadly missiles aimed at American military installations. Maybe if America faced the same consequences that other nations faced from them when they rained down destruction from the skies, a satisfactory compromise could be reached that would finally make the behemoth of oppression yield to justice for those who only wanted to be left in peace to decide their own fate, rather than having America decide it for them.

At the paper mill, they had heard the firing of weapons from the village, and Aaron decided that it was imperative that he return to assess the situation. There was no cell-phone communication on Kwak'wala, so it was necessary to resort to old-fashioned methods of communication. Gary and Tom urged Aaron to return to the village. They snickered a bit and also added, "and make sure you give Huyana greetings from us."

Aaron, as he turned to leave, in a good natured manner, said "assholes."

The engineers put on the chemical suits and began the task of getting the polonium triggers ready for insertion on the missiles that were now being prepared at the dock. Plato Papadopoulos, seemingly gaunt and tired, still exhilaratingly marshaled all his men to perform at peak efficiency and to prepare to weigh anchor as soon as the triggers were inserted. He, himself, would be staying to die, if necessary, alongside those whom he saw as the last relics of a system that was supplanted by the culture of greed of which he had been a part of for far too long. He was the last of a breed of businessmen who genuinely cared about those who worked for him. He saw his success as predicated on the hard work of those who served him. All his employees were given stock in the company, and his will left all his assets, not to his arrogant children, who acted like they were part of that despicable class of people who thought they were entitled by virtue of who their parents were, but to his employees who were the ones truly responsible for his success. Papadopoulos was one the rarest of men, a rich person who had compassion and realized that those who truly did the work were rarely rewarded.

Aaron could not take the boat back, because the others might need it, so he had to trek through the wilderness to the village. All the way, he was frantic about Huyana's safety. The affection he felt for her was as genuine as any he had ever experienced, but it did not fill him with rapture nor carry him away with the power or the fervour he had expected. It was more sedate. After so many disappointments in relationships over the years, at his age, he thought that part of his life was over. He had imagined any future affection as different, and had imagined himself different, too. In dreams and poems everything had been, as it were, beyond the sea; the haze of distance had mysteriously veiled all the restless mass of details and had thrown out the large lines in bold relief, while the silence of distance had lent its spirit of

enchantment. It had been easy as a youth to feel
the beauty; but now that he was in the midst of it
all, when every little feature stood out and spoke
boldly with the manifold voices of reality, and
beauty was shattered as light in a prism, he could
not gather the rays together again and put the
picture back beyond the sea. Despondently he was
obliged to admit to himself that he had been poor,
not just in material wealth, but in spiritual wealth.
Nobody could ever convince him to believe in
God, because Aaron was too smart for that. He
only had faith in what he could see; not in those
things he could not see. Yet, since meeting Jesus
in New Jersey all those years ago, his faith in
humanity had been rekindled. Jesus had taught
him that there were still many redeemable people
in the world who were not imprisoned by the
culture of greed. Jesus had found it on Kwak'wala,
and because of that, Aaron had found it in the
arms of Huyana.

As Aaron trekked onward, the flying boats were
descending on the harbour of the village, landing
in the bay. Large waves of American soldiers were
jumping into rubber landing craft and moving
toward shore. Jesus, looking at the armada,
realized that he may well have led the people into
a battle they could not win, but on their faces he
saw a grim determination to fight for a way of life
far superior to that lived by those who were
determined to conquer them. These people were

prepared to die on their feet, rather than crawl on their knees to submit to those who made slaves out of the masses in service to the moneyed monarchs of the capitalist world who saw all resistance to greed as tantamount to treason against the rightful order of things. Jesus saw the possibility for victory, not physically, but psychologically. The people were on their feet, refusing to submit before those who looked upon them as savages.

As those manning the ramparts scanned the darkness, they could only vaguely pick-out the shadowy figures making their way toward the village. So far, no shots had been fired, and the defenders waited patiently, hoping bloodshed could still be averted. A white flag of truce was boldly waving in the breeze as Jesus hoped to parley with the invaders and arrange for the women and children to be evacuated. The leader of the assault, Colonel Dobson, radioed General Bridgman, who was back at headquarters on Whidbey Island with Canadian General McCabe, who was anxiously awaiting the pacification of the islanders before sending in his Canadian troops to take over the occupation and evacuation.

When Bridgman got word that there was a white flag of truce flying, he, with an acquiescent nod from McCabe, arrogantly replied, "fuck 'um. Raze the place to the ground. These miscreants need to be taught a lesson."

When Jesus Came to Canada to Lead An
Indigenous Rebellion in the Broughton Archipelago

General Bridgman, like so many other U.S. military officers throughout history who had approved the massacres of natives from Sand Creek to Wounded Knee, had given the green light to slaughter these people he saw as nothing but savages standing in the way of progress. Like his heroes, generals McArthur, Patton and Eisenhower, who disdainfully ordered troops to bayonet innocent protesters in Washington, DC in 1932, the general felt a smug satisfaction that he was doing his duty for his country. That was always the excuse of those who committed war crimes, but the war crimes trials were only reserved for the losers. The victors were exempt from justice. People like George Bush and Dick Cheney proved that Americans were never required to submit to international justice. Both of them were murderers and torturers of the vilest kind, but would never pay for their crimes.

However, victory must be measured by more than what land is taken, what people are defeated and what the body count is. The people defending Kwak'wala had no illusions about victory, but they did believe that their sacrifice would encourage other Aboriginals in North America to take a stand against the continuing abridgment of their rights and the confiscation and defilement of their land. This was not a one battle war. This was just one small stand against the genocide practiced against Aboriginals for hundreds of years.

J. Wayne Frye

When Jesus Came to Canada to Lead An
Indigenous Rebellion in the Broughton Archipelago

As the troops edged forward, Jesus realized that there would be no truce. There would be no mercy shown by the military of a nation that thought might always made right. These were the same troops who had decimated Iraq and Afghanistan with weapons of mass destruction while they were there to look for weapons of mass destruction. What an irony. Jesus picked up a loud speaker and proclaimed, "The forces of evil are upon us. The white flag of truce means nothing to these terrorists. Resist with all you have. Victory will be elusive, but regardless of the outcome, make the price they pay so high that they will never again use force to impose their will on a people who had rather die from a bullet than die from malnourishment in a land of plenty or be imprisoned in gulags of torture in that land south of here that hypocritically proclaims itself a righteous and free nation. I say to you, tonight we are all truly free. Do not live as slaves to evil. Die fighting for your freedom."

A mighty roar went up from the people and thus began a battle that was never meant to be, but could not be avoided, because one nation, more than any other, exalted itself as above the law. This was a nation that had crushed freedom movements all over the world, had practiced genocide among its own natives, had callously used the most destructive terrorist weapon of all time in Japan, had wantonly ignored poverty while allowing those at the top of the economic ladder to pile up lavish riches, and had made the Christian religion into an apologist for an economic system based on greed.

While all this was occurring, back at the polonium processing plant, the triggers were being installed in the missiles. Time was of the essence. Jesus knew that they needed a threat of devastation in order to halt the assault on the village. He had to get word to those at the mill to fire a non-nuclear missile into the harbour, so that he could get the commander of the troops to negotiate. They had to prove to the American commander that an assault would be devastating for both sides. Of course, the American troops were considered cannon fodder by their leaders, as they were the poor and middle class kids who were forced to serve in the military because of economic circumstances. So, their lives were not important to a country that based human worth on an economic scale.

As the American troops began to form for a frontal assault, Jesus knew that the only way to avoid further bloodshed was to prove that the costs of taking the village would be too high a price to pay. He understood there was no hope of a military victory, but he knew that by fighting, the people would have a sense of victory even in the bitterness of defeat.

CHAPTER 13
THE CRUCIFIXION OF JUSTICE

The soldiers were poised to attack hope.
There was a deep sense of impending doom.
An intense foulness was in the air.
The invaders thirst for cruelty was insatiable.
Each soldier was a flowing fountain of hate,
Each man harbouring a dark side,
Where compassion ran dry.
Though they claimed fealty to a loving God,
And thought they were serving their country,
Satan was their guide in every conquest.
They were servants to a nation
That had lost its moral compass.

Jesus had assumed that an invasion would have occurred from large ships. As he looked at the assemblage of soldiers preparing to assault the village, he realized he had been naive in placing lookouts at the various approaches to Kwak'wala. It was a waste of manpower and time, but as the moment of truth neared, the defenders of Kwak'wala were prepared to stand against the evil of a world that simply had no tolerance for those who did not bow before the altar of greed. They stoically awaited their fate, prepared for the worst but filled with a soaring sense of self-worth and pride that they had finally decided that they would no longer cower before those who served the rulers of a corrupt system of economic depravity.

When Jesus Came to Canada to Lead An Indigenous Rebellion in the Broughton Archipelago

Sending a runner to the mill with a message that asked for one non-armed missile to be fired into the bay by the village as a warning of what the Aboriginals were now capable of in the battle, Jesus hoped that the fear of a missile strike against their positions might be an inducement to halt the assault. It would take the runner forty-five minutes to reach the mill, and Jesus did not give him a note, and that would prove critical in the way he relayed the message.

Colonel Dobson gave the signal to advance and the troops breached the first barrier with absolutely no resistance. Again Jesus had the white flag raised, and it was violently ignored as furious volleys of bullets were fired at it. The flag was torn to smithereens and with it any hope that a peaceful resolution was possible.

Standing beside Jesus, Luther Blackwater turned to him and said, "We can't win can we?"

Jesus, very deliberately replied, "if you stand against evil and if you stand against tyranny, you may lose a battle, you may lose a war, but you win a victory for self-worth, a victory for dignity, a victory for honour."

Luther, with a half smile, in a determined manner said, "To die beside you is an honour. To die for my people a privilege I lovingly embrace."

When Jesus Came to Canada to Lead An Indigenous Rebellion in the Broughton Archipelago

Jesus, knowing the end was near, turned to those about him and shared one last parable. "Once there was a man named Wayne Frye who used to go to the ocean to do his writing. He had a habit of walking on the beach before he began his work. One day he was strolling along the shore. As he looked down the beach, he saw a human figure moving like a dancer. As he got closer, he saw that it was a young man and the young man wasn't dancing, but instead he was reaching down to the shore, picking up something and very gently throwing it into the ocean. As Wayne got closer he called out with the greeting, 'good morning!' Then he asked, 'what are you doing?' The young man paused, looked up and replied, 'throwing starfish in the ocean.' Wayne asked, 'why are you throwing starfish in the ocean?' The young man replied, 'the sun is up and the tide is going out. And if I don't throw them in they'll die.' Wayne, a bit confused, said, 'but young man, don't you realize that there are many kilometres of beach and starfish all along it. You can't possibly make a difference by throwing the few you save back into the ocean.' The young man listened politely. Then he bent down, picked up another starfish and threw it into the sea past the breaking waves and said, 'it made a difference for that one.' So, we may be unable to save all indigenous people from tyranny, but we can make a difference for a few who will be motivated by this stand against injustice to no longer bend to evil."

When Jesus Came to Canada to Lead An
Indigenous Rebellion in the Broughton Archipelago

As always, the parable had a chilling effect on the people around Jesus. More than ever before, they were motivated to fight those who had come to support the thievery of a corporate world that served the interests of the few at the expense of the many. They were prepared to die, rather than to submit to the terrorism promulgated by one nation in support of a system of corporate slavery in a world where people were nothing but meaningless chattel that could be bought and sold like any other product. These people simply would not go meekly into the darkness of despair like most others who refused to stand against tyranny.

When word of the coming attack got back to Ottawa, the now reluctant Canadian government pleaded with the Americans to halt the assault. However, the pleas were ignored by an American government that had already decided its national security interests demanded that the island be secured and the people evacuated, so once again a corporation's profitability was more important than people. The adage *profits before people* should be the motto of an America that saw its role in the world, not as a protector of freedom, but as protector of profits.

As the Canadian Prime Minister desperately tried to contact the American President to beg for a halt to the assault, he was told the President was busy and could not be disturbed. The PM was now learning the hard way that currying favour with a country that knew no restraint was tantamount to surrendering sovereignty. His miscalculation was about to have dramatic and far-reaching consequences for people in both countries. He hung his head in shame at what he had done, realizing that his miscalculation of American intentions was about to have severe political ramifications. He reached for the phone and reluctantly made a call to General McCabe, who was sitting next to General Bridgman in the Whitby Island Command Centre and said, "Under no circumstances are Canadian troops to assist the Americans. You are to leave immediately, and return to Ottawa. This whole affair is about to blow up in our faces. I have tried unsuccessfully to plead with the U.S. President to halt this insanity. General, this government, my term of office, and probably your career have been sacrificed at the altar of utter lunacy. I am finished. This government is finished."

Thus, the Prime Minister's fate was irrevocably sealed and his government would, no doubt, fall within a few days, as Canadians would become outraged at the subordination of their sovereignty to the will of the U.S. government and its corporate benefactors. However, that was only a minor problem when compared to what was soon to occur on the island that nobody in most of the world had even heard of before. Kwak'wala was about to become a name that would reverberate across the world as a place where a few brave souls took a stand against a behemoth of military might and the corporations that had enslaved the world to a vile system of servitude that snared all of humanity in its evil web of deceit and malicious economic bondage. Of course, a different spin would be put on it by those who manipulated the masses. The American government would unleash its massive propaganda machine to portray those who stood against it on Kwak'wala as terrorists, when the real terrorists were those who represented the U.S. government. Americans could not understand why so many people were willing to strap explosives to their bodies to fight a country that was the self-proclaimed defender of democracy. Patriotic brainwashing had made the American people into apologists for their own terrorism.

Those who flew planes into American buildings were terrorists, but when America dropped bombs on innocent men, women and children in Iraq and Afghanistan, they were great defenders of freedom, not terrorists. Hypocrisy was at the very core of what America stood for in a world that did not envy them, but rather, feared them. However, that fear was no longer present on Kwak'wala. The people there had finally turned their backs on complacency, acceptance and meek acquiescence to the tyranny of submission. No more would they cower before those who wanted to enslave them. They once again knew freedom as did their forefathers. They might die, but they would die on their feet, not their knees.

In the face of evil, resistance is the only truly moral response. The time was now at hand, as death was in the air. All in the village were poised for the coming carnage. The elderly, many of the women and the children were huddled in the bunker that had been prepared to withstand the assault. There was an intensity that permeated the chilly night air.

The earth of Kwak'wala was full of anger.
The sea around the harbour was dark with wrath.
The opposing armies were held in silent harness.
The Aboriginals stood against the evil path.
Ere soon to be let loose the legions of despair.
Ere the army of evil draws the death blade.
Jehovah of the Thunders, Jesus once again
Must pay the price for others who sin.

Aaron and the runner passed each other on the path and exchanged greetings. When Aaron heard of the coming fight at the village, he hurriedly said good-bye and rushed toward the village, so that he might arrive in time to help in the coming battle, and to be by the side of his beloved Huyana. He entertained no illusions about victory, but he would stand with Jesus against all odds.

When Jesus Came to Canada to Lead An
Indigenous Rebellion in the Broughton Archipelago

As the runner to Papadopoulos stumbled through the forest, to his left, he heard a rustling of brush. Unarmed, except for a knife, he reached down and removed it from its sheath, stood still and looked toward the brush, waiting for whatever was there to make its move. He did not have to wait long. From the darkness leaped a cougar, with snarling teeth and a furious cry.

The cougar bit furiously into the left arm of the runner as he stabbed into the furry flesh continuously with the knife in his right hand, burying the blade all the way to the wooden handle. Still, the beast would not let go its grip and with its left paw, mighty claws were ripping the flesh from the left side of the young man's face. Plunging the knife in and out, almost to the point he was thinking that he should just give up the fight and end the pain, the young Aboriginal finally left the knife in the cougar's side as his hand cramped up so badly that he had let go of it.

The cougar, weary from the battle and the loss of blood, collapsed in exhaustion on top of the runner. The two of them lay there, totally drained and sapped of all energy. The runner reached up, pushed the cougar off, looked down at his left leg and realized he had broken it when he fell to the ground. He could not walk. It was still at least 3 or 4 kilometres to the mill site. He would have to crawl there. Looking at the path before him, he sighed deeply and began the slow, painful crawl to deliver the message, a message that now seemed to be fading into the recesses of his mind as he struggled to keep conscious.

Meanwhile, back in the village, the arrival of Aaron was greeted by Jesus with a euphoric hug of recognition, and a smile as he pointed toward the clinic. "The real reason you are here is over there Aaron, and I want you and her to take the back way out of the village, go to the bluffs above us and observe what is about to happen. Huyana has a camera. Take it with you and photograph as much as you can without giving away your position. You must get the truth out about what is going to happen here. This is going to be worse than the My Lai massacre or even Wounded Knee. Those troops out there are thirsting for blood, and the carnage they are about to wrought will be an abomination. You must tell the truth, so that other Aboriginals all across North America will rise to the cause and demand justice. Go to where we have placed the sentries. They have boats. You can get to the mainland and go to the media in Vancouver with the truth. It is your job to get the facts out about what is going to happen here."

Aaron pensively replied, "Is there no other way? Must these people be sacrificed? Would it not be better to surrender, and save the old men, old women and children?"

When Jesus Came to Canada to Lead An
Indigenous Rebellion in the Broughton Archipelago

"Aaron, look around you. These people will not surrender their dignity once again. They have done that too many times. They had rather die than submit to the capricious whims of a society that has no compassion and no heart. They are prepared to meet their fate, to sacrifice themselves to arouse their comrades to make a stand for justice and unite for the common good of all Aboriginals." Jesus then hung his head as if in recognition of what was about to befall him and those whom he loved so dearly.

Realizing that he would ultimately bend to the will of Jesus, Aaron knew that arguing to stay was fruitless. He would reluctantly do as asked. Also, he desperately wanted to save Huyana from harm.

Courage was mine, and I had mystery,
wisdom was mine, and I had mastery.
But my fate was in the hands of tyrants.
I had been crucified many times,
in a myriad of places,
by legions of the angry.
Do not weep or wail in sorrow for me.
Weep for those who know not what they do
to the son-of-man and those who love him.

All about the village, there was trepidation, but no fear. Not even the small children, huddled in the bunker, showed any sign of fright. These were, one and all, people prepared to meet their fate, and determined to yield no more to those who had stolen their birthright. They would spill their blood onto the land of their forefathers, so that it might mingle into the rich soil of their homeland, forever making them a part of the place they loved.

Aaron pleaded with Huyana to leave as asked, but she refused to abandon the people she loved. With earnestness and commitment, she, with stoic acceptance of her fate, placed her right hand upon Aaron's left arm. "My dear Aaron, you must do as asked by Jesus. You are the only one who can get the story out. You alone can see to it that the world knows the truth. I simply cannot abandon those who have come to mean so much to me, even for you, who mean more to me than life itself."

Aaron looked at her with desperation in his eyes. "Huyana, I was born the moment you kissed me. I have lived a few weeks while you loved me. I will die no other way than by your side. I will not obey Jesus. I am here to the end by your side, no matter what that end might be."

They embraced and Aaron turned and walked back to where Jesus was, along with the others, waiting for the coming assault. He picked up a rifle and leaned beside Jesus, staring into the darkness. Jesus shook his head and said, "You dare disobey the son-of-man?"

Aaron, smiling, replied, "Remember, I am a non-believer. If you were the true son-of-man, you'd call upon that illusionary God you revere so much to slay your enemies and save all of us from annihilation. There is no God and there is definitely no son-of-man. You are just a man, but the most extraordinary man I have ever had the privilege of knowing. It will be an honour to die by your side in defence of a way of life that is no longer viable in a world ruled by heartlessness and greed. It is a world I am weary of and can no longer countenance. This is a good night for dying."

"Aaron, we all die, even the son-of-man has died many times. It is not how we die that counts, but how we live. You and these people here have lived a life of compassion and love for the misfortunate of the world. You may be a non-believer, but you are exalted above all believers I have ever known. I love you, Aaron."

Without hesitation, Aaron replied, "and I love you. That is why I am by your side."

Suddenly, tracers lit up the starless darkness and a loud battle cry was heard as a large contingent of soldiers moved over the first barrier. Jesus nodded his head as a signal to push the plungers that were connected to the dynamite that had been buried under the soil at the first barrier and mighty explosions ripped through the lines of soldiers edging their way forward. Men could be heard screaming, and then the hissing sound of grenade launchers penetrated the stillness as the compound was rocked with explosion after explosion, followed by the cries of the wounded. Aaron glanced over his left shoulder and saw Huyana valiantly scurrying from one wounded person to the other, desperately trying to bring them comfort.

Just as hundreds of soldiers reached the second barrier, a mighty volley of fire rang out from the defenders and the faces of soldier after soldier exploded like ripe watermelons being dropped onto concrete. Knowing the soldiers were encased by bullet proof vests, each defender took accurate aim only above the necks of the soldiers to ensure their fire was deadly. The Americans thought they were invincible, but they were facing a foe that had been well-trained to strike where they were most vulnerable. Even an ill-equipped army, if properly trained, could ward off the most vaunted military machine in the world. It had been proved in Vietnam, Afghanistan and Iraq, but still the Americans had not learned their lesson. This battle would end in so-called victory for the American military, but at what cost? Only through a war of attrition could a determined people fight against the overwhelming odds presented by a nation that spent more on the machinery of war than the ten

next nations combined. They thought all that
money and all their high tech equipment
guaranteed a victory, but they had found out again
and again that when a determined people refused
to bend to the tyranny of conquest, there would
never be a decisive victory. There would only be a
stalemate that would continue to bankrupt the
nation and make cannon fodder out of those poor
souls from the ghettos of despair who foolishly
lined up to fight for an a lie promulgated by the
elite to keep the many in bondage to the few. The
sons and daughters of politicians and CEO's
would never be on the battlefield, only those
foolish enough to accept the lies of the elite would
be sacrificed at the altar of deceit. How ironic that
the children of the middle class and poor would
willingly sign-up to sacrifice themselves for the
privileged class. Could they not see that they had
more in common with those whom they were
slaying than those whom they served?

Aboriginals had lost their culture to an intolerant
society. Many had lost their way in a valiant
struggle to survive. But this day was their day to
stand boldly against four hundred gruelling years
of the white man's maniacal tyranny. They were
not just wantonly slaying the invaders; they were
taking deadly aim against the atrocities and
indignities that had been piled upon them and their
ancestors for generations. This day, in stoic,
determined, splendorous perseverance they were

prepared to die rather than submit to inglorious indignity from those who served the vile, depraved God of indifference and conquest.

With their night vision goggles, the soldiers were in awe at what they were seeing. The faces of the defenders had war paint on them. The defenders had eagle feathers in their hair. The defenders were wearing ancient war beads that had been passed down from one generation to the other as a reminder of how noble this great race had once been. The defenders were all in traditional dress, as if to say, "we now proudly and defiantly proclaim that we will no longer adapt to the cruelty of your system that has no place for honour and respect. The defenders were Aboriginals and proud of it. The defenders were not going to submit to a world where the least among men were expected to bow in supplication before the altar of the privileged class. The defenders were all equal and no man or woman was less exalted than another. These were the defenders of dignity and honour for all of humanity. The natives and their few allies were the defenders of virtuous, righteous benevolence against the evil of corrupt, wicked greediness.

This was more than just a battle between one well-equipped, physically superior, fascist military machine and a hodgepodge, rag-tag army of determined freedom fighters. It was truly a battle

where the gates of glory stood between the evil
represented by the soldiers and the magnificent
righteousness of those who refused to bend before
winds of tyranny.

The past is never really dead as long as
memories are alive. The bright days of glorious
harmony, when the Aboriginals were masters of
all they surveyed, had long been blotted out by the
darkness of evil that had made the land of milk
and honey into a gulag of economic slavery. The
white man's insatiable greed for more and more
had devoured the land that had been sacred to the
people who had revered, nurtured and cared for it.

Originally, the Aboriginals had been too
sanguine and friendly. They met the Europeans
with the hand of friendship, when they should
have met them with bow, arrow and tomahawk.
These people's friendly nature was a fatal flaw
that had doomed them to the evils of those who
thought that their Christianity and white skin
colour made them superior. Today, that
friendliness ended. This was what life was like. If
you were not ready to be killed and to kill in
defence of your rights, then you deserved no
rights. For too long, these magnificent people had
accepted a world they did not understand and did
not want to be a part of. Now they had decided
that, if there was to be no justice, there would be
no beauty and no peace.

When Jesus Came to Canada to Lead An
Indigenous Rebellion in the Broughton Archipelago

The final banner of rebellion had been unfurled. Against the hostile fate of generations, a stubborn breast was now bared with a roar. These people had enough and would submit to the capricious whims of the greedy no longer. In the land they loved, they faced the final judgment!

Arising on the tiny island of hope was the chain of the death dance the defenders now gladly embraced. Never would they submit again. By offering their lives in defence of an ideal, they were finally proud and truly free. The anguish of hatred for the years of oppression now led to the clenched fist that would be brought down in all its fury on the evil robotic soldiers of a society that knew no boundaries to the evil spread of a system that locked all into a prison of greed and pernicious vileness.

There was fire at the feet of these glorious defenders of righteousness that was like burning coals of fury. In the background, the old women and men sat in a circle pounding the drums of defiance in a rhythmic cadence. The ancient sounds were reverberating through the darkness, striking fear into the hearts of the arrogant, bombastic soldiers who could not fathom why these peaceful, compliant people had suddenly decided to defy the might of a nation that never wavered in destroying those who dared defy its authority.

When Jesus Came to Canada to Lead An Indigenous Rebellion in the Broughton Archipelago

Old and young alike were now defiantly swaying to the dance of death, showing no fear as they seemed to be filled with the spirit of freedom. Smiting their heads against the dark skies, the thunder of liberty permeated the darkness as a storm of indignation raged within their breasts for the years of suffering they had endured in meekness. They were acquiescent no more. This was the spark that would light a rebellion that would sweep across the North American continent like a plague – a plague that would eventually destroy the system of oppression that had trapped the many into servitude to the capricious whims of the few. Thus the dance of Kwak'wala would be heard in the Aboriginal ears of the world, and the leg would no longer bend as the knee of defiance would strengthen. Never again would the Aboriginal bow in supplication.

All about the compound, the dance of death was embraced, clasped, squeezed and enveloped with the knowledge that the end was at hand, but, ah, what a grand and noble gesture they were making, sacrificing themselves to the glory of freedom, rather than submitting to tyranny. It was the last watch for the night of wanderings in the world. Soon, the invisible scissor blades would yawn open and slice them into shreds as they closed with a mocking creak on the dance of death. Yet, these Aboriginals were true kings and queens of the glorious moment.

J. Wayne Frye

When Jesus Came to Canada to Lead An
Indigenous Rebellion in the Broughton Archipelago

With Jesus rallying them to defend their homeland, from their intrepid souls there were howls of the coming end, but they embraced it like a father welcoming a prodigal son home from the wilderness of despair. Yet, there was no weeping. They knew there would be no deliverance from the curse of greed.

Fate on the scales of battle was suspended as all knew they were to fall there. Yet, in falling, there would be triumph. One by one they were prepared to fall into the abyss of darkness, sacrificing for the cause of justice.

As the soldiers made their way to the last barrier, now infuriated and enraged by the deadly resistance, they observed a scraggily looking man with long, flowing chestnut hair and a beard moving about the ramparts totally impervious to the volleys of fire aimed his way. Why could no bullets find their mark? Was this man immune from death?

Jesus was moderately tall, a comely man, with a seemingly celestial glow that seemed to permeate about him as he defiantly walked from one area to the other. He was not physically imposing, but the soldiers could not help but be mystified by his lack of concern for personal safety. This was a man they desperately wanted to kill, but it was if there was a wall of invincibility all about him.

When Jesus Came to Canada to Lead An Indigenous Rebellion in the Broughton Archipelago

A skilled sniper, with Colonel Dobson by his side, was instructed to take careful aim at Jesus and eliminate the one man who seemed to be the glue that held the people together in rebellious unanimity. As Jesus was lined up in the cross hairs of his scope, the young soldier squinted and strained to aim at the middle of his forehead. Just as he was about to squeeze the trigger, a strange, thick, intensely black fog began to rise from the ground at the third barrier where Jesus was methodically rousing the defenders. It floated upward, completely obscuring Jesus. The soldier said to the colonel, "I have lost him. I can't see the son-of-a-bitch."

The colonel, overwhelmed with anger shouted, "Fire, fire into the fog. Fire every round. Kill that son-of-bitch. Kill him!"

Doing as ordered, the sniper let loose with a series of single shots into the thick fog. After twelve rounds had been fired, the fog lifted and there was Jesus standing tall. As the soldier again got him into his cross-hairs, Jesus seemed to look directly into the scope. There was a faint smile crossing his lips. Again the soldier fired and Jesus tilted his head to the left, the bullet whizzing by his right ear. Another shot and Jesus tilted his head to the right. This time the bullet whizzed by his left ear. The soldier, dumfounded, shouted to the colonel, "I can't kill the asshole."

When Jesus Came to Canada to Lead An
Indigenous Rebellion in the Broughton Archipelago

The colonel, now overwhelmed with anger at the losses his men were incurring, shouted, "If bullets can't kill him, then when we take the compound, we'll crucify the son-of-a-bitch. That would be a fitting end to a man who fancies himself a modern day messiah."

The soldier, a veteran of both Afghanistan and Iraq, where he had ruthlessly killed men, women and children with equal disdain, simply replied. "Colonel, I don't know what it is, but there is something about that man – something strange."

The colonel enraged even more, replied, "The only strange thing about him is his name. He is a fucking rebel-rousing anarchist – just another terrorist with a cause. And like all terrorists, he will feel the wrath of Uncle Sam. He'll be begging for his life when the end comes."

The sniper, realizing disagreement would not be tolerated, kept his thoughts to himself. Yet, in his mind, he was saying, "I don't think so. This is no ordinary man. This is not a man afraid of death. This is a man who bows before no one." In fact, at that very moment, the sniper realized that he had been on the wrong side all along in Afghanistan, Iraq and now, Kwak'wala. He had been fighting for a bankrupt idea of superiority and serving the interests of the elite who had no concern for common people like him. He was now determined to only go through the motions of appearing to fire his weapon. He was through serving the interests of repression. He would no longer be a killing machine for evil. He was fearful of repercussions and did not have the courage to turn his back on a country that was engaged in oppression. Like most of his fellow countryman, he was too fearful to stand-up to authority, but at that very moment, he had decided that he could no longer serve the interests of those who wanted to imprison the world to exploitation by the privileged class. Having Jesus in his sights was a cathartic experience. He could not slay love and righteousness. He was no longer a soldier for America and its fascist-like oppression of the working class. He was now a soldier of righteous indignation who would resign from the army, rather than serve the interests of oppressors.

Colonel Dobson, seeing the soldier's trance-like stare into the distance, shouted, "Sergeant Pierce, get it together. Start popping those assholes, now."

Pierce, having no intention of killing anyone, replied, "Yes sir," as he fired toward the parapets, but intentionally missing. Even in the carnage of battle, Jesus could reach the few of the enemy who could see the wisdom and righteousness of a man who was only standing against those who promulgated a system of economic, religious and patriotic servitude.

When Jesus Came to Canada to Lead An
Indigenous Rebellion in the Broughton Archipelago

As the battle raged furiously, Papadopoulos, hearing the sounds of the battle, wondered if he would be ordered to fire the missiles at the designated targets of Whidbey Island Naval Base outside Seattle, Umateilla Chemical Depot in Oregon and Travis Air Force Base in California. Those were the three places within range of the missiles, as the decision had been made to absolutely not target any urban areas for fear of civilian casualties. Unlike the U.S. military, there would be no attack on civilian areas. In fact, there likely would be no attack at all, as the only purpose was to let the authorities back in Washington know that the capability was there. Having the possibility of destruction had been used by America in country after country. Now, the tables would be turned. Yet, Papadopoulos was getting nervous. Surely, Jesus would have sent a runner with word on what should be done. Of course, Papadopoulos had no idea that the runner was crawling through the wildness, trying to reach him with word to fire a missile into the bay as a warning to the attacking army.

As it became obvious to Colonel Dobson that there would be mass casualties on both sides, he frantically contacted General Bridgman at Whidbey Island, begging for an air strike. Bridgman, contacting the Pentagon but was denied permission, as there was fear of what the reaction of the Canadian public would be to such an act.

It was then that Bridgman made a statement that would be forever remembered as a green light to disaster. "Colonel Dobson, do whatever you must to bring those people to heel. This is your command and your responsibility. Use your 1500 men whatever way will get the job done. Do not allow a rag-tag army of Injun terrorists to defeat the best goddamn army in the world. Get the job done, and obliterate that fucking village from the face of the earth if necessary. We already have a cover story about a massive explosion in a polonium field that will be used as a cover. I tell you that I will accept nothing less than total defeat of these miscreants, and I want that man calling himself Jesus dead. You hear me? I want him dead. We don't need a public trial or detention in Guantanamo where he can be made into a fucking martyr. Dead! You hear me, dead! Just like bin Laden."

Dobson, seeing this operation as his ticket to be made a general, replied. "Got it sir! Dead! Believe me, I have the men who can carry out the task."

"Good colonel. Get it done."

It became obvious that the final wall was about to be breeched. The defenders climbed from the ramparts and all gathered in an area in the centre of the compound. Jesus, bleeding from a slight wound, was helped there by Aaron.

When Jesus Came to Canada to Lead An
Indigenous Rebellion in the Broughton Archipelago

As the remaining 200 men and women prepared to die rather than surrender, from the bunker emerged the old men, old women and children, carrying pots, pans, kitchen knives, anything that could be used as a weapon. Some of the old women even had rolling pins. One old woman, at least 70, shouted, "I've had plenty of practice using this rolling pin on my husband. Now, I will pretend the soldiers are him, and, like him, they will suffer my wrath." A roar of laughter went up, as even in their desperate situation, levity was just another tool used to fight evil.

The children began picking up rocks to hurl at the soldiers. This would be the end of Kwak'wala, but it would never be the end of the story, as in coming years, in Aboriginal village after village, the story of the valiant stand would be told and retold. This would be the Aboriginal Masada, and like the Jewish legend of how a few defenders held off a superior force, this story would serve as a rallying cry for the oppressed aboriginals who had simply suffered too much at the hands of an authoritarian bully nation that knew no restraint.

As the Prime Minister sat idly by his emergency phone at 24 Sussex in Ottawa, ignoring the plight of Canada's most glorious people, the American military machine was set to destroy a tiny bastion of sanity in a world where the insane were running things. The PM realized he was powerless against

the American juggernaut of suppression. He had
no courage to stand up for what was right, rather,
he meekly bowed before tyranny.

Jesus, as the people gathered around the middle
of the compound in preparation for the last stand,
stood tall, his back ram-rod straight and spoke
from his heart one last time to those whom he had
grown to love so much. "My comrades in
sanctified battle against oppressors, I say to you
that today will be a day of infamy every bit has
horrible as Wounded Knee. Yet, the truth will not
be denied this time, for the modern world can no
longer hide the truth from those who seek it. We
who are about to die do it without heavy heart or
fear. We do it in honour, respect for our
forefathers and the belief that what we do here
shall serve as a catalyst to those who rail against
the modern machinery of corporate slavery that is
served by the monolithic military machine that we
face today. In a sense, we are here to cash a check.
When the architects of oppression took your land
and destroyed your way of life, they were signing
a promissory note to which you are all heirs."

Jesus looked toward the huge oak gate that was
the last thing that stood between the people and
annihilation. He pointed toward the gate and
continued. "Obviously, America and even your
beloved Canada have defaulted on this promissory
note insofar as aboriginals are concerned."

He then looked at his friend Aaron, who was standing with his left arm around Huyana and a AK-47 in his right hand. Smiling, he continued. "This man and this woman are just two of those who are willing to die by your side in defence of a way of life that is far superior to that lived by those who look with disdain upon you. They, like you, know that the Bank of Justice is bankrupt when it comes to Aboriginals. Yet, there is great wealth out there in the hands of the few. Their vaults are filled with that which does not rightfully belong to them. We are demanding that the Bank of Justice be reopened with freedom, justice and security for all Aboriginals who have waited too long for their checks to be cashed."

Just as Jesus' last word rang out, a mighty explosion ripped through the main gate and hoards of soldiers stormed forward over the debris, their guns spitting fire at those huddled in the square, cutting down men, women and children indiscriminately. Jesus was one of the first hit, and he tumbled forward, blood flowing from a massive wound in his left side. As he lay on the ground he shouted, "Do not yield to tyranny. Do not yield! Do not yield!"

Huyana ran to Jesus' side, rolled him over and as she was administering aid, a bullet tore through her left shoulder. Aaron, firing rapidly at the advancing soldiers, suddenly dropped his gun and ran to her side. He pulled her toward a nearby building to get her out of the line of fire. As he was doing so, a bullet tore into the back of his left shoulder and he tumbled to the ground, unconscious. Huyana, slowly dying from the loss of blood, reached out and touched Aaron's hand for the last time. She sighed once and took her last breath as she lay beside of her beloved and drifted into that deep, dark abyss that awaits us all.

The defenders fought bravely, but soon their ammunition was exhausted. The children, old men and old women valiantly flung rocks toward the soldier's faces, many scoring direct hits that brought the marauders of mayhem to their knees in excruciating pain. Firing blindly at anything that was before them, the soldiers rained down a volley of death that rapidly diminished the defenders to a few children under the age of ten who were witnessing the carnage from the side of a nearby building. These children picked up rocks from the ground, and together, the thirty or so remaining defenders stood like statues of stone, grimly fighting those who had defiled their land. They were no longer children. They were brave defenders of justice against those who knew no restraint in their savagery, as the soldiers mercilessly cut down hope in service to those who knew no human compassion and looked upon the earth as nothing but a commodity to be exploited rather than revered.

When Jesus Came to Canada to Lead An
Indigenous Rebellion in the Broughton Archipelago

Aaron, slowly regaining consciousness, looked
down at his right hand and saw Huyana clutching
it. Her hand was so cold. She was gone. She was
gone..

She lived as best she could, and bravely she died.
Be careful where you step: her grave is wide.

There where the vines cling crimson on the wall,
And in the twilight wait for what will come.
The leaves will whisper there of her, and some,
Like flying words, they will cry as they fall;
But go, and if you listen, she will call.

No, there is not a dawn in eastern skies
To rift the fiery night that's in your eyes;
She is slain with every leaf that flies,
And hell is more than half of paradise.
No, there is not a dawn in eastern skies.

To the grave will I tell her this,
To the grave I will quench a last kiss,
That blinds me to the way I must go.
Bitter to mine own end, it is she I will miss.
To her grave I come to tell her this.

There are the crimson leaves upon the wall,
Go, for the winds are tearing them away,
Nor think to riddle the dead words they say,
Nor any more to feel them as they fall;
But go, and if you trust her she will call.

When Jesus Came to Canada to Lead An
Indigenous Rebellion in the Broughton Archipelago

She lived as best she could, and bravely she died.
Be careful where you step: her grave is wide.

Aaron, kissing Huyana's cheek, did not have the energy to cry out in pain. As he surveyed the compound, the rising sun cast a crimson glow upon the carnage before him. Torn and mangled bodies lay all about, and the few who remained alive cried out in agony. The soldiers, almost laughing with sinister glee, were dragging the survivors to a nearby gulch and tossing them in.

Dead and wounded women and children, even two little babies were scattered all about the bottom of the gulch. The soldiers stood above the gulch, as those in it looked up with defiance. Not even the children pleaded for mercy, nor shed a tear in despair. As they were being murdered by volley after volley of deadly fire, they defiantly stood proud and unafraid. As a little baby suckled on its dead mother's bloodied breast, a soldier aimed directly at its head. It exploded; brains flying all about. Two brave little boys, no more than ten, still clinging to life with wounds all about their frail bodies, bent down and picked up rocks from the gulch and flung them toward the soldiers. The soldiers laughed as they dodged the rocks and purposely aimed at areas of the body where they would only inflict pain, rather than immediate death. They seemed to get sadistic pleasure in watching them suffer.

When Jesus Came to Canada to Lead An
Indigenous Rebellion in the Broughton Archipelago

Men, women and children were heaped and scattered all over the flat area around the gulch. Some of the soldiers fixed their bayonets and started stabbing those who remained alive. One woman, about seven months pregnant, gasping for breath from numerous wounds, looked on helplessly as a soldier cut out her child, skewered it on his bayonet and proudly waved it above his head like it was a trophy signifying a great victory. The mother, barely breathing, defiantly kicked at his shins until he finally plunged the bayonet into her chest and she went still.

As Aaron observed the slaughter, he wished he could die too, but he wanted revenge, and for that, he needed to live. As he slowly crawled toward the nearby forest, he looked back and saw a group of soldiers who had found Jesus, who was still alive, but had a huge hole in his left side from a gapping wound. The soldiers mockingly called him Messiah as they built a cross out of old boards and nailed him to it, finally propping it up against the side of a building. Then, they walked away laughing and shouting, "If you are the messiah, I suppose we'll see you in three days."

The sniper, Sergeant Pearce, the only soldier refusing to take part in the abominable behaviour, took his canteen from his side and reached up to give Jesus a drink. This was the act of a man who had realized that he was in service to evil.

When Jesus Came to Canada to Lead An
Indigenous Rebellion in the Broughton Archipelago

Through tears, he said, "I am sorry. Please forgive me. Please forgive me."

Jesus, with a barely audible voice, replied, "It is not for me to forgive you. You must forgive yourself through acts of atonement. Do this in my name."

The sunshine was bathing the compound in light at the time Jesus uttered those words. But as he took his last breath and sighed "it is over," a dark cloud blotted out the light, plunging the whole village into a veil of darkness as the sun was vanquished from sight. The intense darkness made it possible for Aaron to crawl into the forest completely undetected. Looking back, he felt that he had witnessed the crucifixion of justice.

J. Wayne Frye

PROLOGUE
REAP WHAT IT SOWED

As the light slowly returned to the village, Colonel Dobson, who was prancing about among his men like a peacock with full plumage, congratulated them on what he termed a great victory. Aaron, in the safety of the woods could hear his bombastic, boastful, arrogant exhortation. "Gentlemen, you have achieved a great victory for the American people today. Hold your heads high, because you have defeated terrorists of the vilest kind. You bring your nation great glory, and the people will forever be in your debt for this moment of glorious vindication of the American way of life that was threatened by these heathen anarchists."

A mighty roar went up from the soldiers, as a few faint moans of agony could still be heard from the remaining defenders who were alive. The moans were ceasing one by one as Aaron heard the firing of single shots from the guns of the soldiers who were walking through the village methodically killing the few survivors of the carnage. Aaron hung his head in shame for being alive, but he would spend the rest of his days finding those responsible for this abominably heinous act of cold-bloodied murder. This was what happened when a nation lost its moral compass.

When Jesus Came to Canada to Lead An
Indigenous Rebellion in the Broughton Archipelago

As Aaron lay in the forest, the runner he had passed on the way to the village had finally managed to crawl near the missile batteries manned by Papadopoulos. Exhausted from his ordeal, he could hardly speak as Papadopoulos bent over him. It was then that the lack of a note from Jesus with specific instructions would prove fatal for the military installations on Whidbey Island, Washington; Umatilla, Oregon and Fairfield, California. The runner did not say that one lone unarmed missile should be fired into the bay by the village as a warning. Anyway, it was now far too late for that ploy to work. All the runner could get out before he died was "fire the missiles."

Papadopoulos gave the order and nuclear missiles were launched toward the three designated targets. A nation that lived by destructive policies was going to suffer the devastation it had made other nations suffer. America was about to reap what it sowed!

J. Wayne Frye

When Jesus Came to Canada to Lead An
Indigenous Rebellion in the Broughton Archipelago